THE PAIR DADENI

BOOK 2 OF THE MAQLÛ

JC HOLMBERG

Library of Congress Control Number: 2021924766

This is a work of fiction and is a product of the author's imagination. Any references to historical events, real people, or real places are used fictitiously.

Learn more about the history and background of this book at:
www.JC Holmberg.com

Names: Holmberg, J. C., author.

Title: The Pair Dadeni / JC Holmberg.

Description: [Pine Knot, Kentucky] [Tist Fiction], [2022] | Series: The Maqlû ; book 2 | Interest age level: 12 and up. | Summary: "After ruining his sister's chance to move on in the afterlife, Alex Scire vows to find one of the Maqlû--alien objects of immense power. But all he has to aid him is his dad's magical ankh and a mysterious dragon's vague directions to the Fountain of Youth. He sets out on the dangerous quest alone and is shocked when his Druid friends, Jane and Diana, join him in boarding a pirate ghost ship, where they manage to convince the captain to help them find the object"

Identifiers: ISBN 9781956342079 (paperback) | ISBN 9781956342062 (hardback) | ISBN 9781956342055 (ebook) | ISBN (9781956342086) (audiobook) ISBN (9781956342062) (large print/dyslexic friendly)

Subjects: LCSH: Magic--Juvenile fiction. | Brothers and sisters--Juvenile fiction. | Future life--Juvenile fiction. | Pirates--Juvenile fiction. | CYAC: Magic--Fiction. | Brothers and sisters--Fiction. | Future life--Fiction. | Pirates--Fiction. | Ghosts--Fiction. | LCGFT: Ghost stories. | Fantasy fiction.

Classification: LCC PZ7.1.H6466 Pad 2022 (print) | LCC PZ7.1.H6466 (ebook) | DDC [Fic]--dc23

To Suzu

My extraordinary book travel guide

And technology consultant

And beta reader

And …

CONTENTS

"**"And in the end,
it is not the years in your
life that count,
it's the life in your
years."**

Unknown author

Commonly attributed to Abraham Lincoln, but there's
no evidence supporting that claim.

CHAPTER 1
THE COURAGE TO CONTINUE

Alex Scire scanned the charred meadow, looking for ghosts in the early morning light. When he saw none, he sighed in relief, leaned back against the cave wall, and returned to planning how to get back to the dig site at Lamanai.

He'd seen the vast unbroken jungle around Lamanai from atop the High Temple a couple of weeks earlier, and knew it would be nearly impossible to make his way back to the Druid encampment without help. He also knew no one was searching for him, as the Viking ghost who'd helped him battle ghosts in the Mayan afterlife had told him everyone assumed he was dead – buried beneath a collapsed hillside.

It seemed like his only chance of survival was to find the New River that cut through the middle of the Belizean jungle and hope to catch a ride on one of the many tourist boats plying the river. But, the problem was that he had no idea which way the river lay. He hoped he was still on the west side, but he'd been wandering underground for over a day and wasn't sure where he'd come out. And, even if he was lucky enough to head the right way, he wasn't sure whether he'd have enough energy to fight through the jungle to reach it as he was battered, exhausted, and hungry. Overwhelmed by his predicament, he gave up trying to figure it out and fell back asleep.

Sunlight was streaming into the cave when a noise woke him with a start. Nervous that vengeful Mayan ghosts might be after him, Alex slapped his Tilley on, grabbed his pack, and looked around the clearing, ready to flee.

Relief flooded over him when he saw the spirit of his old dog coming out of the jungle. "Sport," he cried out. But instead of coming towards him, his former dog turned and headed down the small game trail he'd seen the previous day. Alex started running after him but quickly slowed to a shuffle as every part of his body ached.

He'd only gone a short distance when he remembered he'd nearly died at the bottom of a cenote the last time he'd followed his dog and came to a halt. His ankh necklace tugged at him to keep going, but instead of following its lead like he usually did, Alex pulled out the small metallic looped cross with the alien symbols on it and stared at it.

Before he could decide whether it was trying to help him get back to Lamanai or lead him into some new trouble, a jaguar leapt out of the forest. An instant later, the mysterious opalescent colored creature who'd been following him around Lamanai, flashed in front of him, taking the big cat with it. Alex heard a brief scuffle, some cries of pain, then nothing.

He stepped towards where the two creatures had disappeared and called out, "Is that you, Chrys? Are you okay?"

The same voice he'd heard in the Mayan underworld sounded inside his head. *"I'm fine, little one. But please, don't come any closer. You can't look at me."*

"Why are you so worried about what you look like? You've saved my life three times now," Alex said. "Do you really think I'd be that petty to judge you by your looks?"

"It's not that. Humans can't handle looking into my specie's eyes – they go catatonic when they see us."

"Nothing happened when I saw your eyes before."

"That was in the dark when I doubt you could see me clearly."

Alex ignored the warning and pushed through the bushes at the edge of the trail. He froze when he saw a mouth full of huge sharp teeth inside a twenty-five-foot-long winged creature that stood over ten feet tall at its shoulders. Just as startling were the bright opalescent-colored scales covering its entire body.

Chrysophylax groaned. *"I knew this would happen. Why didn't you listen to me?"*

Alex shook his head and stepped back. "I'm fine. I'm just surprised because I thought dragons were myths."

"Only humans call us dragons. We call ourselves Berellians. The reason we're in so many of your myths is that my ancestors came to this world over 13,000 years ago to help humans. And just like humans, we come in many different shapes, colors, sizes, and temperaments. That natural variation is why many of your Eastern cultures depict our kind as snake-like, and the western cultures tend to depict us like me – with four legs and wings."

"So why did all of you disappear?"

"Your species repaid those who came to help them, first by stealing nine powerful devices we brought, then killing many of them – all because your kind was greedy, power-hungry, and scared of the differences between us. As a result, those of my ancestors who

survived left your planet millennia ago and have let you deal with the messes you keep creating for yourself."

"Then, why are you here now?"

"My uncle, Nabu, developed a plan to retrieve those devices, which we call the Maqlû. He gave one of your ancestors the ankh that you wear. He's been monitoring the wearers of that device ever since, waiting for the right person to retrieve the Maqlû for him. But it suddenly stopped working. So, he sent me here to investigate."

Alex reflexively clamped a hand over his chest in a vain attempt to hide the little looped cross hanging underneath his t-shirt. "Why do you think I have it?"

"I wouldn't have traveled 1200 light-years to find out what happened to it if I didn't have a way of finding it. All I had to do was search for its unique signature. It got me close enough to sense your aura, which I investigated. I saw you looking at it once and have been following you ever since.

"But you're not at all what I'd pictured the wearer of the ankh to look or act like. And you seem to have a real knack for finding trouble."

"Hey. That's not true," Alex replied. "Trouble finds me." He dropped his gaze and began kicking at the ground. It was some time before he spoke again. "Well, that's not a totally correct statement. My troubles began when I mistakenly took the ankh from my dad. My entire family died that day, and it's been non-stop crazy since then."

"I'm sorry to hear that. If you don't mind my asking, would that have been about eight months ago? That's when my uncle lost contact with it."

Alex nodded but didn't look up.

"I'm curious, though. I've noticed you talk to yourself a lot and act very strange at times. Why is that?"

Alex started laughing.

"What's so funny?" Chrysophylax asked.

"I just find it odd that you can fly, travel across space, communicate telepathically, and despite your size, can hide well. You even know about the ankh and the Maqlû. But you can't see ghosts."

"Ah. Spirits. I never thought of that. That would explain a lot of your stranger actions. And by the way, I don't think it's odd we can't see spirits. From what I can tell, no one in either species can. So how do you do it?"

"Apparently, it's something that happens to everyone who wears the ankh, because I've been able to see ghosts as soon as I put it on."

"But none of what you've said explains why my uncle suddenly lost contact with it."

Alex shrugged. "I don't know what to say, except that your uncle's wrong about it not working. It's very active. Sometimes it drives me to go places and do things I'd never do in my right mind. At other times it protects me. If it weren't for this ankh thingy, I wouldn't be out here in the middle of nowhere, wondering who's going to try to kill me next. It's turned my life into a living hell."

"I don't understand. If so many bad things have happened to you, why do you still wear it?"

"It's got some hold over me. I get anxious every time I take it off, so I wear it all the time now."

"Interesting. I'm curious, though. Why did you destroy the Palantir?" Chrysophylax asked. *"Everybody else wants to use it."*

"I didn't mean to, but I don't regret what happened," Alex replied. "I went searching for it because I thought it would help my sister move on in the afterlife. But I discovered that it did nothing but cause trouble – driving everyone who knew it existed a little crazy. And even though I broke my promise to my sister that I'd use it to help her move on in the afterworld, I'm glad I destroyed it."

"Your perspective is – different. My uncle thinks the Maqlû are extraordinary devices that could lift humanity from its current mess. Like humans, he, and many of our elders, treasure them." Chrysophylax paused before saying, *"If you still intend on helping your sister, you may want to consider looking for, what your kind calls, the Fountain of Youth. My uncle thinks one of the Maqlû might lie behind that legend."*

"I'm not going anywhere except back to camp, then home. I've had enough of this," Alex said. In a much more uncertain tone, he added, "Besides, the Fountain of Youth is a fable."

"What about your promise to your sister? If you think finding one of the Maqlû can help her, shouldn't you should search for it? The ankh can guide you." There was a pause, then Chrysophylax said, *"I've told you too much. I should go."*

Before Alex could stop him, the Berellian disappeared into the jungle. He waited to see if Chrys would return, but gave up after several minutes and stepped back onto the trail where he'd seen Sport earlier. But he found his dog had disappeared too.

Even though he had no idea which direction the path went, Alex decided to stay on it as he was too tired to fight through the jungle. A few minutes later, he was surprised to find the path emptied onto the banks of a small creek where Sylvanus Morley was standing next to a dugout canoe with two Mayans in it.

The unexpected sight of three ghosts in the middle of the jungle startled him. "What are you doing here?" Alex asked.

Morley took his pith helmet off and scratched his head. "I'm not sure exactly. Right before sunset last night, I felt an urgent need to prepare this boat for you – like some invisible hand was directing me."

"Where am I?" Alex asked.

"A long way from Lamanai. Far enough that I doubt you could make it back through the jungle on your own, especially in the condition you're in."

"I can't thank you enough for being here," Alex said. He looked around the small clearing and asked, "By the way, have you seen a big yellow lab ghost dog? He led me here, then disappeared."

Morley shook his head. "Nothing's come down that path except you."

Alex nodded towards the canoe. "Is it safe?"

Morley nodded. "Yes. The canoe is real, and you can trust the guides. I've known them for a long time and can vouch for them. The man in the bow's name is Itzamm. Kukulcan is in the stern. They'll understand what you say, but they can't respond, as the Conquistadors cut their tongues out."

Morley didn't notice Alex's grimace and continued talking. "I've taken the liberty to stock the canoe since I figured you'd be hungry. There are bananas, some chicken, rice, and fresh water."

Alex's thoughts drifted to imagining how his grandfather and cousin would react when he finally returned to the reservation. He glanced down at his raggedy t-shirt and torn camo pants and wondered what he looked like. Absent-mindedly tugging on one of his braids, he stepped into the canoe.

As his guides paddled down the tributary, he watched Sylvanus Morley slowly shrink from view. Alex sighed and turned to face forward when the spirit archeologist and former spy disappeared at the first turn, surprised at his sudden hesitancy about returning home.

Half an hour later, they reached the New River and turned south. They'd only gone a short distance when Alex shook his head, shocked by what he'd decided to do. He called out to his ghostly guides, "I'm sorry, but can you turn around? I need to find the Fountain of Youth."

CHAPTER 2
HOPE AND A FUTURE

Diana Bennet sat outside her mother's tent, numbly watching the other members of the archeological expedition restore the camp. It had only been a day and a half since the Mayan spirits had kidnapped her, but it seemed like an eternity. Alex was gone, buried under a million tons of rock. Her mother, Sophie, was inside, still recovering from injuries she'd sustained in the ghost attack.

She didn't notice Jane Roland running towards her, the older girl's mass of ginger-colored hair wildly flying around, until Jane called out in her slight Scottish accent. "We need to talk."

Diana looked up and was surprised to see a wide grin splitting Jane's freckles.

"I'm sorry. You know I don't hear well. What did you say?" Diana asked in her thick accent.

Instead of replying, Jane grabbed Diana's hand and headed for the open-air dining shelter overlooking the New River. When they were alone, Jane took a deep breath and blurted out, "Alex is alive."

"That's impossible. There's no way he could've survived that hillside collapsing on top of him.

Jane put a finger to her lips. "Quiet down. I don't want anyone to hear us. Ye know how I get premonitions sometimes? Well, I thought I sensed his presence yesterday when we were at the site."

"So, that's why you weren't upset."

Jane nodded. "I lost track of him shortly after that and didn't say anything because I didn't want to get my hopes up if I was wrong. But, this morning, I sensed him again and came to see ye."

Diana furrowed her brows as she looked sharply at her fellow Druid. "If it were anybody other than you, I'd say you're deluding yourself. But you have an eerie ability to know what will happen long before everyone else. I just don't understand how you do it, since you say you don't have any magical skills – unless you've been hiding something from us all these years." She thought she saw a fleeting look of fear in Jane's eyes but immediately dismissed the idea, thinking she'd imagined it.

Trying to cover up the ensuing silence, Jane added, "I think he's somewhere downstream. In case I'm right, we should check it out. What's the worst thing that could happen? We spend a couple of hours on the river."

"It wouldn't be the first time he surprised us. How do you think he got there?" Diana asked.

"How should I know? But ye know him. He manages to get into all sorts of odd situations."

A wild idea popped into Diana's head. She tried to dismiss it, unwittingly talking to herself out loud. "It couldn't be."

"What?" Jane asked.

"Do you think that was the Palantir he grabbed while we were down in that Mayan temple?" Seeing the puzzled look on Jane's face, Diana said, "Think about it. Who found the *Sibylline Book* for the Palantir? And who's the only person who can open that book? I bet you that's what he found and is now trying to escape with it."

Jane frowned. "But he doesn't have any magical powers."

"That's what he says. How can any of us know for sure? What if he's been playing us all along? Everything about him screams to me that he's a warlock. If I'm right, then we've got to stop him and get the Palantir away from him before he learns how to use it."

"That's crazy talk. For all we know, my hunch is wrong, and he's dead beneath that temple. Even if I'm right, and he escaped, he's probably lost and hurt. And anyway, it doesn't matter which of our theories is correct. I'm going to search for him. If ye want to come, meet me down by the river in a few minutes. I'm going to pack some supplies." Before Diana could reply, Jane was gone.

It took her only a minute before Diana decided to join her friend. Ten minutes later, she was standing with Jane in front of the stone wall near Lamanai's dock, waiting for the tourist boats to come. It wasn't long before the first two pulled up and let out their sightseers. As soon as the tourists had left the dock area, Diana approached the pilot of the nearest one and asked, "Sir, can you help us? A friend of mine is lost downriver, and I need you to take us to find him."

The pilot shook his head. "I can't. I've got a bunch of tourists I have to take back in a couple of hours."

Jane stepped forward and said, "Ye don't understand. The boy is the grandson of a wealthy woman back in the States. She's the one who's paying for all the people working on the dig here. Ye'll get a large reward if ye help us find him."

Diana elbowed Jane in her side and hissed, "You can't say that. My mom's in charge down here and would never approve charges like this."

The pilot of the second boat called out, "What the girl says is true, Elio. I heard there was a big accident here yesterday and some boy is missing. This is your chance to make some real money. I've got plenty of room in my boat and can take your group back. Just remember me, though, when they pay you."

Elio took his hat off and scratched his head thinking about the opportunity. When he put his hat back on, he motioned for Diana and Jane to get on board. Several minutes later, he gunned his boat's engines and headed downriver.

Unable to hear over the roar of the engines, Diana sat staring out at the jungle, not caring that the wind was whipping her curly brown hair all around. All she could think about was how Alex had betrayed her and stolen the Palantir. As the minutes ticked by, her anger slowly drained, and she began wondering if her emotions were truly about Alex stealing the object or if she was upset he was gone.

Her hopes rose fifteen minutes later when she spotted a boat in the distance, but she slumped when she saw it was only a small fishing boat. Shortly after passing Orange Walk, she decided it was a waste of time to continue searching for Alex. She tapped their pilot's shoulder and shouted for him to head back to Lamanai.

Jane shouted, "Please don't give up now. Let's give it a little more time."

Diana shook her head. She dropped her chin to her chest and surreptitiously wiped the tears from her face as the boat slowed and made a wide turn. A motion on the bank caused her to look up in time to see a dark-skinned boy standing on the river bank near a dugout canoe.

Diana jumped up, shouting and waving to get Alex's attention, astonished that he was still alive. Elio turned to see what was happening and accidentally gunned the engines. Unprepared for the sudden motion, Diana tumbled overboard.

CHAPTER 3
IF TROUBLE MUST COME

Alex stared numbly at the passing riverbank, wondering if he was making another big mistake. Wanting to re-think his hasty decision to search for the Fountain of Youth, he asked his spirit guides to pull over.

For the next half hour, he paced back and forth on a tiny patch of grass along the river, trying to decide whether to keep going or turn around. Every few minutes, he would pull out his ankh and look at it, hoping it would guide him on what to do next. When he realized it wasn't going to give him an answer, he picked up his pack and was about to head back to Lamanai when he heard a woman's voice in his head, saying, *"Why have you stopped? Your quest lies beyond."*

Alex spun around in a circle, trying to spot who was talking to him. He cried out, "Who are you?"

"I prefer to remain anonymous. And it's no use trying to see me," the voice said. *"I don't intend to show myself to you as other spirits do."*

"Why? Aren't you the same person who shrieked in horror when I first touched the ankh? The same voice who urged me to risk my life in the Mayan Underworld, then screamed in delight when I accidentally destroyed the Palantir? What do you want?"

"That's what I'm trying to decide. I spent my entire life studying the Maqlû, helping Nabu with his plans, but now I'm wondering if that was the right course."

"What does that have to do with me?" Alex asked.

"Maybe everything."

Alex was so deep in conversation with the unseen woman that he didn't hear the roar of an approaching boat until the engines throttled down and someone called out his name. He looked up just in time to see Diana fall into the river.

Seeing his two Druid friends caused Alex to forget about the conversation and watch as Jane stretched out her hand to Diana, who, with her usual stubbornness, ignored the proffered help and swam for shore.

A splash off to his right caused him to turn. He gasped when he saw a large crocodile slide into the water and head for Diana. Alex waved his hands to get her attention, but Diana misunderstood the gesture, stopped swimming, and waved back. He glanced from the rapidly approaching crocodile to the boat to see if it could reach her in time but saw it was too far away.

Without thinking, Alex pulled a knife off his pack and was about to jump into the river when he caught a flash of opalescent color on the other side. He watched in mute fascination as Chrys, despite his size, slipped into the water without a ripple, and raced across the river towards Diana.

A couple of seconds later, the crocodile let out a guttural roar, flipped its mighty tail, and swam away. Alex looked for Chrys, but the dragon had disappeared once again. Snapping out of his daze, he ran to where Diana was lying on the shore.

Jane jumped out as soon as the boat pulled up and ran towards Diana, reaching her at the same time as

Alex. She reflexively checked Diana's pulse and asked, "Are ye all right?"

"No," Diana groaned.

"I can't see anything wrong with ye," Jane said. "Where are ye hurting?"

"I'm fine." Diana slapped her pants. "My phone was in my pocket when I fell into the river. Now it's gone."

"A cellphone. That's what ye're worried about?" Jane shrieked. "That crocodile could've killed ye."

Diana sat up. "What crocodile?"

"It's gone now," Alex said. "Besides, you probably had nothing to worry about. Remember what Constance told us about the crocs here? He was probably just curious and wanted to take a bite or two out of you to see what you tasted like. Now, if we were in Guatemala, it would be an entirely different story."

Diana took a playful swing at him. "Smart aleck. Besides, I'm sure Constance was yanking our chains."

As he helped her stand, Alex asked, "What are you two doing here?"

Diana stared at him in disbelief. "I can't believe you're asking that question. We saw you tumbling to your death right before the temple collapsed. You should be dead – crushed beneath a million tons of rock. How did you escape?"

Before Alex could reply, the pilot shouted, "Are you okay, miss? I'm sorry about causing you to fall overboard."

"I'm fine," Diana replied.

"I'm assuming this is who you're looking for," the pilot said. "Get in so we can head back to Lamanai. I need to be back soon, or my boss will have my head."

"Come on, Alex," Diana said. "You can explain how you survived certain death on the way back. Knowing you, it should be quite a story."

Alex surprised himself when he replied, "I'm not going back. There's something I've got to do."

"What could be so important that ye're charging off in the opposite direction of camp?" Jane asked. "Besides, yer in no state to go anywhere. Ye look like death warmed over. I'm surprised ye're even standing after what ye've been through."

Feeling that his secrets were becoming unbearable, Alex blurted out, "I promised somebody I'd help them, and I can't go back on my word."

"What are ye talking about?" Jane asked.

"You'll probably think I'm crazy," he replied.

"We've been around ye for a few weeks now. I doubt there's much ye can say that'll shock us. Remember, we've grown up around magic, something most people think is a fantasy." When he didn't say anything, Jane stared intently at Diana and said, "We won't tell anyone. I promise."

There was a long hesitation before Diana said, "Fine. I promise I won't tell anyone either."

Alex looked hesitantly from one girl to the other before leaning forward and whispering, "I promised my sister I'd help her move on."

Diana nervously laughed. "You realize she's dead, don't you? We need to get you back to camp and have Mary look at you."

"See. I knew you wouldn't believe me. Well, I'm not going back. If I did, your mom or my grandma would think I'm crazy and send me to a psych ward. No matter what, I'm going to do what I can to help Deborah. When you return to camp, would you tell my grandfather what I'm doing? Even though you don't understand, he will." Alex picked up his pack, stepped into the canoe, and waved his hand downriver.

Elio made the sign of the cross and muttered a silent prayer, while Diana stared in astonishment as the canoe moved away from the shore with two paddles digging into the water, held up only by air. With a blank look, Diana turned to Jane and asked, "How's he doing that?"

Coming out of her shock, Jane held out her hand and yelled, "Stop. What are ye doing?"

"Go back to camp," Alex shouted back. "Everybody will be happier that way."

Jane looked from Diana to Alex, then back again. "Ye know what I have to do. Lady Yvaine told me to keep an eye on him and ensure he doesn't come to harm. So, are ye in?" Getting no reply from Diana, Jane shouted, "Wait up. I'm coming with ye."

Alex swung around in the canoe, staring at the rapidly dwindling figures on the shore. He could see Jane waving her arms, trying to get him to come back, but he turned his back on her, hoping to shut out the second-guessing in his head. His stubborn determination to go it alone lasted for all of five seconds before he told Kukulcan to turn the canoe around.

Seeing Alex coming back, the pilot called out, "Hey, miss, you've found what you're looking for, so let's head back."

Not hearing the pilot, Diana looked at Jane for several tense seconds before saying, "He's nothing but trouble, and following him would be foolhardy."

Jane shrugged. "I'm going with him, wherever that is."

Diana threw her hands up in the air. "Fine. You win. I hope I don't regret this." She turned back to the pilot. "My mother's the site leader. Ask for Sophie Bennet. Tell her we found the lost boy and will be back shortly. She'll pay you well for your time."

The pilot cursed and backed his boat away from the bank. A minute later, he gunned the engines and headed back upriver.

Alex didn't get out when the canoe reached the shore. "If you're coming, get in," he said. "But you should know I've only got a little food, so we'll have to stop downriver to get supplies."

"Where are you going?" Jane asked.

"To find the Fountain of Youth," Alex replied. "I think one of the Maqlû objects might be there."

Diana rolled her eyes. "That's a myth." Distracted by the site of the two paddles stuck in the river bottom to keep the canoe from floating away, she couldn't help but switch the subject. "What type of magic are you using to control those paddles? I've never seen anything like it."

"I keep telling you that I don't have any magical abilities. But hey, since you know everything, you figure it out. Anyway, I've wasted enough time here and need to get going. I'm sure you're smart enough to figure out how to get back to camp."

"That's mean," Diana said, putting her hands on her hips. "I can't help but get freaked out by all the strange things that happen around you. If you were in my shoes, what would you think?"

Alex looked at Itzamm and Kukulcan before replying. "After everything you've seen, why won't you believe me?"

He was about to tell his spirit companions to take off when Jane blurted out, "Ye can see ghosts. Can't ye?"

Realizing he couldn't hide the secret anymore, he nodded.

"Have ye always been able to do that?" Jane asked.

"No. I started seeing them right before the accident that killed my family. But it wasn't until I came to Salem last month that I ever spoke to one."

Diana shook a finger at Alex. "I knew you had some sort of power. You were too lucky not to have had something helping you. Is that how you found that horrid temple?" Diana asked.

"A young Mayan slave girl named Ixchel, who the king sacrificed over a thousand years ago, asked me to help free her and others."

"So, all those people in the cave were ghosts?" Diana asked.

Alex nodded. "The ghosts you saw were using you as bait to lure me down so they could kill me."

"Why would they want to kill ye?" Jane asked.

"I'm not positive, but I think it's because they wanted to stop me from finding the Palantir."

"Was it that red and black orb the king was using?" Diana asked.

Alex nodded. "Your mom would never have found the Palantir – not even if she'd dug around Lamanai for the rest of her life."

Diana turned to Jane. "See, I knew he found it." She turned back to Alex and said, "So where is it?"

Alex winced, expecting an outburst. "I accidentally destroyed it."

"What! Why would you do that?" Diana screamed. "You threw away hundreds, no, make that thousands of years of our order's efforts to find and protect magical objects like that."

"I told you it was an accident. I was planning to use it to help Deborah, who is stuck in the afterlife and thinks that if I find one of your precious Maqlû, then she can move on. But, Stoughton, that Puritan ghost you saw, wanted to take it, and I couldn't let him. That's why I'm heading to the Caribbean – so I can find the Fountain of Youth and the magical object at the heart of it. And don't worry. If I find it, I'll gladly hand the blasted thing over to you after she moves on."

Seeing the disbelief on Diana's face, he said, "I don't know why I'm telling you all this. I can see you don't trust me, so we might as well go our separate ways."

Trying to calm him down, Jane asked, "Do ye know where the Fountain is?"

"Not really, but I believe I can find it – just like I did the Palantir."

Jane glared at Diana as she asked, "How can we help? Because I'm going with ye."

"I can't let you do that," Alex said. "You've seen what happens around me. It's too dangerous. Besides, I have no idea how I'll do it, nor how long it will take."

"Which is all the more reason why ye need our help," Jane replied.

Alex slumped in the seat. "I'm not lying when I say it would be great to have your company, but …."

"But nothing. I'm coming with ye."

Jane started to step into the canoe, but Diana grabbed her arm before she could get in. "You can't be serious," Diana cried out.

Jane pulled away. "Are ye coming, or not?"

"You sound almost as crazy as he does. Most adults couldn't survive what he's planning to do." Diana turned on Alex. "You have no money and no gear.

"I've got credit and debit cards in my pack for expenses."

"Well, but there's no way you can cross the Gulf of Mexico and the Caribbean to search for the Fountain of Youth in nothing but this canoe. It would be suicide."

"I can't expect you to understand, because I don't understand it myself, but I'm sure I'll get help when I need it. At least I want to believe it's true. Otherwise, I'd be too scared to do anything."

Before Alex could stop her from sitting on Kukulcan, Jane stepped into the canoe and sat down on the front seat. He thought about saying something but decided against it since she couldn't see or feel him.

"Are ye coming?" Jane asked Diana. "We better get going while we still have daylight."

Diana took a deep breath. "I can't believe I'm going to do this. But if you're going after one of the Maqlû, then I'm duty-bound to go after it too." Diana stepped in and sat down on Itzamm, adding, "I might not be comfortable with everything that's going on, but I have to admit I've never felt more alive. So, let's go."

CHAPTER 4
LIGHT DESPITE THE DARKNESS

Constance Marley returned to Lamanai shortly before sunset and climbed the hill to Sophie Bennet's tent. The lead archeologist on the dig was resting outside and looked up hopefully as she approached. Constance shook her head at the hopeful look from her boss and said, "The boat pilot showed me where he dropped the girls off, but the jungle is so thick there that I'm pretty sure they didn't go inland. After that, we went to Corozal – but I didn't see any sign of them along the way. I don't know where he's taken the girls, but since he's got a canoe, he can go almost anywhere."

"What could that boy want with them?" Sophie asked.

"I don't know, but from what the guide said, he tried talking the girls out of going with him. It was Jane who encouraged your daughter to join him in whatever scheme he's got going." Constance gently laid a hand on Sophie's shoulder. "I promise you; we won't stop until we find your daughter. I've alerted the local authorities and arranged for several boats to be at our disposal first thing tomorrow morning to continue the search. Now, get some rest – you need it."

As soon as Constance left the tent, Sophie dropped her head into her hands, trying to deal with the shock of her daughter running off. She instantly regretted the movement as fireworks seemed to explode inside her head. Sophie slowly sat up, closed her eyes, and waited until the pain subsided before she picked up a hand mirror to look at her bruises. She winced when she saw her face had turned into an ugly collage of bandages, broken by splotches of swollen purple and yellow skin.

Knowing she couldn't hide the news any longer, Sophie pushed herself up and shuffled over to the small scrying dish she kept in her tent. Forcing her nausea down, she pulled off the white linen cloth covering it and chanted the words that brought the silvery waters to life.

"By Water, Earth, Fire, and Air
I call for Elizabeth to answer me."

She only had to wait a few minutes until Elizabeth Adler, the High Priestess of the Salem Grove, appeared on the surface. Elizabeth took one look at Sophie's ghastly pallor and said, "You should be lying down. Constance could have updated me."

"I'm too worried about Diana to lay down. I'll be fine once we find the girls."

Elizabeth studied Sophie's haggard face briefly before saying, "What have you learned?"

"The good news is, they were fine a few hours ago. Apparently, Jane talked one of the riverboat guides into taking her and my daughter downriver this morning. From what I can tell, it was Jane who convinced Diana to go with her, but I'm sure it all has something to do with your grandson.

"Constance has been out all day looking for them but had to stop the search because of darkness. All we know for sure right now is that the girls asked the boat pilot to stop along the river where a dark-skinned boy with a pair of long black braids was waiting. It had to be your grandson. The pilot said that despite repeatedly urging the girls to come back with him, they chose not to."

"How could he still be alive?" Elizabeth wondered. "An entire hill collapsed on him. And if he did survive, then what's he doing running away with Jane and Diana?"

"I don't know." Sophie paused, her eyes growing wide. "Unless he set all this up as a diversion to mask his real intentions. Maybe he found the Palantir and is trying to escape."

"How could he have found the Palantir and created such an elaborate cover-up? He's not even fourteen."

"Well, he probably didn't do it by himself. Think about it. How did he break into your study? How did he find the *Sibylline Book* for the Palantir? Even stranger, how did he open it? He must be getting help from some powerful warlock." Sophie paused, a steely-eyed look coming into her eyes. "I'm warning you, if that boy harms my daughter, I'll kill him. I don't care what you or Lady Yvaine say."

"You won't get any argument from me, but let's hope it's just a misunderstanding because I shudder to think what would happen if you're right." Elizabeth took a deep breath as if to fortify herself. "Do whatever you have to do to find them. Cost is not an issue. I'll speak to Lady Yvaine about this and see if she has any connections that might help you. For now, let Constance do the work. You need to get better, so you can be prepared for whatever lies ahead."

Sophie nodded before waving her hand over the scrying dish to break the connection.

***

Elizabeth stood for some time thinking about what she'd learned. Her feelings were torn between fears her grandson was a warlock and relief that her only living relative was still alive. She took a deep breath, then called Lady Yvaine, the leader of the Bandruí order.

She never tired of watching the yellow, magenta, and blue colors shooting into the scrying dish, bringing the silvery liquid to life. Elizabeth stared as the mixture swirled in a counterclockwise direction, forming a whirling rainbow for a few seconds before slowing to show Lady Yvaine's youthful face.

"What news do you have?" Yvaine asked.

Elizabeth twisted her hands nervously as she gave an update on what she'd learned about the latest events in Lamanai. She ended by saying, "I'm confused about what to do with my grandson. I talked with his grandfather Ignacio, who surprised me. He wasn't nearly as concerned about the boy's disappearance as I thought he'd be. In fact, for just a second, I thought he sounded pleased. But I could be imagining it. What I'm concerned about is, what if Sophie's right and he's found the Palantir? That would mean he has to be working with some warlock."

"We've talked about this before," Yvaine said. "Although the circumstantial evidence is pretty damning, you still don't have any proof he's a warlock. And even if what you fear is true, what would he do with the object? The Maqlû are nearly impossible to master, and Sophie has the book. I don't think your grandson stealing the Palantir is our most immediate concern."

"I hear you," Elizabeth said. "But I don't see how all of this could happen unless he's a warlock."

"What if he's just different?" Yvaine countered. "We must continue studying him rather than taking any irrevocable actions."

"You're the only one who thinks that."

"That might be, but I insist that we follow our rules about warlocks. I want to see how this plays out."

The two women stared at each other through the scrying dish until Yvaine said, "Let's get back to our top priority – finding the girls. Do whatever it takes to find them, but I insist that no harm comes to your grandson. I want you to bring him to me when you find him. I must know the truth, and I can't do that unless I see him face-to-face."

"As you wish." Elizabeth bowed her head, then waved her hand over the scrying dish to close the communication.

CHAPTER 5
THEY'RE HERE

Brother Robert Stafford could not have looked less like his older brother. With his short, stout stature, tonsure haircut, and plain brown robes, he was the polar opposite of Sydney Carton, who was tall and trim, with thick grey hair and glasses.

"Do you think she'll see us?" Carton asked. "You two didn't exactly part on good terms."

"It's been a long time, but I'm sure she's gotten over it," Stafford replied as he banged the lion head brass knocker on the great oaken doors. A couple of minutes later, one of the doors silently opened, and a middle-aged woman appeared. She stared at the two brothers but said nothing.

"We'd like to see your mistress," Stafford said.

"Lady Yvaine knows you're here," the woman replied.

Stafford nodded. "Ah, so that's what she's calling herself now. Well, we'd still like to talk to her. We have some urgent business with her."

The door opened, and a tall, olive-skinned woman with dark brunette hair and haunting grey eyes appeared and said, "I'll take care of this."

Yvaine waited until the other woman was out of sight, before saying, "You have some nerve to come here. What do you want?"

"May we come inside?" Stafford asked. "We have something to discuss of mutual interest."

"Your brother can come in, but not you. Whatever you have to say, you can say it out here."

Stafford clenched his hands to control his anger. Then he took a deep breath and said, "Fine. I believe you have a book of mine, and I'd like you to return it."

Yvaine sniffed. "The book isn't yours. You stole it."

"If I remember correctly," Stafford said, "you helped me. Besides, that was a long time ago. It belongs to me now, and I want it back."

"If it's so precious to you, why did you give it to the boy in the first place?"

Stafford blushed. "I was so flustered that he broke through my security measures that I wasn't thinking straight, which is why I'd like you to return it now."

"Enk…, I mean Robert. Get over your ego. You'll be more likely to get what you're looking for if you tell her the truth." When his brother didn't respond, Carton said, "The truth is, Lady Yvaine, he has no idea how the boy talked him out of the book. His only explanation is that the boy used some powerful black magic to overcome him – something that he hasn't seen in ages."

"I'll admit that the boy has a knack for sowing chaos wherever he goes, but I assure you the book is in safe hands," Yvaine said. "He gave it to his grandmother, just as you asked him to. Sophie Bennet has it now on a dig site in Lamanai."

"No. That's where you're wrong," Stafford said. "It isn't in safe hands if that boy is around it. He's dangerous. I'm sure he's out to get the Palantir. If he can put a spell on me, and weasel into your order's good graces, then I wouldn't put anything past him. Just think of what he could do with one of the Maqlû."

The implication of Yvaine's words suddenly hit him, and he said, "Wait. Go back. What is your order doing with the Palantir book in Lamanai?"

"That's where the book indicated the object was," Yvaine replied.

"Are you saying you were able to open one of the *Sibylline Books*?" Stafford asked.

Too late, Yvaine realized she'd disclosed more than she'd intended. Trying to seem nonchalant about it, she replied, "There was a map in the back of the book that indicated we could find the Palantir in Lamanai."

"But how did you open it?" Stafford asked. "Nobody's ever been able to open one of them."

Yvaine raised an eyebrow as if to say it was an impertinent question.

Carton, who'd been intently studying Yvaine throughout the conversation, said, "The boy managed it. Didn't he?"

Surprised at his brother's question, Stafford studied Yvaine, looking for a reaction. He was disappointed, though, when she didn't bat an eyelash. After a long silence, Stafford said, "This just reinforces our concerns about that boy. What are you going to do about him?"

"You have concerns about him, little brother," Carton said. "I know nothing about him and don't want to make any decisions until I know him better. Besides, he's only a boy. How dangerous can he be?"

"Have you heard nothing of what I've said?" Stafford asked. "Remember, he broke into Elizabeth's study. Then he circumvented my defenses and bewitched me. And to top it all, he unlocks one of the *Sibylline Books*. Aren't you worried that someone like

Gilgamesh is manipulating him? Only he would have this type of power." Stafford turned back to Yvaine. "Look, we're on the same side. Let's work together on this. I believe the boy is dangerous, and we need to stop him before he can do any more harm."

Carton shook his head. "I still disagree with you, brother. I know I have no data to back me up, but I feel like there's something else afoot. Rather than charging off and destroying things, I strongly suggest we proceed with caution. Let's learn more about him, and whatever else is going on, before we take any irrevocable action."

"This may all be a moot issue," Yvaine said. "The boy has disappeared from our dig site and taken two of our apprentices. We have no idea where he is."

No one spoke until Stafford said, "I know two men who have a knack for finding people and objects. I can ask them to help in your search."

Yvaine hesitated before replying, "No thank you. Your methods tend to be a little rougher than I like."

"We used to be aligned very closely. Can't we renew that partnership?" Stafford asked.

Yvaine blushed but quickly regained her calm. "You have different memories of our parting. We split because you continued to pay allegiance to Gilgamesh, even when it was clear that all he wanted was more power. I'm not sure he ever truly believed in our avowed goal of stealing the objects to help humanity."

"If you remember, I came to regret the alliance too and split with him long ago," Stafford said. "Ever since, I've been silently on your side, trying to stop that ego maniac's delusions of grandeur."

"Funny. I don't recall you ever showing up on any battlefield, fighting him like we did."

"We have chosen to fight the battle differently," Stafford replied. "We have recruited and sheltered those he would have manipulated and used for his purposes."

Yvaine rolled her eyes and abruptly changed the subject. "Which of our former acquaintances are you suggesting track him down?"

Stafford smiled for the first time since he arrived at Stormhold Mansion. "I'm talking about Utnapishtim and Urshanabi. You can't have objections to them."

"Of course not. They're the most decent people in our whole lot. But I'm surprised you'd pick them. They don't seem to be an obvious choice, given your concerns. They're somebody I'd trust."

Stafford smiled. "Exactly. So, will you help us by providing information on the boy's whereabouts?"

"I'll consider it."

"Fair enough. Here's my card. Contact me any time." Stafford bowed and said, "Good day, Milady."

Yvaine dipped her head in response and stepped back inside, closing the door behind her.

As they walked away, Carton said, "You surprise me. I thought, especially hearing what else the boy has done, that you'd be even more set on eliminating him."

Stafford smiled grimly. "I am."

"What about what you promised, Lady Yvaine?"

"I will do as I promised and ask Utnapishtim and Urshanabi to track the boy down. I have full confidence they'll find him. However, that doesn't mean I won't be simultaneously using other resources to eliminate him."

CHAPTER 6
MARCO POLO

For the next few hours, the trio headed steadily north, ducking into the heavy brush beside the river every time they heard a motorboat approaching. Alex held his breath each time he saw Constance pass by, worried she'd spot them and force them to return. But the only times they encountered anyone was when they came upon local fishing boats. Then, Diana and Jane would hastily grab the paddles from the two Mayan ghosts and use them until they were out of sight.

They reached Corozal, at the mouth of the New River, by mid-afternoon. Seeing a cell phone tower, Diana said, "If I hadn't fallen into the river, I could call my mom and tell her we're all right. I guess I'll have to find a pay phone so I can call her."

Alex shook his head. "You can call her if you want, but I'll leave you behind."

"Are you kidding? Why can't I tell her we're all right?"

"Because, as soon as you call her, she'll have someone come searching for us and stop me from going on. I've gone through too much already to give up so soon. Why do you think we hid every time we heard engines?"

Diana didn't reply. When they pulled up to a small dock, she cleared her throat and said, "If I'm going to do this, I need some things. I wasn't planning on being gone for days. Can I borrow some money?"

"Don't worry about it," Alex replied. "I'll pay for the supplies. What do you need?"

Diana's face turned bright red. In a nearly inaudible voice, she said, "I'd like to do my own shopping."

Alex was about to say something when Jane laid a hand on Alex's arm. "I think it would be best if ye let us get everything while ye stay here with the canoe. We need some things like, uh … toothbrushes, sunscreen, water, toilet paper, and, uh … other personal items. We'll be back soon," she said, holding her hand out for money.

As they left the dock, Diana whispered, "Thank you. I didn't know what to tell him. I'm too used to being at an all-girls school where you don't have to worry about what boys think.

"No problem, but ye need to decide if ye're all in on this quest. As crazy as it sounds, if we're going to search for the object at the heart of the Fountain of Youth legend, then we need to trust him. And unfortunately, that means ye can't call your mom. Are ye willing to do that? There's no shame if ye don't." When she didn't get an answer, Jane said, "I'll take that as a yes. If it makes ye feel any better, I can't believe I agreed to go on this escapade. It's like I'm being swept up in his madness."

Diana smiled. "Hearing you say this is crazy makes me feel better. But as much as I like the freedom and excitement of this, I hate keeping my mom in the dark. I'm sure she's already going out of her mind with worry about us."

"Maybe, but I'm sure the boat captain has already told her what happened when we found Alex. Besides, if we can find one of the Maqlû, she'll forgive everything." Jane jerked a thumb back towards the canoe. "Except him."

Diana blushed at the criticism of her mother but didn't argue.

As they were getting back in the canoe after buying supplies, Jane said, "The money won't last forever. What are we going to do when ye run out?"

"It's not a problem. Like I've told you before, I have a credit card and plenty of money in the bank, thanks to my parents' life insurance policy. Plus, my grandpa's putting all the money I get from social security survivor benefits in there too, so we're good," Alex replied.

After crossing Corozal Bay, they headed east, pulling into a small cove with a long sandy beach some time later. Diana looked around and asked, "Why are we stopping here?"

"It's getting late," Alex said, "so I thought we should find a place to sleep. The sand is soft here and should make a decent bed."

"I think we should find a sheltered area," Jane said. "Remember, this is the rainy season. We've been lucky not to get soaked today, but I don't want to keep tempting fate."

It was dark by the time they found a small thicket with a grassy opening underneath it. Alex pulled a raincoat out of his pack and attached it to the top of the branches, finishing just before a brief rainstorm hit.

As he crawled into the makeshift shelter, Alex asked, "Why couldn't you do some of your magic and make us a shelter?"

"We can't just create things," Diana replied. "Remember when I told you that what you call magic is just us manipulating the environment around us? It's like my hand-held fire. All I'm doing is pulling enough heat out of the atmosphere where it can mix with the oxygen in the air, and voilà, I have flames."

"Can ye talk about this tomorrow? I don't know about ye two," Jane said, "but I'm exhausted and want to sleep. And this place is surprisingly snug."

Neither Alex nor Diana argued, and soon all were asleep.

They left early the next day and continued along the bay's shoreline until it turned south. It wasn't long before a manatee came alongside their canoe and playfully swam with them for some distance. When it finally turned away, Diana tapped Alex on the shoulder. "If you're searching for the Fountain of Youth, why are you heading this way? Almost every myth about it has placed it east of here, including Africa, India, North America, the Caribbean, especially Florida, and the Bimini Islands."

"This feels like the right direction," Alex replied. "Don't ask me why. It just does."

"Assuming you know where we're going, there's another issue I'm worried about," Diana said. "We're still inside Belize's barrier reef. It's the second-largest reef system in the world and is protecting us from the bigger ocean waves. Once we get outside of it, then we're in the Gulf of Honduras, and I hate to break it to you, but this canoe can't handle the deeper waters. Which leads me to wonder if you have any idea how dangerous this quest of yours is – because nobody in their right mind would wander around like this, trying to find some myth."

"I'm looking for a different way to get there, so bear with me."

He was silent for some time, and when he spoke again, it was in a much more somber tone. "I have to tell you guys that I feel guilty about not stopping you from coming. But I was too scared to do this on my own."

"I can't imagine what ye're going through," Jane said. "But, we're here for ye."

Diana grumbled something, but Alex ignored it and said, "My mother gave me only one piece of advice in her life – right before she died. She told me to make sure I could live with the consequences of my choices. So, you should know that since I destroyed the Palantir, ruining Deborah's chances of moving on, I feel compelled to make it up to her by finding the Fountain of Youth."

"I think that's very noble of ye," Jane said. "And I have to say that, so far, this trip isn't all bad. It's like we're going on some great adventure while simultaneously getting us away from all that boring dig work in Lamanai. If ye don't find a ride to the Caribbean, we can at least head to Belize City, where we can easily get a ride back to Lamanai."

As if the fates were mocking Jane, Alex felt the ankh suddenly yank him towards the shore. Ignoring the girls' questions, he directed the Mayan ghosts to put in a small cove they were passing. Alex jumped out as soon as the boat ran aground and pointed towards a small trail that led inland. "We need to go this way."

"I thought ye wanted to go to the Caribbean," Jane said. "Why are ye changing course all of a sudden?"

Alex started reaching for his ankh but stopped before giving away its existence. He looked up at the small hill before them and replied, "I can't explain it, but my instincts tell me we should go this way."

"That's a scary thought," Diana said. "Aren't you afraid of what's up there?"

"Of course, I'm scared. But I've found that in the last couple of months, I'm usually better off following my instincts and learning what troubles are ahead rather than being surprised."

"Well, in case you see something scary that I can't see – don't tell me about it," Diana replied. "That way, I can still pretend everything's okay."

Jane piped up, saying, "I'd prefer to know, so maybe ye can tell Diana to close her ears."

Alex chuckled. "Deal."

"Be serious for a minute," Diana said, halting. "I don't want to keep looking for some myth unless I know more about what you've been doing. Why should I trust you'll find the Fountain?"

"What do you want to know?" Alex asked.

"How did you survive back in Lamanai? Jane and I barely had time to get out before the temple collapsed."

Alex shrugged. "I thought I was a goner when that boulder slipped off the stairs, but I was lucky and survived the fall."

Jane snorted and mumbled, "I bet there's more to the story."

"What did you say?" Diana asked.

"Nothing. Go on, Alex. Ye were saying."

"Well, then Ixchel, that Mayan girl I told you about, and a Viking ghost named Thorfinn, the owner of the sword we found, helped me escape."

"Why would ghosts do that for ye?" Jane asked

"They hoped I could help them move on."

"But why you?" Diana asked.

"Good question, but I don't know the answer. It's been happening to me a lot lately."

"Is that how ye knew where Diana was a couple of nights ago?" Jane asked.

"No, that was a different ghost. An archeologist slash spy named Sylvanus Morley warned me of the attack…."

"What attack?" Diana asked.

"The one where a bunch of the Mayan ghost king's soldiers destroyed the camp and kidnapped you," Alex replied.

Diana's eyes narrowed. "Everybody I talked to thought it was a freak storm."

Alex shook his head. "Nope. The king and that Puritan ghost were trying to get my attention. They kidnapped you, so I'd chase after them. I think they thought it would be easier to get rid of me on their turf than in the world of the living."

"How can that be? My mom said you stayed with her until the medic arrived. There's no way you could have followed them.

"I didn't. I saw the ghosts kidnap you but waited until Mary Seacole arrived and stabilized your mom before I went after you. I figured the ghosts had taken you to the Moon Temple, so I headed there. Jane caught me as I was leaving camp."

Diana scowled at Alex. "I don't want to believe any of it, except it explains a lot of the strange stuff that's happened. I'm dying to know, though, where did you learn to speak so many foreign languages? My mom made me listen to some audio of the Mayan language on the way down here. I'm no expert, but it sounded like you were speaking fluent ancient Mayan down in the cave and with our ghost guides. You also spoke some language that sounded like one of the Scandinavian tongues."

"I have no idea what you're talking about," Alex replied. "I talk to them just like I am with you."

"Well, that's not what comes out of yer mouth," Jane said.

Alex frowned. "That doesn't make any sense. The only foreign language I've ever taken was Spanish, and I sucked at it. This isn't getting us anywhere, though. I think we should keep going and find out what's ahead. You can ask me more questions later."

Diana looked like she was about to prolong the discussion, but all she said was, "You're not off the hook yet, bub. I still have lots of questions."

Alex grinned. "I would have expected no less from you."

The trio moved inland and were just starting to ascend the trail when Jane asked, "Where are the spirits leading us?"

"They're not coming," Alex replied.

"Are they just leaving us out here in the middle of nowhere?" Diana asked.

"They're going to hang around for a while, in case we need them again." He resumed heading up the path but quickly noticed that neither girl was moving. Alex stopped and turned. "It'll be okay. I never expected them to come all the way with us."

Diana rolled her eyes and grumbled, "Of course not. That would make things easier." Seeing Jane glaring at her, she shrugged and headed after Alex.

The trail rose gently in elevation, running parallel to the coastline until it dead-ended in a small opening surrounded by sheer rock walls. A ten-foot-high waterfall shot straight out of the wall on the far side, emptying into a pond that took up most of the open area. The waterfall's roar echoed off the rocks, making it hard to hold a conversation.

Thinking of how grubby he felt, Alex shouted, "Last one in gets thrown to the crocodiles!" He dropped his pack, kicked off his boots, and dove in. Alex swam over to the falls and pulled himself up onto a rock ledge at the base, where the thundering water hammered at him.

Diana swam up beside him and shouted, "What's the matter? Are you too wimpy to go into the waterfall?"

Alex gave her a playful splash. "Who are you calling a wimp, slowpoke?"

Without replying, Diana grabbed his arm and pulled him into the pond.

By the time Alex surfaced, sputtering and wiping the water out of his eyes, Diana had pulled herself onto the ledge.

Alex grinned and pulled Diana in, then crawled up onto the shelf. Despite the torrent pounding on him, he pushed through the wall of water and tumbled into darkness.

It took him a few seconds before his eyes adjusted to the dimly lit conditions. When he could see again, he stood up and looked around in wonder at the small grotto he was in. It was almost ten feet high and twice as deep, with a perfectly smooth floor. He made a slow circuit around, finding openings at the side and back of the room.

Diana surfaced a second after he'd disappeared behind the falls, coughing up water and laughing. She wiped the water out of her eyes and looked around for Alex but didn't see him.

"Alex?" She blinked. "Alex!" She spun around; nothing. She dove back into the pond, looking to see if he was drowning, but didn't see any signs of him. When she resurfaced, she looked at Jane and shouted, "Where did he go?"

Jane, who was sitting on the bank, kicking her feet in the water, pointed at the waterfall.

A few seconds later, a grinning disembodied head poked out of the waterfall. "You gotta see this!" Alex shouted.

"Wait for me," Diana called out, but Alex had already disappeared again. She headed to where his head had appeared, crawled onto the ledge, and followed him in. Diana glanced around, but the temperature difference from outside was so great she wrapped her arms around her side and said, "It's cold in here. I'm going back into the sunshine to warm up."

Alex didn't see her leave as a blast of frigid air distracted him. He saw a head pop through the pounding water, look around, then disappear. Worried that someone had followed them, he ran towards where he'd seen the head but tripped and fell into the pond, scraping his leg on the sharp rock edge. When he resurfaced, he tried swimming to the shore, but the pain was too intense for him to kick.

Seeing blood spreading through the pond, Jane let out a yelp and jumped in. She helped Alex to the side, then got out and pulled him ashore with Diana's help. The movement caused Alex to see stars momentarily. When he opened his eyes again, he saw Jane kneeling beside him, looking worriedly at his bloodied hand covering the wound.

Jane nodded at his leg. "Pull yer pants down so I can see yer cut."

Alex reflexively put a second hand over the cut as if it would shield him from embarrassment.

"Relax," Jane said. "Ye don't have anything I haven't seen before, but I need to see yer cut, and I can't do it if yer wearing yer pants. Now drop 'em."

Blushing, Alex pulled his pants below his knees.

When he saw Jane grimace, he asked, "What is it?"

"You've got a two-inch-long slice that will need a few stitches, but I think I can take care of it without too much problem." Jane searched through the medicine kit she had brought with her, but a minute later, she threw her hands in the air and yelled, "Damnations!"

"What's wrong?" Diana asked.

"I forgot to pack the antiseptic when I was putting this kit together yesterday morning and didn't think to buy extra medical supplies in Corozal. Well, I'll jest have to make do." She pulled a water bottle from her pack, rinsed off the cut, and placed Alex's hand over the gash. "Put pressure on your thigh while I get something to stop an infection from happening. I saw some plants a little way back on the trail that I can use as an antiseptic and a numbing agent. I'll be right back."

"Is she really going to bandage me up with plants?" Alex asked Diana.

"Relax," Diana said. "Even though she's only a couple of years older than us, everyone considers Jane the best healer in our order. She's gifted. It's almost like she's somehow figured out how to use magic in her healing methods."

"Wait, you don't use magic on wounds? Why not?"

"Magic is like a blunt instrument compared to the complexity of a human body," Diana replied. "It's why healing is such a respected skill in our order, and as I said, Jane's the best. You're lucky she's here."

Jane was gone for only a few minutes. When she got back, she poured some more water on the wound. Then she ground the leaves and flowers she'd collected between two rocks, mixing them into a fine paste, before sprinkling her poultice on the wound.

Alex felt a tingling sensation around the wound and was about to ask what was causing it when Jane shoved a rubbery stick into his mouth and said, "Clamp down on this while I sew ye back up. It will sting a little, but I can't help it. I wasn't prepared for this type of emergency. Now hold still."

Alex's eyes widened when he saw Jane threading a sharp hook with a fine thread and realized what she was going to do with it. The pain from the needle digging into his flesh, again and again, was almost too much to bear, causing him to clench his fists and arch his back.

Without looking up, Jane said, "I know this hurts, but try to relax. The more you tense up, the worse the pain. Just focus on the fact that it'll all be over soon."

True to her word, Jane was winding some gauze around his leg before he realized she was done sewing. After tying it off, she picked up the bottom of Alex's shirt and tried ripping a strip off.

He grabbed her arm and yelled, "What are you doing? That's my favorite t-shirt. And right now, it's also the only one I have."

"I need to put more pressure on the wound," Jane said. "Since I don't have a lot of gauze and don't know when I'll get more, I'm conserving it and using your shirt."

"What will I wear?" Alex wailed.

Jane ignored his question and asked Diana to find something sharp to cut with.

Diana nodded and started rummaging around Alex's pack. Without looking up, she said, "Hey, I've already lost two cell phones chasing after you. The least you could do to repay me is give up some of your shirt." She found a knife and cut off the bottom couple of inches of his shirt before handing the strip to Jane.

After sliding the strip underneath Alex's leg, Jane tied the ends of his shirt into a knot over the bandaged wound. Looking at her handiwork, she said, "As long as we keep yer bandage and wound clean, yer cut should heal with no problems. Let's hope this place has supercharged mineral water to aid in yer healing. But ye need to be more careful in the future. Ye can't go around thinking you're immortal."

Alex grinned. "Yes, Mom."

Shaking her finger at him, Jane playfully responded, "Ye say that again, and I'll leave ye to fix yer own cuts and bruises. From what I've seen, that won't end very pretty."

The three sat on the grass for a while, letting their clothing dry. After a few minutes, Diana asked, "So now what, oh fearless leader?"

"I saw an opening behind the waterfall," Alex replied. "I think that's where the path goes,"

"Exactly what are you looking for?" she asked.

"I don't know, but it feels like the right way." He stood up and winced as he pulled his beat-up camo pants over the wound. Grabbing his gear, he led them through the side entrance of the waterfall he'd noticed earlier and then through the back opening.

They'd gone only a short distance when the trail leveled off into a large open area with a thick green carpet of plants. Alex could hear the faint sound of waves breaking on rocks but didn't think anything of it as he stepped out onto the green mass. To his surprise, he found it was spongy and difficult to walk on, as his feet kept sinking into the ground cover. A vague uneasiness came across Alex. "Stay where you are," he called back. "This place doesn't feel right."

Diana stood at the edge of the opening and called out, "What's wrong?"

Alex waved off her question as his thoughts were on the ankh, which had suddenly turned cold against his skin. Figuring something was wrong, he decided to turn around and go back. As he did, his foot slipped below the surface.

Feeling like he was sinking into a vegetative quicksand, Alex twisted around and grabbed a vine to stop from falling further into the ground. His motion, however, had the effect of sending him further into the living mass. His feet suddenly slipped through, and he found himself lying on the ground cover, hanging onto a thick vine with his feet dangling in midair. "Get back!" he shouted. "There's some sort of hole under this stuff."

CHAPTER 7
DOWN THE RABBIT HOLE

"But I'm already on the open space," Diana wailed as one leg sank into the green mass.

Jane called out, "Listen to me, Diana. It'll be okay if ye do what I tell ye to. The first thing I want ye to do is slowly sit down and lie back. Then, when yer lying down, slowly roll onto yer stomach and spread yer arms out, so ye can distribute yer weight better. Then crawl back towards me."

Diana completely forgot about Alex's situation as she followed Jane's instructions. It seemed like forever before she left the shifting green mass and crawled back onto solid ground, where she collapsed, relieved her ordeal was over.

She only got a couple of seconds reprieve, though, before Jane grabbed her shoulders and shook her. "Ye've got to get up and use yer magic to help Alex. He's barely holding on, and it's not safe for us to go out there to help him."

Diana struggled to her knees and turned around to Alex. She gasped when she saw him hanging onto a vine, with only his torso above the mat. "Give me a second. I've got to recall a growing spell," Diana said as she reached into her pouch to pull out her talisman. Closing her eyes, she stretched out her senses, searching the plants for something she could use. Finding a large vine, she threw out her arms and chanted,

"Water, xylem, energy flow
flourish faster,
vine, please grow."

She pulled all the energy, moisture, and nutrients from the plants around it and sent them into the large tuber, encouraging it to grow towards Alex.

Not understanding what Diana was doing, Alex shouted, "I need some help. Is there a rope or something you can throw me?"

"Hang on. Diana's trying to help ye," Jane yelled.

Unwilling to wait, Alex tried to get more of his weight on top of the green carpet. He reached as far as he could on the vine and pulled. Instead of holding fast, though, the vine loosened. Panicked, Alex kicked his legs, hoping to get his hips up onto the surface, but the kick caused him to slip backwards even more. He jerked to a stop with his armpits at the edge of the hole.

Diana opened her eyes to check on the progress of the vine's growth. She was pleased to see her spell was working but worried it was still several feet away from Alex. Diana stared into his hazel eyes and called out, "Grab onto the vine I'm sending you. I'll pull you out."

Chanting the spell under her breath over and over, Diana watched as the woody tendril continued its slow movement towards Alex. She started relaxing when she saw it coiling around his wrist but screamed when Alex suddenly jerked his hand away and plunged out of sight. Without thinking of the implications, she started crawling back onto the mat.

Jane grabbed her legs and pulled her back, saying, "Ye can't go out there. It's too dangerous."

Diana slumped on the ground and silently cried. She didn't get to wallow in misery long, as seconds later Jane shook her shoulders, saying, "Get ahold of yerself. We need to help Alex, and ye are the only one who can do it. I need ye to do the same spell as ye did for Alex, but do it with me on the end of the vine."

Diana stumbled to her feet. "What are you talking about?"

Jane, who was looking around for a sturdy vine, didn't answer immediately. Spotting a long vine thicker than her wrist, she picked it up and leaned back, tugging at it as hard as she could. It barely budged. Relieved it could hold her weight, she bent down and looked Diana in the eyes, asking, "Do ye think you can grow this vine another hundred feet?"

"Probably, but you're crazy to go after him. You don't know what's down there."

"I know, but I've got to try. I figure it can't be too far down. It's probably only a cenote."

Diana hesitated before nodding. "What happens if you find him? How are you going to get back up?"

"I was counting on ye pulling us up one at a time with yer magic. Do ye think ye can do that?"

Again, Diana hesitated. She looked around and spotted a large tree a short distance away. Talking more to herself than Jane, she said, "I can if you take the vine you have on now and wrap it around the tree, then around you. That way, I can lower you down with it securely wrapped around something that won't move. When it's time to pull you up, I'll wrap the vine back around the tree. Are you sure it'll hold your weight?"

"Pretty sure. When I get down there, we'll have to communicate by tugging on the vine. So, keep yer hand on it at all times to make sure ye get my signal."

"What's the signal?"

"I'll tug it twice to let ye know when I've reached the bottom, three times to pull me up. Got that?"

Diana nodded, then chanted the same spell she'd used to help Alex. Jane waited till there was some slack in the vine, then walked towards the tree trunk as fast as the vine grew. After wrapping it around the tree, she returned to the mat and backed on. As the vine lengthened, Jane kept stepping back until her feet hit the hole Alex had disappeared into. She looped the vine around her forearm, then slipped below the mat.

It seemed like forever before Diana finally felt the two tugs letting her know Jane had reached the bottom of whatever was below. A growl caused her to whirl around so fast that she tumbled backwards into the matting. She looked for where the sound had come from and didn't find anything. It wasn't until she heard a second growl that she spotted a jaguar lying in the crook of a tree ten feet up. Before she could move, the big cat jumped to the ground and crouched, as if waiting to pounce.

Wanting to escape the jaguar, Diana grabbed a thick vine next to her and chanted the same spell she'd already used twice. The tangled vines around her started moving as if they were in a cobra dance, separating from each other until she could see the hole Jane and Alex had disappeared through.

Diana looked the jaguar in its eyes as the vine grew into a pile at her feet. Seeing the big cat inching forward, she hurriedly wrapped the end of the vine around her waist and arm. Then, before her courage failed her, she ran towards the opening and jumped through.

52

CHAPTER 8
THE FANCY

Alex jerked to a stop, nearly losing his grip when he saw he was hanging fifty feet above a large body of water. Feeling the vine dangling between his feet, he wrapped his legs around it and started clambering up. But he only managed to climb several feet before it loosened, and he dropped again. The vine hit its full extension and jerked to a sudden stop. Alex bounced, and for a moment, felt weightless. Then gravity caught up, and he resumed his descent.

The vine snapped when it hit its full length, sending Alex plummeting. He struggled to right himself, managing to straighten his legs and clap his arms to his sides just before he slammed into the water. His momentum drove him far below the surface until the natural buoyancy of the seawater had time to stop his descent.

He opened his eyes to orient himself but quickly shut them against the stinging saltwater. With his lungs bursting, he kicked to the surface and tried gulping in air, but a wave hit him in the face and caused him to swallow a mouthful of water. His stomach recoiled, causing him to throw up. Alex turned around and waited until the next wave broke over him before he tried breathing again.

When he finally caught his breath, he swam for the beach. He tried standing as soon as he ran aground, but a wave caught him and knocked him over. Two more waves slammed into him before he finally stumbled ashore, where he promptly collapsed.

It was some time before he managed to sit up and look around. His heart momentarily sank when he didn't see a way out of what looked like a small cove with towering fifty-foot-high cliffs on three sides and a giant green curtain, with the same matting he'd fallen through, blocking the fourth side. But what caught his attention was a large, three-masted sailing ship, rocking peacefully at anchor in the middle of the cove.

Images of sailing the seven seas flitted through his mind for a few seconds before he quickly realized it was more probable that he'd accidentally discovered a drug cartel's secret hideaway. The thought sent Alex stumbling across the narrow white sandy beach, frantically looking for a hiding place. He found a small cave, crawled in, and studied the ship, looking for activity. After several minutes, with no sign of movement, Alex decided it was safe to come out and explore.

He'd only taken a few steps when he noticed Jane slowly descending into the cove. Alex called out and ran towards the beach, near where she was coming down. When she was a few feet above the water, she let go. Jane quickly surfaced, gave the vine a couple of hard tugs then swam ashore.

Alex called out as she emerged from the waves, "What are you doing down here? There's no way of getting out. Besides, I fear we might have accidentally stumbled onto some drug smuggling operation."

"What are you talking about?" Jane asked. "It doesn't look like there's anybody around."

He was about to point out the sailing ship a hundred yards away when a scream from above distracted him. Looking up, he saw Diana falling through the same hole he and Jane had come through. The vine she'd wrapped around her hit its end, causing Diana to bounce up a few feet before resuming her plunge. When she hit the end, the vine split and she plunged into the water. She quickly popped above the surface and started swimming for shore. A minute later, Diana plopped down onto the sand at their feet.

Jane was the first to get over the shock of Diana's sudden appearance. "What are ye doing down here? I thought ye were going to stay on top and pull us up."

Diana looked up. "I would have, except some jaguar wanted to snack on me."

"I appreciate you two trying to help me, but we've got to get out of here," Alex said. "We're in danger."

Jane did a slow turn. "What are ye talking about? It seems pretty idyllic, except we're stuck down here."

"Can't you see it?" Alex pointed to the ship, gently rocking with the waves. "There. They've got to be drug smugglers, pirates, or something."

"Are you feeling all right?" Diana asked. "There's no one here but us."

Jane looked to where he was pointing, then turned back and gently took hold of his head. "Let me take a look at ye," she said as she bent over him. "Did ye hit your head on something when ye fell?" Jane didn't wait for an answer as she lifted his right eyelid and examined his eye, then did the same to his left eye.

When she finished her exam, Jane said, "I don't see anything wrong with ye. Maybe it's all the stress ye've been through."

Alex pulled away. "I'm not crazy. Don't you see it? There's a three-masted wooden sailing ship in the middle of the bay. It's even got the name *Fancy* painted on the bow."

Jane continued eyeing Alex. "Maybe ye got a concussion during the cave-in at Lamanai. I would never have let ye talk us into this journey if I knew ye weren't well."

"I'm telling you, I'm okay," Alex protested.

"Then why did ye purposely let go of the vine up on top," Jane asked.

"I freaked out when I saw what looked like a snake slithering towards me."

Diana smothered a giggle. "I didn't mean to scare you. I was using magic to help the vine grow. It was all I could think of to help you."

"Look, I'm fine. But we need to be gone when whoever owns that ship comes back," Alex said.

Jane put a hand on his shoulder. "Alex, I'm telling ye, there's no ship out there. Ye're jest imagining things. Why don't ye rest while Diana and I look for a way out?"

When he didn't budge, Jane slipped her arm through his and led him over to the cave, where she deposited him. Then she walked with Diana towards the entrance, scanning the cliffs for some way out. When they got to the green curtain, they found the same type of thick vegetation as above.

Jane tried wiggling through, but the vines were so tightly woven that she couldn't pull them apart. Diana tried several magic spells to get the vegetation to unwind, but was equally unsuccessful.

They headed back to where Alex was relaxing and sat down beside him. As she took another look around the enclosure, Diana said, "I have to admit that this place does look like a perfect hideaway for smugglers."

"I've been thinking about that some more," Alex said. "The ship is too old, so there's no way it could outrun anything nowadays. I'm starting to wonder if we've stumbled into some land before time type place."

Seeing Diana look askance at him, he laid one hand on her shoulder and pointed towards the ship. "I'm not imagining it. Maybe some sort of magic is hiding it. Can't you see it?"

Diana's eyes popped open, and her jaw dropped. "Oh, my god. Where did that come from?" she exclaimed.

Alex's relief was palpable. "I'm glad you can see it, as I was beginning to think Jane was right, and I was going crazy." He dropped his hands and leaned back.

Diana turned to Jane. "Did you see that? It just appeared out of nowhere."

"What are ye talking about? I still don't see anything," Jane said.

Diana turned back to where she'd seen the ship and pointed. Her mouth dropped open. "Wait. It's gone. What happened to it?"

"Nothing. It's still there," Alex said.

"Then why can't I see it anymore?"

Jane's eyes narrowed. "I have a theory. Alex, point to the ship and touch me as ye did, Diana."

He did as she asked. An instant later, Jane gasped. When he pulled his hand away, she said, "Ye say ye don't have any magical powers, but ye do. It might not be anything like we're used to, but nobody can make things appear by touching a person, unless they have magical abilities. Besides, we've already learned that ye can see ghosts."

Diana snapped her fingers. "Oh, oh, oh. You know what this might be?" Not waiting for a reply, she said, "It's kind of like that quantum physics stuff where they say the only way to explain some of the inconsistencies of the laws of physics is that there have to be parallel worlds."

"I'm not sure what that means, but why don't we go check the ship out?" Alex suggested.

"Before we do that, I want to do an experiment," Jane said. "Give me yer hand." As the *Fancy* came back into view, she nodded. "Yep, either ye're creating an illusion with yer touch, or ye're enabling us to see something that isn't in this world. I wish there was time to check it out, but we need to figure out how to get back to the canoe. All our food and water are in it."

"I was thinking about that while you were off exploring," Alex said. "There might be a way out, but you're probably not going to like it."

"I'm afraid to ask. What are you thinking?" Diana asked

Alex pointed towards the vegetation curtain. "Maybe we can push our way through, in the middle, where it's weakest."

"That's a long way back, and none of us know how dangerous the shoreline is. What happens if it's a lot tougher to swim than you think?"

"Who said anything about swimming?" Alex asked. "I was thinking we go aboard that ship and see if there is a boat on it, or something else we can use."

Diana looked skeptically at where she'd seen the ship. "If I can't see it, how do we know it's real?"

"But you can see it, at least sometimes. It's worth a shot. Besides, it's better than doing nothing."

"All right, let's go before I chicken out." Without waiting, Diana plunged into the water and started swimming to where she'd last seen the *Fancy*.

Before he could get to his feet, Jane had followed Diana in. Marveling at the courage it took for them to swim towards an invisible ship, Alex dove in after them. He reached it first and found the steps built into its side. When Diana got near, he climbed up a couple of steps and stretched out his hand to help her aboard.

Diana treaded water short of where Alex was and shook her head. "Are you sure there's a ship there? You look as if you're hovering a few feet above the water with no visible support."

Alex grinned. "Trust me. It's solid. Besides, the worst thing that can happen is that you fall back into the water."

Diana reached out to touch the ship, but all she got was air.

"Grab my hand," Alex said. "I'll pull you up."

Diana reached out and grabbed Alex's hand. Out of nowhere, the ship appeared. She sighed in relief as she scrambled onto the first step.

Alex swung to one side to let Diana pass. "Go on, so I can help Jane up."

"I'm not going up there until you check it out," Diana replied.

Jane, who was treading water below Diana, said, "It's strange seeing ye both hovering in midair, but I'm with Diana on this. I'll come aboard after ye make sure it's safe."

CHAPTER 9
INDEPENDENCE IS HAPPINESS

Alex climbed the rest of the way up, then turned to help Diana over the gunwale. Once she was on board, he went back down to help Jane onto the steps. As soon as all three were on the main deck, Alex headed towards the raised quarterdeck. He'd only taken a couple of steps when Diana grabbed his arm and hauled him back to where she and Jane stood. "Don't you dare leave us. We don't know what will happen if you walk away. What if this ship disappears while we're on it?"

Despite the tropical temperatures, Alex shivered. "Sorry about that. I assumed it was safe since it feels solid to me. Besides, the worst that can happen is we all get dunked back into the sea, and we swim back to shore."

"Are ye cold?" Jane asked.

"Aren't you guys?" When both girls shook their heads, Alex said, "Well, I'm freezing. Which means this is probably a ghost ship because it feels just like the Mayan Underworld in Lamanai."

Diana looked around. "Wait, are there ghosts here?"

"I don't see any," Alex replied.

"Is this what ye were thinking about using to get out of here?" Jane asked as she stepped over to the longboat standing in the center of the deck. She pounded her fist along its hull, then said, "At least this seems sturdy to me. Even if it isn't, the probable worst case is that we'll have to bail a lot."

Diana walked over to where Jane was examining the longboat and said, "This is too big for us. We could never manage it by ourselves."

Spotting the ship's dinghy, Jane said, "How about that? Maybe that's our way back to the canoe."

"That might work, but what will we do when we get there? Go back to Lamanai?" Diana asked. "So far, the trip hasn't inspired me with much confidence that we'll find the Fountain of Youth."

Before Alex could defend their progress, he saw a face peering down at them through the spokes of the ship's wheel. He held a finger to his lips, sidled over to the stairs, then ran up to the quarterdeck.

The unknown person was about the same height as Alex but wore a tri-corn hat, a long scarlet dress coat with a row of brass buttons running down the front, and a brace of pistols tucked into his belt. Putting his hand on the cutlass at his side, he took a menacing step towards Alex and, in a heavy British accent, growled, "Get off my ship."

Diana reached the top of the quarterdeck just then. Seeing him, she shrieked, "Ahh! What have you gotten us into now, Alex?"

Alex ignored the ghost's demand and looked at Diana in surprise. "You can see him?"

"Is he a ghost?" Jane asked when she'd joined the other two on the quarterdeck.

"I said, get off!" the man yelled. "I don't want to hear a bunch of living people discussing whether I'm real or not."

Turning his attention back to the ghost, Alex said, "I'm sorry if we're trespassing, but we're looking for a boat we could use to get out of this cove. By the way, I'm Alex, and these are my friends Diana and Jane."

Flustered by the kids' nonchalant attitude towards him, the ghost screamed in frustration and disappeared.

"That's amazing," Diana said, a smile widening across her face.

"What? Seeing ghosts?" Alex asked.

"No. That you have the same talent for riling ghosts up as people."

"It's no time to make jokes. We need to get out of here, but I don't want to risk taking one of the boats without his permission. I wish we had a computer to discover who he is and why he's hiding from the rest of the world on this ship. That information might help us convince him to help."

Diana grinned. "I'm shocked. I didn't think you liked computers. Besides, I think I know who he is."

"How can you know that?" Alex asked.

"Given all the man's weapons, I think it's pretty safe to say that he is, or at least was, a pirate," Diana replied. "It took me a while before I remembered where I'd heard of a pirate ship named *Fancy*."

"Only ye could remember a trivial piece of data like that," Jane said.

"Well, I've always been fascinated with pirates. If I remember right, Henry Every was captain of the *Fancy* and is one of the most interesting pirates ever because of three facts. First – he survived. Most famous pirates either died in battle or at the end of a gibbet. And even though the British caught and hung most of his crew, Captain Every just disappeared. Second – he is the first person in history to have a worldwide manhunt for him.

He took the Grand Mughal of India's ship, the *Ganj-i-Sawai,* and all its treasure. The Indians were so mad that they threatened to cut off all trade with the British East India Company. Rather than lose their lucrative spice trade, they posted a huge reward for his capture or death. And third – by some accounts, his treasure haul was the largest ever."

"How big?" Alex asked.

"Some estimate his haul at close to half a billion dollars in today's money. But there are so many other cool stories about him, like; how he led the mutiny to take over a British frigate and use it for his own. I mean, how many people have ever stolen a ship right out from under the British Navy's nose. He also talked the other pirates in the Indian Ocean fleet to trust him with the Grand Mughal's treasure. His exploits inspired many-a-man to take up pirating. In a way, he and a pirate named Thomas Tew created the Golden Age of Piracy."

Before Diana could say anything else, a voice came out of the shadows. "What the lass said is true, as far as it goes. But there's a dark side to my story."

There was an uncomfortable silence as Captain Every stepped out into the open, then started pacing the deck with his head bowed. "I came back because I wanted to know how ye found me but had to set the record straight when I heard the glamorized version of my life that the miss was telling ye.

"I've done very little in my life I'm proud of, especially in my early days. As for pirating, yes, I led a mutiny to capture this ship, but we had all signed on to be privateers. Instead of taking us out to earn a living, the captain had us stay at anchor in Corunna for months with no pay. Many of us counted on our wages to send home to care for our families. So, we got desperate, took over the ship, and fled to the Indian Ocean, where we joined four other pirate ships. After capturing the Grand Mughal's ship, we sailed to Nassau. Some stayed and led a life of drunken debauchery, while others headed home, where most died on the gallows.

"When the warrants for our arrest finally caught up with us in Nassau, I fled with what remained of my crew. A hurricane hit as we were rounding the western tip of Cuba and drove us here, where we started making repairs. Soon after we anchored in this cove, though, a bunch of natives attacked us. I was the only survivor.

"I believe it was divine punishment. I had a ship but no crew and no way of escaping. The vegetation covered the cove and sealed me in. I died long after my natural life should have ended but never moved on in the afterlife. I figure I'm still here because I have to pay for my many sins. Now go. Leave me alone."

"We can't do that. We need your help," Alex said.

"Boy, ye must be mad. There's no way ye could've known I existed until a short time ago, so ye couldn't be looking for me. Besides, I'm a shell of the man I used to be."

"A little while ago, ye spoke of the divine. We came here looking for help on our quest and found ye. That can't be chance," Jane said.

The captain furrowed his brows. "Tell me more."

Alex told the captain snippets of what had happened in Lamanai and about their quest to find the Fountain of Youth.

The captain didn't immediately say anything after Alex finished his story. He looked around the cove for a while before saying, "I've sensed something was brewing, but I never thought it'd involve me." He paused and looked up at the top of the masts before saying, "Maybe fate is giving me an opportunity to atone for my sins." He slapped his leg. "By gad, I'll do it. Let's get ready to sail."

Diana's jaw dropped open. "How are you going to sail this ship? There are only four of us, and three of us don't know anything about sailing."

Every grinned. "There are a few benefits to being a spirit. For instance: I can fly, I can't feel hot or cold, I don't get hungry or thirsty, and I can move objects without touching them. All I need is that curtain down and a little breeze to get me out of this cove."

"Have ye ever tried cutting it down?" Jane asked. "It seems impossible to get through."

"Aye, but I also thought an outsider couldn't find me. Fate brought ye here for a reason. If so, then there's got to be a way to get through it."

"I'll take care of the breeze once I open the curtain," Diana said. "You'll have to be patient with me, though, because it might take me a while to get the right spells."

The captain stepped back, looking askance at Diana. "Are ye really a witch?"

Alex balled his hands and stepped forward. "What if she is?"

"Black magic is the mark of the devil," replied the captain.

"It seems hypocritical to speak ill of her after what you've done. She's done nothing wrong, except have powers that we need to get out of here," Alex said.

Captain Every bowed his head and said contritely, "I apologize. How can I be of assistance?"

A rumble in Alex's belly drove him to say, "For starters, we need to get out of here and get the food and water from our canoe."

CHAPTER 10
REVENGE IS LIKE A GHOST

For millennia, Pythia had used the Cup of Jamshid to see into the future. But ever since William Stoughton had attacked Alex's family, the cup had worked only intermittently. It wasn't until the boy unexpectedly appeared in her cup that she realized he was the cause of her problems and not his sister that she'd feared.

Pythia had gone to Boston to persuade Stoughton to try again to kill the boy, but it had been nearly six weeks since she'd returned to her home near Delphi, Greece. She'd occasionally been able to use the Cup of Jamshid to reach across the astral plane to get updates from Stoughton but was still awaiting word that the Puritan ghost's mission had been successful. Pythia hadn't been too upset at his early failures, as she knew there was a learning curve to mastering the magical staff Gambanteinn that she'd given him for his mission. But as the days turned to weeks and his misses continued to mount, her frustrations grew.

Even the cup seemed to sense the situation, as it worked more and more sporadically until it went an entire week without stirring at Pythia's call. Just when she thought the cup was irrevocably broken, it came to life, but instead of Stoughton's face, she saw a three-masted sailing ship with the name *Fancy* written on the bow. The image lasted only a few seconds before the cup went dark again. She knew it was giving her a warning, but she couldn't figure out what an ancient sailing ship had to do with her.

Pythia continued staring into her darkened cup for some time until a horrible thought entered her mind – that the boy had somehow defeated Stoughton. Wanting to clear her head, she got off her tripod stool and went outside to gaze at the stars.

Sometime later, the flashing lights of a plane flying overhead roused her out of her reverie. Realizing she was being too old-fashioned in her problem-solving, she rushed inside, where she sat down and searched the internet for information on the *Fancy*.

It was long after midnight before Pythia finally pushed back from her computer and stared at the cavern ceiling, wondering what she should do next. She still had no idea what had happened in Lamanai, but she had the uneasy feeling that events were rapidly spiraling out of control. Pythia returned to the cup, stuck her index finger into the silvery liquid, and chanted,

"By Water, Earth, Fire, and Air
What was past, and what will be
Show me what I need to see."

Pythia sighed happily when the liquid stirred to life. Her relief was short-lived, though, as once again, the cup only showed an image of the *Fancy*, rocking peacefully at anchor. Frustrated by the seemingly random image, she began pacing around the room, talking to herself to help sort out her thoughts.

"I asked the cup to tell me what I need to know. And what I'm most concerned with is the cup's original warning about the boy's family. Yet it showed me Captain Every's ship, the *Fancy*. Why? Is it because I'm supposed to get its captain to help me? Or is it because he's helping the boy? If I assume Murphy's Law is in effect, it would mean the boy is working with Every. But how is he doing that?"

She sat back down in front of the computer and drummed her fingers on her desk while staring at the blank screen. Suddenly, she sat up, slapped her forehead, and exclaimed, "I'm a dummy. Why did I think a preacher and politician could defeat someone the cup warned me would be dangerous? I need to fight fire with fire. If the boy has joined forces with Every, I need someone who would go to the ends of the Earth to kill Every." She stuck her index finger back into the silvery liquid and chanted,

"O' great Cup of Jamshid
Guide my spirit across the great void
Open the astral passage to the world of the dead
And call Thomas Tew to me."

She wasn't sure whether the former Rhode Island Pirate had moved on in the afterlife, but the circumstances of his death gave her hope that he was still around. Minutes later, a man's scowling face appeared on the cup's surface. "I can hear a voice, but I can't see anyone. Who's there?" Tew demanded.

"My name is Pythia, and I'm calling to offer you something that might interest you."

"What type of witchcraft is this?" Tew asked warily.

"I'm not a witch, so be quiet and hear me out," Pythia said.

"What could ye possibly have that would interest me?" Tew replied.

"I'm guessing that you're still in the afterlife because Henry Every tricked you out by talking you into attacking the Grand Mughal's convoy, and letting you do all the dirty work. As a result, you died in battle while he ran off with the greatest pirate haul of all time."

"That lying, two-faced scoundrel. I knew I shouldn't have trusted him."

"I can tell you how to find Henry Every."

The scowl on Tew's face disappeared, replaced by an eager look. "And where might that be?"

"I'll tell you, but I want something in return."

Tew's eyes narrowed. "Aye. I should have known I wouldn't get something for free. What do ye want?"

"It's nothing much – just kill all the humans around Every, especially a young boy. What you do with your former associate is up to you."

"I can think of many things I'd like to do when I find him, but ye're making no sense. Why would a spirit be associated with the living?"

"I'm not sure why, but I know I don't want Every to help the boy."

"Since ye can talk to the dead, why don't ye go after the boy yourself? Why do you need me?"

"I can only see spirits through this method, but I believe the boy can interact directly with your kind. So, it makes sense I send other spirits after him. I want you involved because you also have the advantage of knowing Every and his habits. Besides, you were a forward thinker. You made the Pirate Round famous. And after your early successes, you returned and managed to ingratiate yourself to powerful officials. If you're going to hunt Every and the boy, those are skills that will come in handy. But time is of the essence. The longer you take, the harder it will be to track them down. Are you interested?"

"If this were so easy, ye'd already have done it," Tew said. "There must be something about this venture that ye're not telling me. What is it?"

Pythia paused for a moment before replying, "I hired someone else to dispose of the boy, but he failed. I can only surmise that the boy is quite resourceful."

"Now that I know Every is still around, why should I help ye?" Tew asked. "I could go after him myself and never bother with ye again."

"Don't flatter yourself that you're the only person I'll be talking to. I don't know you, nor if you'll be successful. I'm talking to you first because I think you have the biggest incentive to eliminate Every."

Tew's eyes narrowed. "Gaining revenge on Every doesn't seem to be worth all the trouble and danger this expedition will entail. What's in it for me?"

"I'll be talking to every cutthroat, pirate, and adventurer near where the ship is located and let whoever kills the boy keep the magical staff he has with him. What's more, if the boy has a crimson and black orb, and you bring it back to me, then I'll use it to bring you back to life."

"If I do all that, what's to stop me from taking both objects," Tew asked.

Pythia smiled. "If you double-cross me, I will find you like I did today. And then, I promise you, your suffering on Earth will truly start. I have magic at my disposal that will make Hell look like a tropical paradise."

Tew swallowed nervously. "We have a deal," he said. "Now, where's the *Fancy*?"

"Off the coast of Belize in a hidden cove. Please remember that the boy has shown he can be quite cunning. If I were you, I'd study him before doing anything rash."

"I'll find them, but ye need to give me more to go on."

"I'd suggest you start in Salem, Massachusetts," Pythia said. "He's caused quite a ruckus there, both in the world of the living and the dead. I'm confident you'll learn something there that will assist your search. Now go. Find the boy and kill him."

CHAPTER 11
THE BROKENNESS OF HUMANITY

Boston Public Library's McKim building was dark, having closed an hour earlier. The only sounds were the ventilation system and the nighttime security guards' footsteps echoing through the halls as they made their rounds.

Ichabod Crane silently opened a protective glass case in the Department of Rare Books and Manuscripts and pulled out a copy of an ancient Akkadian incantation text. He'd been studying cuneiform every day since he'd seen Alex open the Palantir's *Sibylline Book*, hoping that reading *The Maqlû* in its original language would give him an insight into the namesake objects.

Pushing open the department's double doors, he wound his way down into the cavernous Bates Hall reading room from the third floor, carefully placed the book onto an oaken reading table, and turned on a small green reading lamp. He took off his tricorn hat, flipped up the tails to his black coat, sat down, and continued reading the ancient magic text.

He didn't notice the other ghostly intruder until a hand clapped him on the shoulder. In a noxiously sweet tone, the second spirit whispered into Ichabod's ear, "And what might ye be doing with a book like that, eh, matey?"

Ichabod froze. He turned around and saw a spirit dressed in a black tailcoat, grey waistcoat, and a white cravat standing over him. "Wha… what do you want? Who are you?"

"I'm Captain Thomas Tew, although some call me The Rhode Island Pirate. I'm here because I understand you're acquainted with a boy named Alex Scire. Some friends of mine were looking for him, but they're missing now. So, I wanted to chat with the boy to see if he knew where they might be."

Hoping to escape from the specter in front of him, Ichabod tried flying away, but Tew grabbed him by his shoulders and slammed him back into the chair. Tew circled around until he faced Ichabod. "Ye can't escape me. Wherever ye go, I'll hunt ye down, and any future discussions between us will be much less pleasant than this one. So, I'll ask ye one more time. Where might I find the boy?"

Ichabod looked into Tew's eyes and shuddered. "I don't know. The last I heard, he was in Lamanai, in Belize."

Tew stood up and stroked his chin while continuing to stare at Ichabod. Then he leaned towards Ichabod and said, "Tell me what ye know about him. I need to understand the lad and how ye came to know him."

"I, I can't tell you much," Ichabod replied, his teeth chattering. "Originally, I sought him out because I was curious about his aura – which is so strong that you'll easily be able to track him once you get close. I also know he has a way of disconcerting those around him by doing odd things from time to time. Who has he upset now?"

Tew plopped in a chair across from Ichabod. "What do ye mean?" he asked.

"It seems to me that someone sent you. Who was it?"

"It be none of yer business," Tew replied. "Besides, I'm the one asking questions here." He stared at Ichabod for some time before abruptly saying. "Ye should know that the boy is running around with some pretty unsavory company, and good men are missing because of him. We can't allow someone like him to wander among us in the afterlife wreaking havoc, now, can we?"

Seeing Tew glaring at him, Ichabod stammered, "No, no, no, sir. But please believe me. All I know is that he went to Lamanai some weeks ago, and now there's a big uproar over something that's happened there. If I were a betting man, I'd wager he's involved. But I don't know what he's done."

Tew stared at the ornate coffered ceiling of the reading hall and mumbled, "This isn't good. What's his game? If my hunch is correct, he's defeated, maybe even killed, Stoughton and Corwin. But what's he doing now?" Tew snapped out of his musings. "If I don't find him, I'll be back and expect ye to have better information on him than ye did tonight. So, it behooves ye to learn more about the lad. If ye don't, well, let's say there are ways to turn yer death experience into a hell far worse than ye can imagine."

Ichabod turned even paler than his usual ghostly pallor. "You don't need to prove your point, sir. I'll find out what I can and let you know." Ichabod disappeared from the library in the blink of an eye, and for the first time in his life, didn't put his library books away.

CHAPTER 12
WHERE THE WAY IS HARDEST

"Where's your canoe?" Captain Every asked.

"It's a little ways up the coast," Diana replied.

"Why don't I lift you through the hole ye came down, and ye could walk back," Every said.

"I appreciate the offer," Alex replied, "but no thank you."

Diana rounded on him. "Are you serious? Why not? It's the only way we're going to get out of here."

"First of all, remember the jaguar?" Without waiting for Diana to reply, Alex said, "Besides, the captain's already agreed to help us search for the Fountain of Youth, which means it's not chance that we found this ship. It's fate – stepping in to help us."

"But all of our supplies are in the canoe," Diana said.

"I'm not saying we don't get the supplies," Alex replied. "I'm suggesting we take this ship to get them. Then we could head straight out to the Caribbean to start searching for the Fountain."

"I'm willing to go on this quest of yours, but I'm not sure yer friend can get us through that curtain," Every said. "I tried and failed a long time ago when it was new. It's grown even more impenetrable since then."

Before anyone could respond, Jane cried out and pointed into the air. "Are those our guides?"

A moment later, Kukulcan and Itzamm landed on the deck. Both ghosts dropped their bundles of supplies from the canoe and rushed over to Alex, gesticulating wildly.

Alex held up his hands and tried to calm them, but it didn't help. He looked from Diana to Jane and said, "I can't understand anything. Do either of you understand them?"

Kukulcan pointed up to the cove's living ceiling, then pointed at Alex and moved his arms as if shooing him away. When no one reacted, he pointed to the curtain and made the shooing motion again.

"It seems like they're trying to tell us that someone is following us, and they want us to leave," Diana said at last.

Every looked from the vegetative curtain above to the one in front of the ship. "Ye managed to break in here, so ye must have some ability to get us out."

"It was an accident," Alex said.

"It couldn't have been," Every replied. "Nobody has entered here in three centuries. So, if you got in, then there must be a way out."

"As I mentioned earlier, I can try different spells," Diana said. "But if I open a hole, and I conjure up a wind, how do we sail out of here?"

"Leave that to me." Every turned to the two Mayans and said, "Help me lower the topsails." Then he flew to the middle of the foremast without waiting for his recruits.

As the Mayan spirits flew to join Every, Alex asked Diana, "How are you going to open the curtain?"

"Let me worry about that. You two need to help get the ship ready to sail while I concentrate on unraveling the vines."

Alex headed for the foremast with Jane, where the ghosts were already lowering the topsails. Halfway there, he stopped to look back and saw Diana sitting on the deck with her legs crossed. She'd closed her eyes and was singing in the same strange language Alex had heard at his mother's funeral. He reached the mast, grabbed one of the ropes the captain had tossed down to Jane, and helped her pull the sail down.

For the next half hour, he didn't pay any attention to what Diana was doing as the captain had him hustling about, doing the multitude of tasks necessary to sail a ship. The last topsail on the mizzenmast dropped with a snap just as a ray of light pierced the front curtain for the first time in three hundred years.

The captain flew by and shouted, "Join us at the capstan so we can weigh anchor. I want to get underway as soon as the opening's big enough. Yer girlfriend, though, needs to go to the wheel so she can steer us out of here."

"Jane's not my girlfriend," Alex said. "We're just friends."

"Pardon me. I meant no disrespect," Every said. "Miss Diana appears to be a capable young woman too."

"You've got it wrong. Neither one is my girlfriend. They both volunteered to help me search for the Fountain of Youth."

"Well, whatever yer relationship, we need to be ready to sail soon. I'll join ye and yer servants…."

"Kukulcan and Itzamm aren't my servants. They're volunteers too."

"I'll be interested in learning more about ye later, but right now, we need to get underway. Follow me to the capstan."

Alex ran after the captain but felt useless as the three spirits did most of the heavy work. When the anchor finally cleared the water, he could feel the ship move slightly.

When they'd hoisted the anchor up, he noticed Diana slumped on the deck. He let go of his spindle and raced back to check on her. "Are you all right?" he asked.

Diana managed a weak smile. "I just need some rest. All this spelling is taking more out of me than I expected."

Alex looked at the vegetative curtain and could see it was thinner, but even though rays of light were piercing through it here and there, it was still mostly intact.

A series of howls and screams caused him to look up. He gasped when he saw Mayan warriors dropping through the hole above. They waited until over a dozen had entered the cove before swooping towards the ship.

A spear clattered on the deck as Every flew to Diana and yelled, "I need you to conjure up some wind to get us underway. Hopefully, we can punch a hole through the curtain because we need to get out of here quickly."

Diana struggled to her feet. "I might not be able to whip up a storm right now, but I think I can do a breeze," she said as she hurried to the stern. Leaning back against the railing, she chanted,

"By wind, water, earth, and fire.

I call upon Gaia to bring the winds I desire."

Nothing happened. Several more spears rained down, two splashing harmlessly in the water while the rest clattered onto the deck, luckily missing everyone.

Captain Every turned to Alex. "Ye probably haven't been in battle before, but I need ye to help defend the ship so yer friend has time to get us out of here. I hope they'll turn back once we're in the open water."

Alex ran towards a spear lying on the deck, reaching it just as a pair of Mayan spirits landed nearby. The ankh thrummed against his chest, giving him a shot of courage, just like it had in the battles in Lamanai.

The next few minutes went by in a blur. Alex barely had time to pick up the spear before he was ramming it through one ghost warrior's heart. Out of the corner of his eye, he saw Every, Kukulcan, and Itzamm dispatching spirit after spirit to another part of the afterworld. But he couldn't spare a thought for them as he was busy defending himself from an attack by another warrior. He dodged the first spear thrust but slipped and fell, hitting his head against the teak deck.

Alex saw a warrior looming over him, with a lance aimed at his heart. But he was too dazed to react. Out of nowhere, a pike suddenly plunged into the Mayan's heart, causing his attacker to turn into a cloud of dust that gently rained down on him. It took Alex a few seconds, before he realized that Jane was saying something to him.

"Are ye all right?" Jane asked a second time, raising her voice to get through the din of battle.

Just as Alex tried standing, a breeze sprang up. The ship trembled as it got underway, causing Jane to lose her balance and tumble onto him. It took them a few seconds to get disentangled, but before they got to their feet, the ship came to an abrupt halt, sending both crashing back to the deck.

Jane jumped up and ran towards Diana, shouting, "Use yer fire spell to burn the curtain down."

A second later, a fireball hit the curtain. The flames spread across the green vegetation but quickly petered out. A cry from above caused Alex to look up and see more Mayan spirits pouring through the hole.

With Diana's magic seemingly their only hope to escape, Alex reluctantly pulled his eyes away and got to his feet. He stumbled over to a nearby spear and prepared for the swarm of Mayan ghost warriors flying at the ship.

Then, it was like a miracle occurred – Chrysophylax popped through the opening and sent a massive ball of fire rocketing towards the curtain.

The shock wave of the fireball's passing was so powerful that it knocked everybody down – both the living and the dead. It hit the curtain and exploded like a bomb, leaving only a few charred remains of what had trapped the *Fancy* inside the cove for centuries. But seeing the Mayan spirits fleeing the scene was an even more welcome sight.

He got up, then turned towards the hole where he'd seen Chrys, but the dragon had disappeared again. Not knowing whether he could hear him, he thought, *"Thank you for saving my life again."*

To his surprise, he heard the faint sound of Chrys' voice in his head, *"I will not forsake thee, little one."*

Alex felt the ship moving and was relieved a short time later when he felt the sun's rays beating down on him. He heard Jane calling for him and went to where she and Diana were standing, watching small white waves form at the bow.

"Did ye see that fireball Diana conjured up?" Jane asked. "Wasn't that amazing?"

Alex smiled. "Yeah, it was. I don't know what we would've done without you, Diana." He looked over the vast expanse of water ahead of him, enjoying the gentle roll of the ship under his feet, savoring the breeze hitting his face, and surprised he was still alive and on his way to the Fountain of Youth.

CHAPTER 13
TO GO IN HARM'S WAY

An hour later, Captain Every called Diana, Jane, and Alex onto the quarterdeck, where he was steering the *Fancy* through the barrier reef outside Belize. "Ye'll need more supplies for a voyage than what yer friends brought on board," Captain Every said. "I might be able to make a few sallies to get supplies, but we need to put in somewhere to resupply properly. Plus, I need more sailors to manage this ship. We've only got two of the topsails unfurled and won't make much progress until we can use all the sails. And forget about maneuvering. It'll be nigh impossible without experienced crewmen."

"Where are ye thinking of putting in?" Jane asked.

Every pushed his hat back on his head. "It depends on where we're going."

Diana looked at Alex. "Have you given any more thought to where you think the Fountain of Youth might be?"

"Nope, but I'm confident I'll know it when we're there."

"I thought you were just being secretive when you said it's somewhere to the east. But there's a lot of world east of here. It sounds like you don't have any plan at all," Diana said.

"I told you I was counting on unplanned help," Alex replied. "And look where we are. We've already found more than I'd imagined."

"I have an idea." Jane knelt, then reached into the leather pouch at her side. She pulled out a runestone, glancing at it before quickly putting it back in the bag. "Some people think runes are mere superstition, but I've found they can be helpful at times." She pulled out three polished brown stones and placed them in a row on the deck.

Alex knelt beside her and asked, "Why did you make that weird face when you pulled out the blank stone?"

"It's a little unnerving to pull that one out," Jane said. "It's a fairly recent addition to runes, so some believe that the blank rune stone shouldn't be in our bags and ignore it. Others believe it can portend a death, although it could be metaphorical, like giving up my old life to go with ye on this quest. At the very least, it means Fate has taken a hand in my life."

"What about the other runes?" Alex asked.

"They provide an overview of the situation, the challenge I face, and the action called for. You read the runes from right to left. The first one is *Algiz*, the rune of protection. It's a reminder that new opportunities and challenges are ahead of me. For instance, it could be referring to our search for the Fountain of Youth. It may also mean that doing the right thing is our only true protection.

"The middle symbol is *Uruz,* or strength. It's the rune of terminations and beginnings, telling me that my life has outgrown its old form. I'm interpreting it to mean that the only way to discover my true future is to help ye find the Fountain. The symbol on the left is *Laguz,* or flow. I'm interpreting it to mean that there are unseen powers here, and I should immerse myself in this problem."

"That sounds like a lot of ifs, ands, and maybes," Alex said.

"This is more art than science."

"I'd say it's all nonsense, but you have an uncanny knack for predicting the future," Diana said, "So, I'll suspend my doubts and hope you have something good to tell us, like which way we should go."

Jane grimaced. "I'm afraid to say that my reading of the runes is that we trust Alex's intuition."

Diana groaned and turned to Every. "You said we need to find someplace to get supplies. From what you just heard, where would you suggest we go?"

"Assuming yer supplies hold out long enough, I think our best bet is Kingston, Jamaica," Captain Every replied. "We can recruit experienced sailors there, and it'll be a good place for getting supplies. It's also to the east, where you say we'll find the Fountain of Youth."

Diana did a quick calculation in her head. "But that's almost a thousand miles away. You really think that's the best place?"

Every nodded. "We can't sail west without a crew, so east is our best bet. At least the winds should be with us."

Diana looked from Jane to Alex, but when neither one said anything, she rolled her eyes and said, "Fine. Kingston, it is."

They saw several smaller boats plying the Gulf of Honduras' waters over the next few hours, but after passing by them without any acknowledgment, Diana turned to the captain and said, "I'd have thought somebody would have come close and checked us out. I'm sure they don't see many sailing ships like this."

"Aye, but remember, this is a ghost ship," the captain said.

"What are you saying? I know you're a ghost, but the ship seems pretty solid to me." To emphasize her point, Diana stomped on the deck.

"I don't fully understand it myself because no other living person has ever done what ye three are doing," Every said. "Usually, the living and spirit realms are separate worlds that overlap but don't touch. People enter the spirit world only when they die but can still see the world of the living. Since this ship only exists in the spirit domain, no living person can see us."

"Ah, so it's like a two-way mirror," Diana said.

"Can you explain why I'm always so cold around ghosts?" Alex asked. "We're in the tropics, and I'm freezing. But neither Jane nor Diana seem affected."

Every shook his head. "No. I can't explain the temperature differences."

"I've been thinking about why things affect ye so differently," Jane said, joining the conversation. "I think whatever has given ye the ability to cross between the worlds has also sensitized ye to everything in this world."

Diana, who'd been growing quieter as the swells grew, suddenly couldn't take any more of the movement and ran over to the railing, where she threw up.

When she returned to the wheel, Jane put a hand on her shoulder. "Don't feel so bad. They say Admiral Nelson used to get seasick during every storm, which means you're in good company."

Captain Every nodded. "Why don't ye take her below where she'll be more comfortable. Ye'll find hammocks stored there, so she can sleep off her queasiness. Ye also might want to scrounge around below decks for a bucket for her – jest in case."

Alex was about to head off to do what the captain had suggested when Jane put a hand on his arm. "Ye stay here. I'll take care of Diana."

He nodded and waited until after the two girls had disappeared into the cabin before asking, "You wanted to chase us off your ship when we first met you, so why did you stay and fight back there? You could easily have escaped from those warriors."

The captain was silent for a bit before replying. "God wouldn't capriciously give out a gift like yers, which means there's a reason ye can see our world. I'm hoping that if I help ye on yer quest, then maybe it'll offset enough of my past misdeeds that I can move on. But I see something else is troubling ye. What is it?"

"I already feel guilty for having placed Diana and Jane in mortal danger several times," Alex said. "And now they're on a ghost ship in the middle of the ocean headed to who knows what new danger. I'm afraid of what will happen to them if they come any further with me, and I don't want the responsibility of having someone else's life hanging on the choices I make."

"Have you ever considered that maybe fate wants ye three together?" Every said.

"Then it sucks to be them. At least I've got a personal stake in all this, as I feel I'm partly to blame for my sister's death, and I owe it to her to help her move on."

"But they chose to go with ye. They appear to be very intelligent, thoughtful girls. Do ye really think they don't realize the danger they're in? Don't sell them short."

When Alex didn't respond, Captain Every added, "Maybe ye're right, and none of ye deserve this fate. But God has chosen ye. So, it's up to ye to make the best of it."

The captain abruptly changed the subject. "It's getting late, and the seas are calm. Why don't ye go below and get some rest."

Alex stifled a yawn and went below. Diana was already asleep, but Jane had been busy opening some of the portholes on the gun deck to get a cross breeze and was quietly making up hammocks when he arrived. She slipped into one and motioned him towards one across the deck. He was so tired that he flopped in and was instantly asleep.

It was still dark when Alex woke the next day. Not hearing anyone moving about, he thought he'd try to go back to sleep, but his mind was already racing. Knowing it was futile to try to sleep anymore, he climbed to the quarterdeck, where he found Captain Every at the wheel looking eastward. Alex stood silently beside him, watching the sky slowly turn from a dark purple to a faint blue.

He nearly jumped when Captain Every said, "I've seen almost a hundred thousand sunrises, yet I still find them awe-inspiring.

For the next half hour, the two stood silently facing east as the sky gradually turned to a brilliant orange-red. The spell broke when the sun finally peaked over the horizon, and Alex sighed. "Wow. I could get used to this."

Every smiled for the first time in almost three centuries. "Aye. Thank ye for sharing the sunrise with me. I've been alone for so long that I'd forgotten what it's like to experience a moment like that with someone else."

"This brought back a lot of memories for me, too," Alex said. "When my dad was alive, we'd often go camping in the Rockies. He'd wake me up early, and we'd watch the sun as it rose over the peaks. I'd freeze my butt off, but it was always worth it. I stopped watching them once he died." He was quiet for a moment before he looked around the deck and asked, "Where are Kukulcan and Itzamm?"

"They stood watch most of the night while I rested, heading off to the netherworld just before ye came up. But don't worry. They'll be back later today. I figured I need to be at the helm during daylight hours since that's when ye three will be awake."

It was some time before Alex spoke again, "I've been wondering. Do you think I'm crazy for doing this – going after a fable? I mean, what's the strangest thing you've ever seen in your years at sea?"

"That's easy – ye three showing up. Although yer question reminds me of one incident that still haunts me."

"What's that?" Alex asked.

"We were fleeing the Bahamas, on our way here, when we were becalmed in a thick fog bank, about a hundred and fifty nautical miles northwest of Nassau. A longboat came alongside us, with a bunch of sailors who must have had a nasty case of scurvy, because they looked like they had one foot in death's door. They told us they'd found the Fountain of Youth and would be willing to show us where it was if we promised to take them back to civilization afterwards. Just about every man jack in the crew wanted to go with those poor souls and become immortal, but something about them felt wrong, so I answered them with a shot across their bow. They rowed away, and we never saw them again.

"Later on, I got to thinking and realized the incident reminded me of a conversation I'd had with an old mate of mine in Nassau some months earlier. We were in a tavern and got to swapping yarns. As the night got long and the whiskey got short, our tales got wilder. Old Billy Bones told me about an incident he'd had that, in retrospect, sounded a lot like mine. His captain made a different decision, though. Billy and a few of his shipmates didn't like the feel of it, just like I didn't, and asked for a longboat so they could sail to another island. The captain granted their wish, and off they went. No one ever heard from the crew again, except for one strange incident. A few years later, Billy said he was on another ship in the same waters. You can guess what happened next; the same fog and the same offer. Billy believed he recognized one of the men in the longboat that greeted them as a shipmate from his previous encounter. He called out, but the man never looked his way. Old Billy swore his former shipmate looked like he hadn't aged a day, but he had no life in him. He was like the walking dead.

"Most people would put those tales down to the effects of whiskey, but then ye come along and say ye're looking for the Fountain of Youth. It seems too coincidental. This whole situation sends shivers running up my back." The captain tried smiling, but his attempt looked more like a grimace. Seeing the shocked look on Alex's face, Every hastily added, "I shouldn't have said anything, as it's probably jest a sailor's tale." He shook his head to clear his mind and asked, "Would ye like a tour of the ship?"

"I'd love it. When can we go?"

"Right after yer breakfast," Every replied.

Alex didn't wait to hear what else the captain said as he was already racing below, calling out to Jane and Diana, "Get up, sleepyheads."

Diana groaned. "Why do you want to drag me out of bed this early in the morning? I was sound asleep – like you should be."

Undeterred by her response, Alex said. "I was just talking with the captain. He's going to take us on a tour of the ship right after breakfast, so you have to get up."

Diana pulled her pillow over her head. "I've already seen as much of this ship as I want to. Now go away."

"Oh, come on. I tell you what. I'll serve you breakfast if you promise to get up."

Diana glared at Alex with one eye. "You don't have to threaten me. I'll get up because I've seen you trying to cook."

After they'd finished breakfast, they went to see the captain on the quarterdeck. "Who's going to steer the ship while you're showing us around?" Alex asked.

The captain looped a short rope attached to the railing in front of the wheel over the top middle handle. "We're in calm deep waters with no one in sight. We should be good for a while. Now follow me."

Before they headed down to the main deck, Alex stepped back, craning his neck to see the tops of the masts. "Exactly what type of ship is this?"

"Originally, they called it a great frigate, but when they started building bigger ships, it got reclassified as a brigantine, or brig. It's smaller than the big ships of the line but much faster. It has two gun decks with 62 cannons on board. She's 80 feet long, displaces 150 tonnes, and was one of the biggest pirate ships in my day."

From there, the captain took them down into the hold. Diana looked at the drums lining the sides and pushed on one. "Were these barrels for molasses?"

The captain shook his head. "Not this ship, but I regret to say that I was part of the rum trade before I took to privateering. I believe it's one of the many reasons God is punishing me for my sins. There's no other way to explain why I've been in solitary confinement back in that cove for three centuries. As I was telling Master Alex this morning, I'm hoping this quest is a chance at redemption."

Alex held up his hand. "What's the rum trade?"

"In my day, European countries would send their manufactured goods down to Africa to trade for slaves," Every said. "The same ships would then head for the

Caribbean or the American colonies to trade them for commodities like sugar cane molasses, lumber, or tobacco. Then they'd use the molasses to distill rum which they traded to the Europeans. It was so profitable that the plantation owners needed more and more slaves to produce enough sugar cane to meet the demand of Europe and the Americas."

"So, what were these barrels used for?" Diana asked.

"All sorts of things," Every replied. "Some we used to store water, others salted pork, biscuits, and gunpowder. I always tried to keep full stocks of essential supplies on board because ye never knew when ye were going to need them."

"Do you think any of this is still good?" Diana asked.

"Normally, I'd say no, but everything was different in that cove," the captain replied.

"Would you show us how to fire one of the cannons?" Alex asked.

"After we finish the tour. Now, let's go up to the main gun deck, where ye'll get to see the cannons and how the crew lived."

When they arrived on the gun deck, Diana looked around and said, "I don't get it. All I see are cannons and our hammocks. Where did the crew live?"

"Here. We didn't have much room, so this area did double duty."

Diana grimaced as she asked, "Where are the bathrooms?"

"Did ye notice the two holes up near the bowsprit?" Every asked. "We called it the head and used the holes in fair weather to take care of business. If not that, we'd hang out on the rigging. In rougher weather, we'd use buckets."

Diana groaned. "I was afraid you'd say that."

"There were a lot worse privations," Every said. "For instance, to prevent the food from rotting, we heavily salted the meat and ate dried biscuits that often had weevils. Then there was the water, which would become so putrid it'd turn yer stomach. It's why we'd always dump our old water and refill our water barrels at every chance. A partial fix to that problem was carrying rum on board, so they had something other than stale water to drink. Of course, we had to ration it out and post guards over the kegs of rum to prevent sailors from breaking into them and getting drunk. Disease was pretty common here in the tropics too. Sailing the seven seas might have sounded like a glamorous life to landlubbers, but it was a tough life once ye got on board. Between the harsh life and the boredom, we would always have a few men jump ship anytime we got near shore."

"If it was so tough, why did you spend most of your life at sea?" Diana asked.

"At first, it was for adventure. Later on, it was how I supported my family."

"What happened to yer wife?" Jane asked.

"I don't rightly know. Her name was Dorothy Arther. She was a periwig salesperson."

"What's a periwig?" Alex asked.

Diana smiled. "It's an old-fashioned term for a wig."

"I never understood why they did it," Alex said.

"Well, their history goes back over 5000 years, all the way to the ancient Egyptians. They used to shave their heads for comfort, then wear wigs to protect themselves from the intense sun, eventually becoming a vanity thing," Diana said. "I think it was one of the French kings in the early 17th century who popularized it in Western culture. He wore it to hide his bald spot. But you know people. They have to keep up with the Joneses, or in that case, the royals."

"Oh," Alex replied.

He wasn't paying attention as they returned to the main deck and bumped his head against the bulkhead. As he rubbed the sore spot, the captain said, "Ye'll need to get used to walking bent over. That's the end of the tour. Are ye ready to learn how to fire a cannon?"

"Sure," Alex shouted.

Diana was more cautious. "Will it still be safe after all these years?"

"I'm not positive, but it should be. Jest in case, we'll put a small charge in for the first shot and try it out," the captain said. "Now, the first step is to bring up some powder and supplies from below."

Diana and Alex started racing below when the captain stopped them. "Hold on, ye two. It doesn't take much for dry powder to explode. Alex, ye need to take off your belt, and Jane, ye need to take off your jewelry.

"Since we'll be using one of the small bow chasers. Ye'll find a couple of racks with equipment that ye'll need on the gun deck right below us. I want ye to bring up two small swabs since we'll be using the bow chaser, one of the buckets with a rope attached, a dozen pieces of wadding, a quill, and a slow fuse. One of ye will have to go one deck below that to the powder magazine and get a powder horn and a bucket of charges. Get the smallest cartridges ye can find. There's no light in there, so ye'll have to use one of those torches ye have. When ye've got all that, meet me on the fo'c'sle.

"What's the fo'c'sle, and what's a torch?" asked Alex.

"The forecastle is on the top deck at the bow," Captain Every replied. "And the torch is that black thing I saw ye with last night."

"You mean my Maglite. Got it. But why do we have to use buckets? I can easily carry a couple of charges by myself," Alex said.

"This is a wooden sailing ship, and fire is the worst disaster that can befall her," Every replied. "If ye're using a bucket and the charge leaks, then ye won't trail a line of gunpowder through the ship and..."

Alex didn't hear the rest of what the captain said as he felt the ankh beating hard against his chest. He looked out and saw three single-masted ships off in the distance heading straight for the *Fancy*. "What do you think they're doing?" Alex asked.

Every flipped his spyglass to his eyes and studied the oncoming boats. A few moments later, the captain lowered the spyglass. "Hurry up, ye three, and get everything I asked ye to. And bring up as many powder charges as you can. I fear we're going to need them."

CHAPTER 14
SPEAK SOFTLY
AND CARRY A BIG STICK

The three hurried about their assigned tasks, returning to the fo'c'sle a few minutes later. As they laid out their materials behind the bow chaser, Captain Every pointed below. "Alex, I need ye to start bringing up the smallest cannonballs in the shot racks. Then, alternate your trips between shot and powder. Hurry, but be careful."

As Alex ran off, Diana asked, "Are you sure these are bad guys, Captain? What would they want with us?"

"This is not the time to ask questions," Every replied. "If I'm right about those ships, ye'll need to learn the steps of firing a cannon as we go. So, ye'll have to do exactly what I tell ye. Got that?"

Diana and Jane both nodded.

"First, untie the rope that runs behind the cannon that's tied to the metal rings on the deck." When Jane and Diana had an end in each of their hands, the captain said, "Now, pull the gun into the ship so ye can load it."

It took some effort to move the small gun several feet backwards, so when the captain told them to stop, they both stood up and wiped the sweat pouring off their brows.

The captain didn't give them time to rest, however. Instead, he started barking commands at them in a rapid-fire manner. "Jane, use the bucket with the rope to bring up some seawater. Ye'll use it to douse the gun after firing. Diana, take out the tompion, the plug at the end of the barrel. Then run the swab down the barrel a few times to ensure it's clear."

When they'd finished their first tasks, the captain said, "Diana, place a charge and a piece of wadding in the muzzle. Jane, use the swab to push the charge firmly down the barrel. Make sure ye seat it snugly at the back of the cannon. When she's done with that step, Diana, I want ye to place a cannonball in the barrel, wait till Jane pushes it down before placing another piece of wadding over the muzzle. Jane, when the wadding's in place, I want ye to shove it down the barrel."

Captain Every waited until they had completed those steps, then said, "Now, I want each of ye to grab one end of the rope that ye've already untied and pull towards the center of the deck. This will run the gun out and get ye ready to fire."

When they'd tugged the cannon to its firing position, Every said, "Now we need to aim the cannon. Ye'll have to center it in the opening by tugging the ropes one way or another." When they'd finally centered the gun, the captain said, "Now, Diana, get the quill and run it down through the small hole near the back of the cannon. Make sure you pierce the canvas charge cover. Ye'll know ye've done it when the quill sinks easily into the powder."

When Diana had poked a hole into the charge, the captain said, "Ye're almost ready to go. Get the powder horn and pour in just enough to fill the hole but be careful not to overfill it." When she finished, the captain inspected her handiwork and said, "Jane, I want ye to stand several feet away from the cannon and off to the side. When Diana lights this thing, it will jump backward and do most of the work to get it in position so ye can swab it and be ready for the next shot."

Captain Every inspected everything one more time, then sighted along the cannon towards the set of three ships – now only five hundred yards away. "Diana, light the slow fuse several feet away from the powder charge," he commanded. "When ye've got the fuse burning, walk towards the cannon, extend the fuse, and light the powder at the top of the cannon. Make sure ye stand an arm's length away from the cannon because I don't want either of ye to get hurt."

"We're not going to fire on those ships, are we?" Diana asked. "They haven't done anything to us."

"I'm sure they're unfriendly spirit ships because they're continuing to sail straight towards us. If I'm wrong, and those are ships from the world of the living, then there's no harm done. Our cannonballs will sail right through them. But we can't afford to assume they're friendly. Now, do as I say. If we're lucky, we'll get out of this alive."

Diana struck a match Jane had given her, lit the slow fuse, extended her arm, and put the fuse to the powder hole. The resulting explosion deafened her, temporarily engulfing them in smoke.

"Jane, soak your swab in the water bucket," the captain shouted as he looked out towards the oncoming boats. "Then run it back and forth several times. Make sure you twist it to clean out all the smoking embers in the cannon. Diana, grab another charge and get ready to ram it down the barrel, just like ye did before. Look lively now."

The water sizzled as the swab slid down the barrel. Diana and Jane then followed the captain's directions to reload the cannon. A couple of minutes later, it was ready to fire again.

"Can you tell if they're ghost ships, Captain?" Diana asked. "If they are, how can you tell whether they're our enemies? I'd hate to be firing on innocent spirits."

Every peered at the oncoming boats. "Aye. I'm sure they be unfriendly. They're sloops, loaded with some pretty rum-looking men. What I don't understand is why they haven't attacked yet."

Alex, who'd been continuously bringing shot supplies up on deck while Jane and Diana were working the cannon, set two more charges down and studied the oncoming ships.

"Do ye know who they are or why they're after ye?" Captain Every asked.

"No, but I'm guessing it's someone who thinks I still have one of those magical objects," Alex replied. "The good news is, they probably won't want to sink us."

"Yeah, but they're still coming straight at us," Diana said. "If they don't want to sink us, then that means they intend to board us, which sounds a lot worse to me."

The captain nodded. "True." Turning to Alex, he said, "We have enough shot supplies to last us a while, so I suggest ye get a cutlass and prepare for action. Ye'll be more help repelling them than running gun supplies now. I jest hope yer Mayan friends come back soon, though, although two won't be enough."

As Alex ran below to get a cutlass he'd seen stored on the gun deck, Every made an elevation adjustment, then nodded at Diana. The cannon roared to life, once again engulfing them in a swirl of smoke.

When it cleared, Diana could see one of the three sloops had fallen back, its single mast lying to the side in the water. She was so excited that she started jumping up and down. The captain shouted, "Calm down and focus. There are still two more sloops headed for us."

The girls kept loading and firing the small cannon for the next few minutes, with Every adjusting the angle ever downward to compensate for the fast-closing boats. On their fourth shot, they put a cannonball through one of the other boats' hulls. The sloop quickly sank, but instead of daunting their attackers, a dozen ghosts left the ship and flew towards the *Fancy*, screaming and waving their swords.

Diana thought she'd fallen into some weird version of *The Twilight Zone* and would die in an alternate world, with her mom never knowing what happened to her. She caught movement out of the corner of her eyes and stopped what she was doing to look. In disbelief, she watched as Itzamm and Kukulcan, followed by almost two dozen Mayan spirits, appeared in mid-air and dove for the oncoming attackers.

She was so entranced by the strange aerial battle that Captain Every had to reprimand her for not paying attention to her tasks. An occasional pirate would escape the melee high in the air and charge the boat, but none ever made it to the ship. As the battle died down, she noticed the third sloop turn and sail away, gradually disappearing into the haze.

Minutes later, it was all over. The remaining pirates flew away while the Mayan warriors circled the ship for some time, ensuring the attackers were gone before abruptly disappearing.

Kukulcan and Itzamm floated down and joined Captain Every on the bow.

As soon as they landed, Diana ran over and hugged each spirit in turn. "Thank you. I can't believe what you guys did," she said. "You saved our lives." When Alex came up, she hugged him too.

Surprised, Alex turned bright red.

Sensing his embarrassment, she quickly dropped her arms and stepped next to Jane, who had also been thanking the spirits. Diana was surprised a moment later when Alex grinned and swiped a finger across her face, saying, "Your face is black from the gunpowder."

"So is yours," Diana said, playfully swiping back at his face.

The captain's stern voice cut through their celebration. "Pay attention to what ye're doing. The next thing ye have to learn about firing a cannon is how to stow away the gear and prepare for the next attack."

Diana smiled as Alex groaned at hearing the word cleaning.

CHAPTER 15
SURPRISE IS THE GREATEST GIFT

Chrysophylax hesitated outside his uncle's laboratory, working up the courage to share the news he'd brought back from Earth. Knowing it wouldn't get any easier, he entered and thought, *"Is now a good time to talk?"* Hoping he could postpone the conversation, he quickly added, *"I can come back later if it's not convenient."*

Nabu looked up from what he was studying. *"Welcome back. I've been anxiously awaiting your return. Did everything go well?"*

"Uh, I found the ankh...."

"And? Have you discovered why it's no longer under my control?"

"I believe it's because the boy now controls it."

"Why didn't you take it from him?" Nabu roared. *"It's why I sent you to Earth."*

"That's not true. You asked me to find out what happened to the ankh and report back to you. And that's what I'm doing."

"I didn't think I had to be that specific. Of course, I wanted you to bring it back. I need to figure out what went wrong and rework my plan. This disaster has probably set me back centuries, possibly even wrecking my plan altogether."

Chrysophylax hesitated before saying, *"I know I don't have your knowledge, especially about humans and this ankh, but I think there's more to all this than you think. I talked to the boy...."*

"What! Why would you do such a thing? You know we've banned all contact with humans. They're not supposed to know we exist." Nabu paused his rant and shook his head. *"Wait. Did you say you communicated with him? The humans of Earth don't have the telepathic skills to talk with us like humanoids on Irkalla could."*

"What else can I say? The boy is different."

"Could it be the ankh?

"Possibly," Chrysophylax replied.

"If what you say is true, then why can't I communicate with it anymore?" Nabu asked.

"I don't know, but I'll tell you this – the ankh is working because all sorts of strange things have been happening to him since he put it on – like speaking to the dead."

"What! How can he speak to spirits?"

"I don't know that either," Chrysophylax said. *"I couldn't verify his assertion, but it explains some of the strange things I've noticed that happen around him. For instance, I had trouble tracking the boy at times, so I had to follow his aura around."*

"How can he disappear?" Nabu asked. *"Is he using magic we don't know about?"*

Chrysophylax shook his massive head. *"I don't believe so. I think it's because he can interact with the spirit world."*

"What!" Nabu roared.

"When I asked him about some of his strange actions, he started laughing and said he was surprised we couldn't see spirits."

Nabu went silent, trying to understand the implications of what he'd just heard. At last, he asked, *"You're starting to worry me. What else did you discover?"*

"He looked into my eyes twice yet didn't go catatonic. The first time I thought maybe it was because it was dark. But the second time was in broad daylight."

"That can't be. Except for that one girl long ago, we've always had to use a glamour charm to help humans and humanoids avoid fainting if they look into our eyes. And I didn't think you'd learned how to do that spell yet."

"I haven't learned it." Chrysophylax grew silent and shuffled his feet, unable to look at his uncle.

"That's not all. He found the Palantir."

There was a stunned silence while Nabu tried to digest the news. Finally, he said, *"That object disappeared over a thousand of their years ago. How'd he find it?"*

"From what I can tell, he used information from one of the Sibylline Books to get in the general vicinity, then followed his spirit friends, along with his intuition, to the object."

Nabu started pacing back and forth in his lab. After some time, he asked, *"Am I to understand that he opened one of the Sibylline Books? No one's ever been able to do that except their creator, and she told me that she locked them so that only she could open them."* Nabu looked at his nephew. *"Why do I get the feeling that there's something else you haven't told me?"*

There was a long silence before Chrysophylax finally answered. He cringed as he thought, *"The boy accidentally destroyed the Palantir along with a man-made magical object called Gambanteinn."*

"Why would he destroy one of the Maqlû?"

"I believe he was trying to stop someone else from taking the object. I don't know how he destroyed it because I wasn't there when it happened. But I'm encouraged by it. The person who possessed the Palantir was misusing it – just as you feared. The boy, however, seems to be unaffected by its magic." Chrysophylax paused, took a deep breath, and added, *"I also gave him information on where he might find the Pair Dadeni."*

"How could you do such a thing? That was irresponsible of you."

Chrysophylax drew himself up to his full height and, defiantly, thought, *"It was irresponsible for our race to have told the humans about the Maqlû in the first place. It has become my opinion that humans will never be ready for them. Unless we act now and bring all of them back, we are just perpetuating past mistakes."*

It was some time before Nabu replied. *"I still don't have control of the ankh. I still don't know what's going on there. I know I should sound more grateful for what you've done, but this news is so unexpected that I'm in shock."* He looked Chrysophylax in the eyes and said, *"You sound hopeful. Do you think we're better off than before?"*

"I do. The boy shows promise that he may be able to rise above the rabble of his kind. With your blessing, I'd like to return to Earth and shadow him some more. Something's going on, and I want to find out what it is.

It's almost as if Marduk has taken an interest in the situation."

Nabu shook his head. *"The young are always so impetuous; then again, you're not as jaded as us older folks."* He studied Chrysophylax for some time before thinking, *"Fine. Do what you think is right, but be careful. You know the High Council would imprison both of us if they catch you traveling there. And while you're on Earth, be extra vigilant. Never forget that you can't trust humans."*

Nabu didn't hear Chrysophylax's reply as he was distracted by a small dragon-like creature in the corner that blended nearly perfectly with the wall colors. *"Shoo. Get out of here?"*

Chrysophylax couldn't help but inwardly smile, seeing his uncle so flustered because of one of the little furry creatures that inhabited the planet. *"I didn't realize you've adopted one of those things for a pet."*

"I haven't. That thing has been skulking around this place ever since I lost control of the ankh. If I didn't know how dumb those creatures were, I'd think it was spying on me. I've been trying to get rid of it ever since, but the thing keeps returning. Its chameleon capabilities are unlike any of the other pests I've ever seen, so I rarely notice it."

Still smiling, Chrysophylax left his uncle and flew towards the wormhole portals.

The little dragon was so well camouflaged that neither of the larger Berellians saw it follow Chrysophylax into the sky.

CHAPTER 16
THE RICHEST
AND WICKEDEST CITY

Alex, Diana, and Jane didn't finish cleaning the cannon and putting the equipment away until noon. As they ate lunch, Diana asked, "How soon will we get to Kingston, Captain? Our current supplies are pretty limited."

"If the weather holds, we could get there in four days," Every replied. "If ye're careful, ye should have enough food and water for a week, but I'd suggest ye start fishing to supplement yer supplies and collect whatever rainwater ye can."

As it turned out, the captain was overly optimistic. With only a few sails unfurled and unfavorable winds, they put into Kingston harbor shortly after dusk, almost a week later, anchoring near the Coast Guard station at the mouth of the harbor on the Port Royal side.

"Why are we on the opposite side of the harbor from Kingston?" Alex asked.

"I think it's better if we avoid all the dock activity. Once ye leave this ship, ye'll be visible. Plus, what happens if a bigger ship docks in the same place. Ye might be trapped on board, unable to get in or out."

"I wish I'd brushed up on my quantum physics before I left," Diana said half-sarcastically. "Then maybe I could understand what risks we're running while on this ship."

"What are ye talking about?" Jane asked.

"Traditional physics tries to explain how physical matter moves, while quantum physics tries to explain the universe at a molecular level because the normal laws of physics don't explain everything." Seeing the blank looks on her friends' faces, Diana said, "Normal physics deals with physical matter; like if you let go of a ball, it will drop. Quantum physics deals with things like neutrons and protons, which, if you could observe them, act as if they're in many places simultaneously. For instance, if you drop a rock into water, the dropping part and resultant splash are like normal physics. The ripple from that splash is like quantum physics, where the effect is seen in many places simultaneously. That's why some of the most brilliant scientists in the world have theorized that there can be an infinite number of universes. I can't help but wonder if Alex's ability to see ghosts is some form of him being able to go between universes."

Alex scoffed. "That makes no sense."

"Then how do you explain all that's happened?" Diana retorted.

"Well …. I can't. Anyway, it doesn't matter. Right now, we need to come up with a plan for how to get resupplied and help the captain recruit sailors."

"I've been thinking about that," Jane said. "Like the captain was saying a couple of minutes ago, we should try to be as inconspicuous as possible. I don't feel comfortable going around a strange city at night, so why don't we go ashore before dawn tomorrow to get supplies? It's fairly dark over here, but there should be enough light from the city in the morning to get around easily. The big problem will be figuring out how to get our supplies back on board without anyone noticing, but we'll figure that out when we get to it."

Everyone agreed to the plan, and shortly after the eastern sky had started to lighten the next morning, they lowered the dinghy and came ashore near the Coast Guard Station. They hid in the bushes lining the shore until they saw it was clear to step out. Resisting the urge to run, they cut across the concrete lot separating the Coast Guard barracks from the Caribbean Maritime University and breathed a collective sigh of relief when they turned left on Norman Manley Boulevard.

They'd only gone a few steps when Diana looked back and wistfully said, "Do you think we can take some time later today to tour Fort Charles? You know it's part of the Port Royal UNESCO World Heritage site."

"What's so special about a UNESCO site?" Alex asked.

"They're places of cultural, scientific, or historical significance. It's an international program to encourage countries and localities to protect some of our world's most amazing sites. There are over a thousand of them worldwide – places like Stonehenge and the pyramids of Egypt. I doubt if I'll ever see all of them, but I'd like to try and see as many of them as I can in my lifetime."

Captain Every stopped, pulled off his tricorn hat, and scratched his head. "I'm lost. Where is Chocolate Hole?"

"Chocolate, what?" Alex asked.

"I was talking about UNESCO," Diana said.

"I know, but the captain was saying something about chocolate," Alex said.

"Oh. When we stepped out of the dinghy, he disappeared. I thought he'd left us.

"Nope. He's still with us, but I think he's looking for someplace that isn't here anymore."

"We can go to the library and learn about what happened to it," Jane said.

Captain Every shook his head. "It's not important. It's jest, everything has changed so much since I was last here. I don't recognize much of it except for Fort Charles over there."

Alex didn't hear what else the captain had to say as he spotted three children huddled together, standing at the back of a plain white-walled church. The tallest child approached Alex and said, "Please help us, sir."

Before Alex could reply, the captain stepped forward and flung out his arms. "Shoo. We don't need beggars bothering us."

When the three children disappeared, Alex turned on the captain, his face reddened by anger. "Why'd you do that?"

"Do what?" Diana asked.

"Not you – the captain." Turning towards the former pirate, Alex demanded, "Why were you so mean to them?"

Every's face hardened. For a moment, Alex thought he was going to leave them. Then the captain slumped and looked down at the ground. "I'm sorry. I guess I've been alone too long. Maybe we should separate now. I'll look for sailors while you get supplies." Before Alex could reply, the captain disappeared.

"What's going on?" Jane asked.

Alex quickly told them what had happened, then added, "But we need to get going. Kingston looks like it's a long way off, and we still have to find a place to shop."

"What we need to do is find a taxi, but I'm not sure we're going to find one around here," Jane said as she looked down one of the quiet side streets. "At least not at this time of the morning."

A few cars passed as they walked along, all driving on the left-hand side of the road headed out of Port Royal. They walked past the Grand Port Royal Hotel entrance several minutes later, but even that was quiet, with no cars or taxis outside it. The sun was already well up in the sky when a cab finally pulled alongside. Rolling down the passenger side window, the driver called out in a heavy Jamaican accent, "Do you need a ride?"

Alex walked over to the car. "We need to buy some supplies, but I only have American Dollars. Can you take us to an ATM?"

"I'm on my way into the city now, so give me five American dollars now, and I'll take you to an ATM," the driver replied. "When you get more money, I'll take you wherever else you want to go."

Alex looked enquiringly at Diana and Jane, who nodded and hopped in.

The road into Kingston was on such a narrow strip of sandy land that Alex could often see both the harbor and the Caribbean through breaks in the low dunes along both sides. There was also an old fort, several marshy areas with white cranes on the harbor side, and cacti growing on the dunes.

Ten minutes later, the driver pulled over in front of a bank. "Here's your ATM," he said.

Alex looked at the shuttered bank and said, "It looks like the bank is closed."

The driver pointed to a tiny room near the bank entrance. "It's in there. When you get in, though, make sure you lock it. There's a lot of street crime here."

Alex got out but was back a couple of minutes later. "The minimum withdrawal is 3500 dollars," he said. "I can't afford to spend that much money on our first stop."

The driver chuckled. "Those are Jamaican dollars. The exchange rate is about a hundred forty to one."

Red-faced, Alex slunk back into the ATM room, returning to the taxi a short time later, visibly relieved he had cash for their expenses. As soon as they were underway, he asked, "Where can we get some breakfast? I'm treating."

"There's some good roadside stands I know of," the driver replied.

"How about something with a nice bathroom?" Diana asked.

"No problem." The driver looked into the rearview mirror at the three. "There's a KFC not far from here. Is that okay?"

"I was hoping we'd get something more authentic," Diana said. "But a clean bathroom is more important."

Breakfast took longer than usual as all three took advantage of the running water, air conditioning, and comfort food to recharge. When they got back in the taxi, Diana asked their driver if there was a public phone nearby or an internet café.

The driver studied the three teenagers sitting in his backseat through his rearview mirror and said, "The

U.S. Embassy could help you, and it's not that far. It's on the way to the store I recommend you shop at."

"Okay. Let's go," Diana replied.

The driver pulled over a few minutes later and let Diana and Jane out. They walked over to an information window at the embassy, where Diana asked, "Is there a phone or computer I could use to contact my mom? Unfortunately, I ruined my phone and can't reach her."

Emotionless, the woman replied, "Passport, please?"

"I left in a hurry and forgot it. It's back at camp with the rest of my stuff. My name is Diana Bennett, and my mom is Sophie. You can reach her at the archeological dig in Lamanai, in Belize. Can you help me?"

The woman wrote something down before saying, "Do you have any other form of identification?"

"I told you. I didn't bring anything because I left in a hurry," Diana said, a hint of exasperation in her voice.

"This is a long way from Belize. Are you in trouble?" the woman asked as she dialed a number on her phone.

Diana hesitated before replying, "No. I just need to tell her I'm all right, and will be back soon."

"You're awfully young to be out here on your own. Where's your father?" the woman asked.

Jane tugged at her arm and hissed, "If we're going with Alex, we have to leave now. She's probably calling security to bring us into protective custody, and we can't let that happen."

Diana looked helplessly at the woman as Jane pulled her away and said, "Please tell my mom I'm okay."

When they got back into the taxi, Diana crossed her arms and huffed before going silent. "What's wrong?" Alex asked.

"I was worried they'd try to keep us here because we're minors," Jane said. "So, I pulled Diana away before she contacted her mom."

"If you've changed your mind and want to return to your mom, now's a good time," Alex said. "I'm sure the embassy will help you."

"If you'd just talk to my mom," Diana said. "She'd help us find the Fountain of Youth since she has as much interest in finding another one of the Maqlû as you do. You don't have to go it alone all the time."

"I didn't ask anyone along because I've seen what those objects do to people. It drives everyone crazy for power. No one is immune. I'm living proof. Just look at all that I've done because I think one of the objects might help my sister move on in the afterlife. I shudder to think what I'd have done if I still had the Palantir."

"We can talk about this more later," Jane said. "For now, let's get the supplies and get back on board."

When the driver pulled up to a heavily fenced-in parking lot and spoke to a pair of armed guards a few minutes later, Diana asked, "What's with all the security? I thought we were going to pick up groceries."

"I know," the driver replied. "This is Megamart, one of the nicest stores in the city."

After taking a token, the driver moved into the parking lot and said, "This is common at all the nice grocery stores. There's a lot of theft in the city, so armed guards patrol the premises to protect shoppers and ensure no one steals their cars. I can't get out of the lot without giving them the token they gave me." He stopped in front of the store and said, "I'll go park, then meet you at the entrance when you're done."

After the run-down buildings and poverty he'd seen in other parts of the city, Alex expected the store to be similar. But when he walked in, he was surprised at how big, shiny, and well-stocked it was. "I hadn't thought about what we needed until now. What are we getting?" he asked.

"Don't worry. I've got a plan. I jest hope ye have a big enough credit line on yer card because we'll need it," Jane replied. "Both of ye get a cart. We're going shopping."

Getting the supplies wasn't as hard as fitting them into the taxi, as except for the driver's seat, they filled every part of the small car with supplies before heading back to Port Royal. They found exiting to be even more challenging, though.

As Alex handed over the fare, the driver asked, "Are you sure you'll be okay here? This isn't the safest place to be with all this stuff."

"It's okay," Jane said. "Someone's meeting us here soon."

The driver rolled his eyes, then started his car and drove away. Jane turned to Alex and said, "Please don't make a liar out of me. Is the captain, or one of your Mayan friends around?"

As if on cue, Kukulcan and Itzamm appeared out of the bushes and started picking up bags. Within minutes they had shuttled all the supplies on board, leaving the three adventurers milling about onshore. "The captain's not back yet, so what should we do?" Alex asked.

"What are we supposed to do now," Diana fumed. "We're a thousand miles from home, standing around twiddling our thumbs, and counting on a ghost to find something that doesn't exist."

"I know this is all a little freaky," Jane said. "But I'm actually encouraged by our situation. We've got transportation, supplies, and Alex's luck."

"Yeah, well, right now, I'm not feeling it," Diana replied. She growled in frustration, then grabbed a fistful of her hair. "Besides, look at this. Between the humidity, salt spray, and lack of a shower, my hair is a mess. It's all frizzy and feels like matted-down straw."

"Hey, it's only going to get worse," Alex said. "If you still want to come, you've got to promise to stop complaining about everything. I can't do anything about the conditions, so it makes me feel guilty every time you grumble."

Diana looked at the ground as she mumbled, "Deal."

"Good. Now, how about some dinner?" Alex said. "I'm starving."

Luckily Port Royal wasn't that big, and half an hour later, they were sitting on the open-air second floor of Gloria's, looking out at the harbor lights as the sun set over the mountains rimming Kingston.

Alex was downing another Fanta when he saw three children's faces peering at him through the wooden slats of the dining area's railing. Instantly recognizing the ghost kids Captain Every had chased off earlier that morning, he smiled and waved.

"What are you doing?" Diana asked.

Alex's face turned beet red. "Sorry, I forgot myself for a moment. It's the three kids I told you about this morning. They're looking in on us."

"Why do ghosts keep searching for you?"

"It depends on which ones you're talking about. There are the ones who want to kill me. And then there are those who are just curious. Others have a specific request – like that girl Ixchel I told you about in Lamanai. Most, though, follow me around with sad looks on their faces but never say anything."

Jane pushed him on the shoulder. "Admit it. Ye're just a softie...."

Alex didn't hear the rest of what she said as a loud snorting sound followed by the clanking of chains caught his attention. He ran over to the railing and saw a huge black bull with flames shooting out of its eyes and chains hanging from its neck charging up the street. The ghost children screamed and fled with the bull in hot pursuit. Without waiting, Alex shouted, "I've got to go. Money's in my bag to pay the bill."

CHAPTER 17
LIFE IS HAPPENING NOW

Even though it'd been eight months since she'd died, Deborah Adler still didn't understand why her parents had been able to move on in the Afterlife, and she hadn't. She'd been hopeful of getting an answer when her brother had found the Palantir, but had gotten so frustrated when he'd inexplicably destroyed the magical object, her best hope for rejoining her parents, that she'd flown off in a huff.

When she'd finally calmed down and returned to Lamanai, she'd discovered Alex had disappeared, along with Diana and Jane. Uncertain what to do next, Deborah wistfully wandered around the Druid camp until she saw Sylvanus Morley floating by, seemingly lost in thought. Deborah flew towards him, calling out, "Mr. Morley, wait a minute. I need to talk with you."

When she'd caught up to him, Morley said, "If you're going to ask me where your brother went, I don't know. The last time I saw him, he was heading towards the New River. I assumed he was coming back here."

"Do you have any idea where he could've gone?" Deborah asked.

Morley shook his head. "No, but I could see something was weighing on his mind." He took off his pith helmet and wiped his sleeve across his forehead out of habit. "I don't know where he's gone, but I know the spirits I sent along with him haven't returned either."

Deborah thanked him, then took to the air, flying north along the New River. Her hope of finding her brother evaporated when she got to Corozal and saw the wide-open waters of Chetumal Bay. Wondering how she would find him, she landed on one of the thatched-roof vacation homes to figure out her next steps.

The contradictory feelings she had for her brother threatened to overwhelm her. On the one hand, her Druid training had conditioned her to think of him as an enemy, a warlock who shouldn't exist. On the other hand, she felt he was the only one who could help her move on. As she stared over the water, she wondered if Jane and Diana had the same questions.

She stayed in Corozal the rest of the day, eventually fading into the netherworld for the night. When Deborah returned the next morning, she realized she wouldn't get anywhere waiting for him to reappear and headed east towards the Gulf of Honduras. She'd only gone a short distance when she saw a group of ghosts returning to land. Deborah swooped in for a closer look and smiled when she saw their battered boat and shell-shocked faces.

Confident she was on the right track, Deborah continued flying east and was surprised to see a line of spirit ships all heading in the same direction. Spotting one where the crew seemed more light-hearted than the others, she took a chance and flew in close, calling out, "What's going on? I've seen more than a dozen spirit ships heading in the same direction."

A large bearded man shouted back, "Haven't ye heard? There's a bounty out for the head of some boy, who they say is some fierce warlock with mastery over the blackest of magic. Whoever can prove they killed him gets a magical staff. We're not armed well enough to beat the others to him, but watching the battle would be the most fun we've had in over a century."

Deborah thanked the man and flew ahead, wondering who her brother had angered. For the next few days, she flew alongside the flotilla of ghost pirate ships, always staying out of sight. But it wasn't until they reached the western shore of Jamaica that she finally picked up the first traces of her brother's aura. Leaving the pirates behind, she flew ahead, arriving in Port Royal near sunset.

She flew around the outskirts of the small town, hoping to spot him, but a large crowd of ghosts gathered in front of a long, creepy-looking, two-story building caught her attention. Flying closer, she saw a well-dressed spirit, clad in a long scarlet dress coat, standing in front of a rough-looking crowd of sailors, most of whom looked like 17th-century pirates.

It was hard to understand what was happening, as everybody seemed to be talking simultaneously. The man in front held up his arms to quiet everyone down, waiting until the buzz had stopped before saying, "Listen, men. I know it sounds fantastical, but I believe in him. I think we can find the Fountain of Youth. If we do, ye know what that means. We could all be reincarnated and return to the land of the living."

Everyone started talking, and it took some time for the spirit in the red coat to get everyone quiet again. "It's also for a good cause. The boy believes there's a magical object at the heart of the Fountain of Youth legend that can help his sister, who's stuck here in the afterlife just like us, move on."

Deborah could hardly believe her brother had convinced her friends to go on a wild goose chase – searching for another one of the Maqlû. Part of her wanted to get up in front of the crowd and tell them it was a waste of time, but she kept quiet, waiting to see how the rally would turn out.

She dimly heard the man in front calling out, "Who's with me?"

Without realizing what she was doing, she raised her hand. "I am."

The crowd went silent as all heads turned towards Deborah. "And who might ye be, lass?" the man in front said.

"I'm the girl that man was just talking about."

The crowd of men burst into laughter, only quieting when one man raised his voice over the din, shouting, "If this is your idea of shipmates, Every, then count me out. Besides, I don't like that ye ask for help without telling everyone the full story. Every man jack here knows what happens with them that goes searching for the Fountain of Youth. They never come back. There's something evil out there, and I, for one, don't want any part of it."

Deborah knew the man in the red coat had lost the crowd when she heard a general murmur of dissent. She forgot all about it when she heard loud crashing sounds and screams from near the gates. Like everyone else, she turned and flew across the front lawn, looking for the cause of the disturbance.

CHAPTER 18
THE ROLLING CALF

Alex raced down the restaurant steps, nearly colliding with the bull as it followed the three screaming ghost kids down Queen Street. He chased after the beast, but it was too fast for him, and quickly pulled away. Alex was losing hope of catching it until it slipped and skidded across the pavement as it tried turning onto Broad Street. He caught up to it as it struggled to its feet, managing to grab one of the chains trailing behind it.

Leaning back, he put all his weight into trying to stop the rampaging bull, but it was to no avail. It hauled Alex down the street as if he was a featherweight, halting a short distance away in a gravelly area where the children were cowering behind a pair of tall iron gates. Sitting fifty yards behind the brick fence was a large, decaying, two-story building, standing eerily dark against the backdrop of Kingston's bright lights across the harbor.

Alex took advantage of the pause to get a better grip on the chain and tugged as hard as he could, but the bull was unfazed. It turned its massive body towards Alex, fire blazing in its eyes. Then it snorted, dropped its head, and started pawing the ground. Alex's knees turned to jelly as he looked around for some way to stop the bull, but there was nothing to hide behind.

Remembering what he'd heard on a friend's cattle ranch back in Colorado, he slowly backed away, hoping the bull would calm down. He'd only taken a couple of steps when the beast charged. Dropping the chain, Alex dove towards the brick wall. But he wasn't quick enough as one of the giant horns sliced his thigh. A searing pain shot through his leg, but he didn't have time to worry about it as he scrambled to his feet, looking for an escape route.

He watched warily as the bull turned, snorted a couple of times, then started pawing the ground again. Alex wanted to look at the blood he could feel flowing down his leg but kept his focus on the nearly two-ton beast staring back at him. Out of the corner of his eye, he could see the three spirit children huddled a few feet away. He slowly moved away from them, never taking his eyes off the creature.

Without warning, it charged. Alex waited until the last second, then jumped to the side. The bull crashed into the wall, knocking several bricks loose. Unfazed by the collision, the beast just shook its mighty head. Seeing one of the chains lying close at hand, Alex grabbed it, intending to wrap it around a nearby tree. But before he could get behind it, the bull swung its head, sending Alex flying into the air, still holding onto the chain.

He came crashing back to earth, hitting the ground so hard that he got the air knocked out of him. Dazed, he watched the bull charge once more. Knowing he couldn't escape it, he closed his eyes and flung up an arm in a vain attempt to protect himself. Instead of the beast trampling him, he heard a whistling sound followed by a sharp crack.

A few seconds went by, and nothing happened. He cautiously peeked through his arms and saw the bull from hell was backing away. Emboldened, he dropped his free arm and saw a gigantic man, over seven feet tall, with rippling muscles, standing a short distance away, holding a long leather whip in one hand and one of the bull's chains in the other. In a thick Jamaican accent, he looked at Alex and said, "You can let go now. I've got him."

Alex watched in awe as the man picked up the chains, leapt onto the bull's back, and galloped towards the harbor, passing within inches of Jane and Diana running towards him.

"Why did you run off?" Diana asked.

Despite the strong breeze coming off the ocean, Alex wiped the sweat off his forehead before answering. "Are you kidding? Didn't you see that thing that nearly ran you down?"

Jane shook her head. "What are ye talking about?" She spotted his blood-soaked leg and didn't listen to his answer. "What have ye done to yourself this time?"

"I was trying to keep a giant bull from tearing apart those three ghost kids I told you about."

Jane knelt beside him and ripped his pant legs open a little wider to get a better look at the wound.

"What have you got against my clothes?" Alex asked.

"Nothing, but I wouldn't have to keep tearing them open if ye could stay out of trouble. We'll have to get you back to the ship where I have my first aid kit. Luckily, we're close by." She placed Diana's hand over the wound and said, "Keep pressure on it." Then, looking towards Alex, she added, "Give me yer shirt so I can use it as a bandage. It's a warm night, so ye won't be needing it. When we get to the ship, I'll wash it out and return it to ye."

Alex's hands were so shaky that he couldn't grip his shirt tight enough to pull it off. Jane brushed his hands away, grabbed the bottom of his shirt, and pulled it over his head before tying it around his leg.

She helped him up, put his arm around her shoulder, and was heading back to the ship when the eldest of the three ghost children approached him. The girl appeared to be about ten years old but had a mournful look that showed she'd seen too much sorrow in her life. Alex's heart ached for her, so he told Jane, "Hold on a minute."

"Thank you for saving us, sir," the girl said. "If you hadn't distracted it long enough for that man to get control of it, I'm sure it would have gotten us."

"You're welcome, but what was that creature? It looked like it came straight from hell."

"It's a duppy, or what you'd call a ghost. In its form tonight, it's called a rolling calf," the girl replied.

"What's going on?" Diana asked.

He held up a hand to Diana and said, "Hold on a minute. Those three kids I told you about this morning are here." Alex turned back to the girl and asked, "Why was it chasing you?"

"They're mischievous and go after travelers at night."

There was a long pause before Alex asked, "Why are you still here? You're too young to have unfinished business."

"I don't know." The other two children slipped through the bars of the nearby gate and came to stand by the older girl. "Everyone we knew died in the earthquake."

"What earthquake?" Alex asked.

"I'm only catching your side of the conversation, but the earthquake is probably the one that wiped out Port Royal in 1692," Diana said. When she saw the blank look on Alex's face, she pointed to the harbor and added, "This is a UNESCO site because over half of old Port Royal is twenty feet underwater just beyond this old building. The whole town was built on a spit of sand. When the earthquake hit, the sand liquefied. Within minutes half the city had slipped into the sea. But that wasn't the end of the disaster. Minutes later, a tsunami hit, destroying even more of the city, sinking most of the ships in the harbor, and throwing others up on the mainland. Thousands died immediately, and thousands more died from injuries and diseases in the weeks that followed. This town went from being one of the largest and richest cities in the New World to a virtual ghost town overnight."

Alex turned back to the girl. "So, you three have been hanging around here for over three hundred years? What about the rest of the victims? Are they still stuck here?"

"Except for Mr. Galdy, we're all that's left from that time," the girl said. "The others moved on almost immediately."

"Then why are you still here?"

"We're afraid of what's beyond," the girl said.

Alex smiled. "You know, I've been lucky enough to see some of my friends move on. All of them were nervous about what lay ahead, but when the time came, they forgot their fears. I never saw them happier than when they left the Entrance to the Afterlife. You should trust the Great Spirit and let go of this world."

"Here now. What be ye doing talking to the children? Leave them alone, I say." Alex looked up and saw an older man hobbling up Broad Street.

"Mr. Galdy," the girl said. "This boy saved us from a rolling calf. He wasn't hurting us."

"I've told you hundreds of times not to trust strangers. Come along now, children. It's time we get back to the church." The girl and her two companions' heads dropped, and they started after the man.

Alex stood motionless for several seconds, feeling like he had to do something to help the children. He broke away from Jane, hobbled after Galdy, and grabbed the ghost's arm, shivering despite the muggy nighttime weather. "Are you the one preventing these kids from moving on?"

Galdy yanked his arm away. "Leave us alone."

Alex moved around in front of the old man. "You need to let them go. They'll be happier."

"But what about me?" the old man wailed, the anguish visible in his eyes. "I was as much a part of the debauchery of old Port Royal as the pirates were. God sent that earthquake to punish us for our wicked ways."

"Who are you talking to now?" Jane asked.

"A Mr. Galdy. He seems to be protecting the children, which I think is preventing them from moving on."

"Galdy, Galdy. Where have I heard that name before?" Diana murmured. Suddenly she snapped her fingers. "I know who that is. I saw his name this morning on one of those tombstones at the church. It said the earthquake swallowed him up, then spit him out. Somehow, he managed to survive both the earthquake and the tsunami. He died an old man right here in Port Royal."

Alex looked at Galdy in wonderment. "Is that true? Did the earth really swallow you up?"

"Aye," Galdy replied. "I saw it as divine retribution for the wicked life I'd led. I tried making up for it by becoming a god-fearing man until my death."

"So, don't you think you should let these children move on?"

"But then I'd be all alone. There's no way God will ever forgive me for my sins," Galdy said.

"I find it hard to believe God would be so unforgiving as to allow everyone else in Port Royal to move on, except you. Don't be afraid of what lies ahead."

Galdy shook his head and shuffled towards the kids. Alex was so angry at the old man's selfishness that he yelled, "Does being lonely give you the right to punish those kids? Huh? Because that's what you're doing to them. I'm disgusted by the way you're wallowing in self-pity. Shame on you."

Galdy's head sunk lower, till his chin touched his chest. For a long time, there was utter silence. Even the night-time animals stopped their racket as if waiting for the old ghost's decision. At last, Galdy lifted his head and stared across the harbor at Kingston. Alex was about to try again to convince Galdy to accept the unknown when the old man stuck out his arms and said, "Come, children. It's time for you to go."

"But, what about you?" the eldest girl asked. "I'm afraid of what's beyond."

Alex felt a lump grow in his throat. He shuffled forward and placed a hand on the older man's shoulder. In a quiet voice, he said, "It's okay for you to go too. You say you tried to live a better life after the quake. Prove it. Take them to the great beyond."

Galdy half-turned and stared into Alex's eyes. Then he nodded and stretched out his arms. "Come. It's time to go."

Out of nowhere, a light appeared at the gates of the building they were standing in front of. The four lost souls stared at the blinding light, then slowly walked through the lit gates. Galdy turned back to Alex and mouthed, "Thank you." The gates closed, swallowing all traces of the four lost souls.

Alex stood motionless, staring at where they'd disappeared. A tear ran down his dirt-stained face, leaving a clean streak on his cheek. He didn't move until Jane gently shook his arm. "What just happened? Because I got goosebumps all over my body."

"That's weird. Me too," Diana said.

Alex didn't answer as he'd shifted his attention to a couple of dozen rough-looking spirits who had surrounded him while he was talking to Galdy. Despite the pain in his leg, he stepped back, motioning for Diana and Jane to move away.

One of the men said, "It's okay. We're not here to hurt you. We just want to know how you did it."

"Did what?" Alex asked.

"Help them kids and the old man move on," the spirit replied. "We want you to do the same thing for us."

"I don't control those things. I'd have helped my sister move on if I could."

"Nah, man. We heard you talking to them," a second man said as he stepped forward. He looked almost as big as the man who'd corralled the rolling calf. "You did something, and we want you to do the same thing for us."

"I'm telling you – I didn't do anything. These types of things happen sometimes."

There was a buzz among the men, and then as one, they took a step forward. Alex backed up to the fence, unsure how he would get out of the jam. Just then, Captain Every pushed his way through the semi-circle of men, turned around, and faced the crowd. "This is the lad I was telling ye about – the one who wants to help his sister move on. Ye saw what he did for strangers. Think of what he can do for the men willing to help him on his quest."

Alex grabbed the captain's arm and hissed, "You can't promise them that. I have no idea if I can help them."

Every smiled at the men surrounding them and whispered, "Aye. But they don't know that. Now be quiet, and let me do the talking. I'm getting ye a crew."

CHAPTER 19
CLOSE QUARTERS

Feeling a little woozy, Alex was glad for Jane's help getting back to the ship, as it took all his energy to keep putting one foot in front of the other. The blood trickled down his leg and pooled in one boot, causing a squishy feeling with every step he took. Just past St. Peter's Church, he collapsed.

"C'mon," Jane said. "Get under his other arm. We'll have to carry him the rest of the way."

As Diana and Jane carried him across the open area next to the Coast Guard Station, Alex noticed two men, one tall and skinny, the other much shorter and solidly built, staring at him from the shadows of the Maritime University building. He didn't think anything more about them because Kukulcan and Itzamm met them at the brushy area near the shore and lifted him to the *Fancy*, where he promptly passed out from blood loss.

Alex didn't regain consciousness until the *Fancy* was underway with the new crew. He tried sitting up, but his head started swimming, and he quickly laid back down. "What happened?" he asked.

Jane was beside him in an instant, checking his temperature and pulse. When she'd finished her inspection, she said, "I'm not sure exactly. You said something about a bull and three children."

He groaned and said, "The rolling calf. I hope I never meet one of those things again."

"How are ye feeling, Denahi?"

Unused to hearing his middle name, Alex paused before replying, "My leg aches like crazy, and I feel a little weak, but otherwise, I'm fine."

"Ye're going to have to take it easy for a while because ye lost a lot of blood," Jane said. "Right now, though, what ye need to do is get some food and drink into ye, so ye can start recovering. Diana is cooking up dinner now and will be here shortly."

"The ship seems to be rocking too much for us to still be in the harbor. Where are we?"

"We're sailing along the southeastern coast of Jamaica, but the captain says we should turn north to go through the Windward Passage in a couple of hours."

Alex was about to say something when he suddenly saw his pants were missing. "Hey, where…?"

"Relax," Jane said. "I had to pull them off to bandage yer leg wound. It was a pretty nasty gash, but it should heal fine. While I was at it, I changed your other leg's bandage. It's healing nicely, so you should be able to take it off in a couple of days."

Alex's hand shot to his chest, where he felt for the ankh. "Hey, where's my…?"

Jane stopped him from sitting up. "Relax. I have your necklace. I figured ye didn't want anyone to know about it since ye keep clutching at it surreptitiously every time we get in a bind."

"But…?"

"I must have accidentally taken it off when I pulled yer shirt off last night. It landed on the ground, so I snatched yer cross while binding yer leg. Ye were so out of it by then that ye didn't even notice. And since ye had a little bit of a fever, I didn't want to put yer shirt back on until yer temperature came down a bit."

"If you noticed it, who else knows?"

"I doubt if anybody else does. Most people are too absorbed in their own issues to notice other people's problems. And ye'd know if Diana knew because she'd pester ye about it." Seeing he was about to ask more questions, she added, "I probably wouldn't have noticed it either, except I've been paying close attention to everything ye do and have seen ye grab for yer chest and abruptly change topics every time ye try to explain yer hunches. I also saw it glowing when we encountered that boulder down in the cavern in Lamanai. Why are yer being so secretive about it? It's just a necklace."

"No, it's not. I got it from my father the day he died. I think it saved my life," Alex said. "The only other people who know about it are my grandfather and sister. Promise you won't tell anyone."

Jane nodded and slipped the ankh into his hand just as Diana arrived with food and drinks. After they'd finished eating, Diana quizzed him extensively on what happened after he ran out of the restaurant. When she was finally satisfied with his answers, she lay down in her hammock, hands behind her head lost in thought.

Taking advantage of the pause in the conversation, Jane said, "Kukulcan and Itzamm have returned to Belize. They waved goodbye and flew away when we left Port Royal."

"I don't know what I would've done without their help," Alex said. "I'd probably be dead by now. And we definitely couldn't have made it this far."

There was a long silent stretch before Diana said, "I still find it hard to believe we're going in search of the Fountain of Youth. I know I haven't always been positive about this quest, but having a crew and supplies onboard has suddenly made it more real. You know, I've been thinking. The Arawak Indians, some of whom settled here in Jamaica, talked about the legendary land of Bimini, where the Fountain of Youth was. Their stories placed the Fountain in places like Cuba, Hispaniola, and Puerto Rico, which are all north of Jamaica. I think we should focus there but include Florida and the Bimini Islands in that arc of possible locations." She broke off her musings and turned towards Alex. "You haven't talked much about where we're going, except east from Belize. Where do you think it is?"

"I haven't given it much thought," Alex replied. "I've assumed something would happen that would lead us to it, like what happened with the Palantir."

"I was hoping you'd have started taking this trip more seriously by now," Diana said. "You can't keep counting on luck to find it, as the ocean is a mighty big place."

"I am taking it seriously, but you've got to admit it's a bit overwhelming."

"That's an understatement," Diana replied.

The three lapsed into silence again until Jane said, "Ye know, ye've never explained how ye survived the fall in Lamanai. At least yer explanation of how ye got out made some sense, but I don't see how it's possible to fall that far and live."

Alex hesitated, trying to come up with a plausible explanation. At last, he said, "I got lucky. Do you remember the roaring sound we heard down in the second cavern? Well, I jumped off the boulder just in time and landed in that river." He rubbed his shoulder and added, "Well, kind of lucky. I dislocated my shoulder, nearly drowned, then slammed into another boulder that popped my shoulder back into place before I finally managed to crawl out. I was far enough away from the collapse that all I had to deal with was a choking dust cloud. Then Ixchel appeared and led Thorfinn and me out through a back entrance. It was her fellow ghost slaves that defeated the Mayan warriors and allowed me to escape."

"I was wondering where ye got that ugly-looking bruise on yer shoulder," Jane said. "Don't worry, though; I checked it out while ye were sleeping. Everything appears to be fine. It's another reason, though, that ye need to take it easy."

"That's all interesting, but it still doesn't help us find the Fountain of Youth," Diana said.

Alex looked out one of the open ports and, in a faraway voice, said, "A year ago, I'd never seen any magic. A week ago, I'd never seen one of the Maqlû." "Just because I haven't seen it doesn't mean it's not out there. I can feel we're getting closer, so bear with me a little longer."

"Do ye really think it'll help yer sister move on?" Jane asked.

"I don't know. Deb seems to think that all she needs for her to move on is for us to find it and give it to your order for safekeeping." He shook his head. "But I don't trust those things."

"I've heard ye say that before. Why not," Jane asked. "If what ye believe is true, then our order wouldn't exist now, as we've been around some of those objects for centuries. Besides, except for Salem, and Lamanai, ye haven't been around many members of our order. And I don't see that we've given ye that much cause for concern."

Alex lifted an eyebrow. "You haven't experienced the anger, fear, and hatred I've experienced with members of your order, especially the victims of the Salem Witch Trial, who tried hanging me. I believe that the Maqlû, well, at least the Palantir, amplifies those emotions. Or maybe it's just greed and lust for power."

"What! Go back. Ye never mentioned getting lynched by ghosts," Jane said. "I saw a thin purple line on yer throat, but I never imagined that's what caused it. Things like that don't happen anymore."

Alex rubbed his neck where the rope had been. "Well, you're wrong about that because it happened to me. But I don't like thinking about that night. Those spirits, especially the women victims, are still furious about what happened to them – and they tried to take some of their frustrations out on me."

"We're not going to solve this tonight, and I'm tired, so I recommend we hit the sack and figure out our next steps tomorrow," Diana said.

"Before we do," Jane said. "I keep forgetting to ask ye, Diana, how did ye manage to create such a huge fireball back in Belize to burn down that curtain? Have ye ever conjured anything that big before?"

"No," Diana said, scratching her head. "I've been wondering the same thing. I initially put it down to all the magic in the cove somehow magnified my spell, but I can't help but wonder if there isn't a different answer." A thought seemed to strike her, and she swiveled around to stare at Alex. "Did you have something to do with that?"

Alex blushed and looked away while trying to sound indignant. "Hey, don't look at me. I had my hands full fighting off ghosts with a spear. Besides, I've told you I can't do any magic."

Jane furrowed her brows as she studied Alex. Talking more to herself than Diana, she said, "I saw him mid-deck fighting ghosts, so I think he's telling us at least part of the truth." Seeing Alex wince in pain, she changed the subject. "We should stop grilling him. He needs rest." But don't go to sleep just yet, Alex. I've got a concoction that will reduce the pain and fight infection. I'll be right back with it."

"I feel sorry for you," Diana said.

"Why's that?" Alex asked.

"Because Jane is notorious for her concoctions. Who knows what she puts in them. They taste awful, but they work. I'd suggest you gulp it down so you don't have to taste it for long.

Although his leg still ached, Alex felt much better the following morning. He came up on deck early and was surprised to see a fog enveloping the *Fancy*. The white mist was so thick that it coated everything with a fine layer of water and made it seem much cooler than it was. Shivering, he crossed his arms for warmth as he climbed to the quarterdeck where Captain Every was involved in an intense discussion with the new first mate. They were so preoccupied that they didn't notice Alex until he asked, "What are you two up to?"

"It's this blasted fog," Captain Every said. "These things always make me uneasy, even when I used them for my benefit. What makes it worse is that we're heading north through the Windward Passage. Someone could be lying in wait upwind of us and have the advantage in a battle."

Diana and Jane joined them just then, but instead of acknowledging their presence, Every cocked his head to one side and stared out into the mist.

"Is anything wrong?" Diana asked.

"I don't know," Every said. "Everything seems normal. All I hear is the occasional flapping of the sheets, the waves hitting the sides, and the noise of the crew going about their business, but…."

Alex clapped a hand to his chest, where his ankh lay, and stared into the fog for some time before he turned to the captain and said, "You're right. Something's wrong."

Diana grew serious. "I don't like the sound of that. I'm to the point that whenever you or Jane start worrying about stuff, I start to panic."

"I've been sending a couple of scouts out every half hour, but they haven't reported anything unusual," Every said.

Alex held up a hand and shushed everyone. He went over to the starboard side and leaned over the railing. A second later, he stood up and pointed into the fog. "There."

Captain Every flew off the ship and headed in the direction Alex had pointed and was gone for several minutes. When he reappeared, he flew to the side of his first mate and whispered, "Be quiet about it but pass the word – everybody to their stations. A ship named the *Amity* is out there, and I believe their captain is itching for a fight.

"Aye, aye, Captain." The first mate went over to the bosun and relayed the orders. The two spirits then went about the ship, quietly passing the word.

Most of the ghosts went below to man the cannons on the top gun deck. The rest flew up to the rigging with muskets and pistols. In less than three minutes, all activity had ceased.

Every glanced towards Alex, then stared ahead into the fog. "When I agreed to help ye, I never imagined ye were so unpopular. What have ye done to rile up so many spirits?"

Before he could respond, Diana said, "It's a talent, and it's not restricted to spirits. He does the same thing to the living. But what is this *Amity* you mentioned?"

"I used to know a pirate who named his ship the *Amity*. Unfortunately, he died the only time we worked together, so I could see him holding a grudge ever since."

"Are you planning to fight them?" Diana asked.

"I don't want to, as I never planned to go into battle with these men. Even though they're experienced, we still only have a skeleton crew, and we haven't worked together. If Captain Tew is in charge of the *Amity*, he'll have packed his ship full of cutthroats – possibly three times the number of men we have, so we'll need all the help we can get. The three of ye have already had some experience firing a cannon. Do ye think you can handle the bow chaser again without me?"

"Yes, Captain," Diana said

"Good. Fire as soon as it's in sight, and keep firing until we're past 'em. Got that?"

Diana nodded, then motioned for the other two to follow her below to get everything they needed.

As they climbed down the steps to get supplies, Jane said, "Let me know if yer wound opens up, Alex. I'm worried the bandages won't hold up since I never anticipated ye getting involved in a battle."

Still weak from his injury the night before, Alex limped through his duties at half speed. As they were setting down their first load of supplies, Jane offered to switch tasks, but he turned her down, saying, "You two learned how to fire the cannon. I only know how to do the grunt work. I'll take it easy and try to be careful. Now get ready. I'll be back up with another load as soon as possible."

He arrived with his second load several minutes later, just as Jane finished ramming a cannonball in. Alex saw a gap in the fog and paused to look. He gasped when he saw the bowsprit of the *Amity* only a couple of hundred yards away, coming towards the *Fancy*.

Before he could react, there was a muffled crash. The ship shuddered, causing Alex to put down the buckets of powder canisters he'd brought up and go to the gunwale. Looking over, he saw the remains of a small boat the *Fancy* had accidentally crushed.

Diana was so nervous that she immediately lowered the linstock to the hole. Jane, who was standing next to the cannon, was barely able to jump out of the way before the bow chaser roared to life. To their dismay, the cannonball splashed harmlessly into the ocean halfway to the *Amity*. As if on cue, the guns on the *Fancy* went off, rocking the ship backward and sending thick, choking smoke swirling around.

An answering roar from the *Amity* hit the *Fancy*, ripping the canvas sails and sending wooden splinters flying. The screaming and explosions were so deafening they disoriented Alex for a few seconds, and it was all he could do to get his attention back on task. Picking up his buckets, he headed below and was about to step on the ladder when he heard Jane yelling the bow chaser was ready to fire. He paused and watched as Diana bent down and sighted along the barrel. Then she stepped back and looked calmly over at the *Amity* despite the chaos all around her.

Smoke from the cannon fire boiled up and shrouded everything as the two ships passed each other. They were so close that ghosts from each ship started jumping to the other to join in hand-to-hand combat.

Alex wondered why Diana didn't fire and was about to head to the bow when the *Amity's* stern came into sight. As soon as the *Fancy* leveled out, Diana lowered the linstock. The small gun belched fire and jumped backward. He watched the cannonball sail across the gap between the two ships and smash into the tiller, causing the *Amity* to shudder, then suddenly veer away. The noise of sailors cheering caused him to shake out of his daze and head below, on his way for more supplies.

CHAPTER 20
FROM THE DEEPEST DESIRES

Despite a splitting headache, Sophie stared at the rainbow of colors swirling around in her scrying dish. It finally slowed, and Elizabeth's face appeared.

"Any news?" the head of the Salem Grove asked.

"I got a message from the U.S. Embassy in Kingston," Sophie replied. "They said Diana and a red-headed girl showed up there, asking to use a phone, before running away."

"Kingston? How in the world did they get there?" Elizabeth asked.

"I've no idea. Unless you have any objections, I plan on returning to Belize City today and going after her in the *Pequod*. I've already taken the liberty to alert the captain. He'll be ready to leave as soon as we're on board. I've also updated all the detective agencies on their whereabouts and redirected their search areas for the girls, although I don't think your grandson will stay in one place very long."

"Of course. But don't you think you should fly there instead?"

"I doubt the girls flew to Jamaica. Diana left her identification here, and the airlines wouldn't let her board without it, which is why I believe they sailed there. I just don't have any idea how. It might have been by cargo ship, or maybe a passenger ship, although the latter would more likely have docked in Montego Bay – not Kingston." Sophie hesitated, then added, "What I'm most worried about is why they ran away. They're up to something, but I have no idea what. I'm guessing that since they're in Jamaica, they're headed to somewhere else in the Caribbean, which makes it important I have the ability to sail after them."

"What about the dig?" Elizabeth asked.

"The Belizean authorities are asking a lot of questions after the cave-in, but I'm pretty sure they're going to assume it was due to natural causes and let us continue our work. Constance will stay here and lead the effort. I'll take a few of the elders with me but leave most here to continue the search for the Palantir."

"Are you sure you're up to this? You still look pretty wan."

"I'll be okay," Sophie replied. "After I get on board, I'll have a couple more days to recover. Besides, nothing will stop me from getting my daughter back."

Elizabeth nodded, then added, "I know you're worried about Diana and angry with my grandson, but remember, Lady Yvaine has been very explicit that we are not to hurt him. You need to bring him back alive."

"I understand." Fearing a migraine coming on, Sophie waved a hand over the scrying dish and cut the link. She suppressed an overwhelming desire to lie down and willed herself to keep moving.

Two days later, she went ashore in Kingston and took a taxi to the U.S. Embassy. As soon as she stepped out, two black men, one tall and skinny, the other short and stout, approached her. The tall one doffed his hat, nodded, and in a voice with a light French Caribbean accent, said, "Pardon me, ma'am. Might you be looking for a pair of teenage girls and a boy?"

Sophie pulled up, startled. "Yes. Are you from one of the detective agencies?"

"No, Ma'am. My name is Jean Paul, and this is my friend Francis. We're just concerned citizens. We happened to see a group of three teenagers over in Port Royal the other day in, shall I say, strange circumstances. One of the girls was tall, with long, ginger-colored hair. The other was several inches shorter, medium height, dark-skinned, with frizzy brown hair. While the boy…."

Sophie cut him off. "If you've harmed them, there'll be hell to pay."

Jean Paul threw up his hands. "Relax, Ma'am. We haven't done anything to them. As far as we know, they're fine, but I doubt they're in Kingston anymore. The last time we saw them, they were near the Coast Guard Station across the harbor."

"I don't understand," Sophie said. "If you're not working for one of the detective agencies, how do you know I'm looking for those kids?"

"We travel around the world a lot and have seen too many instances of people being where they look out of place," Jean Paul replied. "Unsure if they were all right, we reported it to the police, then came to the Embassy and told them what we saw. We figured somebody would show up soon looking for them, and guessed by the worried look on your face, that you might be the involved party."

Sophie slumped, relieved by what Jean Paul had said. "Do you know where they could have been going or who they were with?"

Jean Paul shook his head. "No. It was a bizarre situation, which is why it caught our attention."

"Well, that certainly describes the boy," Sophie said.

Jean Paul looked questioningly at Francis, who nodded. "I hesitate to say this because I could be leading you astray, but if I were in your shoes, I'd look north for them, in the Windward Passage."

"Why in the world would you suggest that? You've never met them and have already said you don't know where they went."

"True, but call it an educated guess. You can do with my suggestions what you want, but here is my card with my contact information. We're leaving here in a few hours and plan on sailing that way. We'll watch for them and inform the authorities if we find anything. I hope this information is helpful and that you find them safe and sound." He then nodded and walked away with Francis trailing him.

Sophie stood frozen for a minute, trying to understand what had just happened. She realized that if the incident had happened a month earlier, she wouldn't have believed anything the man had told her and probably called the police to report them. But she'd seen too many strange things happen around Alex since then to think Jean Paul's story didn't have at least a grain of truth. Shaking her head in bewilderment, she headed towards the Embassy to check on any updates.

Several hours later, she was back on board the *Pequod* and heading for the Windward Passage.

CHAPTER 21
COMING ABOUT

The din of battle had made Diana's ears ring, making it nearly impossible for her to hear what was happening. She was relieved when Captain Every flew up and shouted, "Well done, girls. That last shot of yers saved us. If ye hadn't taken out the *Amity's* tiller, they'd have been able to cross our stern and take out ours. But ye have to stay alert. We've got to be ready if they come back."

Jane asked, "Is anyone hurt?"

The captain dropped his head. "Aye, we lost a few men, but we can't worry about that right now because we need to take advantage of this fog and get out of here before they make repairs."

Diana looked back to the last place she'd seen the *Amity* and noticed Alex had collapsed onto the deck between the buckets he'd brought up. Too numb from everything that had happened, all she could do was gasp and stagger over to where he lay.

Jane rushed past her, knelt beside Alex, and gave him a quick exam. When she finished, she looked at Diana and said, "We need to get him below so he can rest. I think he'll be fine, but he overdid it."

"I'll have some of the men take care of the cannon while you take him below," Every said.

After helping settle him, Diana returned topside. She noticed a group of men at the bow. Several were hauling the two bow chasers around, while others were standing at the bow with firearms at the ready. She saw the first mate and asked, "What's going on now?"

"There's a cluster of small boats ahead, looking like they're going to try to stop us," the ghost said. "So, we plan on giving them an incentive to disperse before we ram them."

Just then, the bow chasers went off. The smoke made it impossible to see what happened, but a cheer from the men clustered around the small cannons told her they had hit their marks. She rushed forward and saw ghost pirates from the sinking boat flying to the others massed ahead. One of the crew pushed her back, saying, "It's not safe up here for you, miss. You need to move back and get out of harm's way."

As if to emphasize the sailor's point, shots rang out. Seconds later, she felt the same crunching vibration as when they'd run over a boat before the battle with the *Amity*. She dashed over to the rail and looked down but pulled back when a grappling hook came flying up. An instant later, several more soared over the railing.

Knowing she had to help fight back, Diana paused, trying to decide which spell she should use. She thought her fire spell would be most effective but was hesitant to use it for fear of setting the ship on fire. The smoke grew thicker, and the noise grew louder as some of the crew fired muskets and cannons at the blockade ahead while the rest fought off the boarders.

Making up her mind, Diana forced herself to shut out all the distractions and focus on her magic. She pulled out her talisman, conjured up a fireball, and hurled it at the nearest boat, not expecting much to happen. Diana stumbled backwards when it exploded on one of the boats clustered in front of the *Fancy*, catching it on fire. A gust of wind caught the flames and whipped them into an inferno that threatened to engulf the *Fancy*.

Realizing she had created a different and much worse problem, she wracked her brain for a solution. She saw one of the burning boats sink below the surface, creating a small wave that rocked the other burning boats. Knowing she had to do something to fight the fire, she switched course and chanted,

> *"Clouds of black, clouds of white.*
> *I summon thee to show thy might.*
> *Blow by me, oh sea I desire*
> *And drench those ships on fire*
> *Not just here but over there*
> *Just like that at what I stare*
> *Let thy power work the best*
> *So my intent can manifest."*

Diana saw a swell rush towards the burning ships, but it was so small that it did nothing but rock them. She repeated the spell and thrust her arms towards the awaiting pirate boats, now burning fiercely.

A breeze popped up that quickly strengthened into a gale. A wave that had been only a foot high swelled to over ten feet and rushed towards the wall of fire. It washed over the boat blockade and doused the flames. By the time the magical wave had dissipated, the boats were no longer in sight.

She dimly heard the ghostly crew cheering but was so exhausted by all the magic that she thought she should go below and rest. But her first wobbly step convinced her to sit down. The absurdity of all that was happening caused Diana to start chuckling.

Seeing her sitting in the middle of the deck, laughing, Captain Every flew up and asked, "Are ye all right, miss?"

"I think so. It's just that my life was so normal a few weeks ago. Now, look at me. Here I am, having used magic in a battle between dead pirates. Never in a million years could I have imagined this happening to me."

"Ye and yer friends performed magnificently. We can handle the clean-up. Why don't ye go below to be with yer friends and get some rest. Ye'll need it, for I fear we'll need more of your magic before this voyage is over. I'll send one of the men over to help ye go below."

Diana surprised herself by not arguing with the captain's suggestion. A few minutes later, she was swinging in the hammock next to Alex's, telling the others what had happened.

When she'd recounted her recent adventures, she asked, "Do you think they'll be back?"

"I think the better question is, who sent all these ghosts?" Jane said. "Captain Every hasn't been out of the cove we found him in for three centuries. Now, it's non-stop attacks." She turned to Alex. "What haven't ye told us?"

"I have no idea what's going on," Alex replied. "These are much more coordinated attacks than the ones I've seen before."

"What other attacks?" Jane asked. "I thought there was just the one when they kidnapped Diana."

"Don't forget about the thugs in Belize City and the cenote incident," Diana added.

"My sister said there were also some ghosts that tried attacking us in Belize City, but she chased them away before they could harm us."

"Is that all the attacks?" Jane asked.

"Well, there was the one on the way down where Stoughton called up a bunch of ghosts from the ocean and had them attack me. Then there were the witches in Salem, but I already told you about them."

"Anything else you're not telling us?" Jane asked.

"Of course, there was the one where my family died, and then…."

"Okay, we get the picture," Diana said. "There's been a bunch. I think the key questions are, why are they attacking you, and what do we do next."

"The answer to the first question is simple. Whoever is attacking us wants the Maqlû and is trying to stop us," Alex said.

"But why now?" Diana asked. "Why are they coming after you with a vengeance all of a sudden? From what you've said, you didn't even know about the Maqlû until a few weeks ago. We should talk to the captain. He needs to know we're going to see more of this stuff. But given all the unanticipated dangers, we need to decide if we should keep going."

"Alex isn't going anywhere right now," Jane said. "Ye can bring the captain down here while I make sure he rests."

"But I'm cold down here," Alex complained. "If I go up, I'll at least get some sun and maybe even warm up. I'll promise to sit down and do nothing. Besides, I'll be less antsy if I can see what's happening."

Jane glowered at Alex. "Fine, but ye'll be coming straight back here if ye don't take it easy. Understand?"

Alex nodded, and with Jane supporting him, followed Diana topside. As soon as they reached the quarterdeck, Every motioned for them to follow him to the stern. When they were far enough away from the other sailors that no one could hear them, he turned and said, "We need to discuss next steps. I didn't expect any of this, and I can't, in good conscience, keep going without a better plan."

"That's what we came up here to talk about," Jane said.

"We sustained some damage in the engagement, but nothing serious," Every said. "But I fear we haven't seen the last of them. They'll come after us again, and I doubt they'll make the same mistake of waiting too long to attack. I'm guessing they'll try boarding us right away next time because we don't have enough men to fight them off."

"How can they catch us?" Diana asked. "I thought we damaged their tiller."

"Aye, but depending on the level of damage, the *Amity* may be able to make repairs within the day and come after us. And don't forget about all the other pirate ships we've encountered, plus who knows how many more are waiting for us. So, unless I know where we're going, we could sail around in circles until we're right back in their midst."

"Where are we now?" Jane asked.

"We're still sailing northeast through the Windward Passage. Within the next couple of hours, though, we'll have to decide whether to turn and sail northwest along

Cuba's northern coast or head east along Hispaniola's coastline towards Puerto Rico. I prefer going east because we can slip into the Atlantic and go anywhere. They'll never find us out there. Whereas, if we go west, there isn't nearly as much room to maneuver between the Bahamas and Cuba."

"But, most of the probable sites for the Fountain of Youth are to the northwest," Jane said. She narrowed her eyes. "Reaching the open spaces of the Atlantic is not why ye want to head east, though. Is it? What's yer real reason?"

Diana thought Every looked uncomfortable when he replied, "I told ye, there's more room to maneuver if they come after us. Out in the open ocean, we can sit off at a distance and pound them to splinters with the greater range of our cannons."

Jane shook her head. "That might be a true statement, but it's still not yer real reason. Tell the truth now. Why do ye want to head east?"

The captain sighed. "Aye, lass, ye're right. There is something else calling me. I told ye we captured the Grand Mughal's ship and made off with a king's ransom of wealth. Not knowing how dogged the British would be in their pursuit, I hid a large part of the treasure in a seaside cenote in eastern Hispaniola. We tried laying low in Nassau for some time, but as I told ye, we had to leave when the authorities caught up with us and never returned. Instead, we ended up getting stuck in the cove where ye found me. If we go east, I could retrieve my treasure."

Diana gasped. "Are you serious? It would be so cool to find a treasure." She turned to Jane, who stared back impassively. Then she looked to Alex, who was sitting on the deck resting. "You've been quiet about all this. What do you think?"

"I have no idea where the Fountain of Youth is," Alex replied. "For all I know, we could wander the seas like the *Flying Dutchman* for the rest of our lives and never find it, which is why I was counting on luck to give us a clue where to go. But, so far, I haven't found that clue." He looked up at the captain. "Can you find the treasure again?"

Captain Every nodded. "As long as nobody has stolen it. I hid it in a seaside cenote on the northeast shore of Hispaniola in Samaná Bay. It's rugged, inhospitable terrain, and no one used to live there."

"Why are ye taking the captain's suggestion seriously, Alex?" Jane asked. "As exciting as it may sound, I see no benefit in going after a treasure hoard, especially if it's in the wrong direction. Diana and I agreed to go with ye to search for the Fountain of Youth. This treasure is nothing but a distraction."

"Maybe. But if we go west, which sounds logical, all we'd be doing is the same thing everybody else in history has. Look where it's got them."

Jane huffed. "Unbelievable. Ye're seriously thinking of going on a treasure hunt, forgetting the whole purpose of why ye're out here, as well as ignoring the fact there are, who knows how many pirate ships wanting to send us to the bottom of the ocean."

Alex closed his eyes and didn't say anything for a while. Diana was about to see if he'd fallen asleep when he said, "I understand your concerns, but as I think about it, I kind of like the idea. It … feels right. I tell you what. If this doesn't help us find the way, then I'll give up on this whole adventure, and we'll go back to Lamanai. Deal?"

Jane crossed her arms and looked from Alex to Diana.

"Hey, don't look at me," Diana said. "You're the one who told me your focus was to follow Alex and figure out what he's doing. If truth be known, I fear he's starting to rub off on me more than I'm willing to admit. Besides, who wouldn't want to go after a pirate treasure? It'd be so cool if we actually found one."

"Ye know this is like chasing windmills," Jane said.

"We both thought the same thing about the Palantir," Diana reminded her.

"I can't believe ye're taking his side. Besides, this whole situation is different. In Lamanai, we had a book with a map that showed us where to find it."

"Exactly. And who found the book?" Diana replied.

Jane heaved a big sigh. "Fine. Captain Every, where did ye say you hid this treasure?"

The captain walked over to where his first officer stood by the ship's wheel. "Mr. Christian, when we clear the northwest shore of Hispaniola, come about and set an easterly course."

"Aye, aye, captain. East it is."

CHAPTER 22
WHAT YOU SEEK

The *Fancy* entered Samaná Bay early the next morning. Alex, who'd just come up on deck, watched the frigate birds and pelicans flying around for a minute before asking, "How are we going to get to your treasure, Captain? The shore looks like an impenetrable fortress."

"I didn't say it would be easy. I chose this area because there are so many hiding spots that it would be nearly impossible for someone to find the treasure. The whole area consists of mangrove swamps, sinkholes, caverns, and small karst islands."

Two hours later, the captain had the crew furl sails and drop anchor.

"Are you sure this is the right place?" Alex asked.

"I believe so," Every replied. "But we'll see in a bit." He then had the crew lower the dinghy and longboat into the water.

Alex went below to get his pack and was heading up the steps to the main deck when Jane called out, "Where do ye think ye're going?"

"Duh. Treasure hunting. Aren't you coming?"

"Of course I am, but ye need to stay here and rest," Jane said.

"Oh, come on. I've done nothing but rest since we left Jamaica."

"Except for yesterday. Ye still look pale."

"Are you seriously going to stop me from going on a treasure hunt?" Alex asked. "What if I promise that when we get back, I won't do anything until we find the Fountain of Youth."

"I can't believe I'm saying this, but it's useless arguing with him," Diana said. "Besides, what can go wrong now? We've been through the worst part."

Jane threw her hands up in defeat. "Okay, but remember to take it easy. I'll be watching ye. If I see ye struggling, I'll make ye stop."

They got into the dinghy with Captain Every and headed after the longboat towards a steep white cliff with trees and bushes clinging precariously to its side. "Where are we going?" Diana asked.

The captain pointed straight ahead. "In there."

"There's nothing but rock."

Smiling, the captain said, "Aye. That's what it looks like. Now duck your heads. We're approaching the mouth of the cave."

The vines and bushes acted as a natural barrier, digging into Alex, scratching his arms, knocking his Tilley off, and nearly ripping off his pack. As soon as they were through, though, they plunged into darkness. Before Alex's eyes could adjust from the bright Caribbean sun outside, their boat ran aground on a white sandy beach. Diana jumped out and was about to help the ghosts pull it ashore when she gasped and asked, "Where'd they go?"

"Who?" Alex asked.

"The ghosts," Diana replied. "They've vanished."

Jane, who was just getting out, replied, "What are ye talking about? They're still here." But when she let go of the boat, she exclaimed, "They're gone!"

"Everything's still here, but you've stepped off their boat," Alex said. "Remember, you're back in the world of the living. But don't worry. I'll tell you what's going on. Besides, if we find the treasure, it'll be real, and you'll be able to see it."

"Well, lead on," Jane said. "We'll just have to follow ye since ye can see what they're doing."

Alex nodded and followed the captain deeper into the cave up to the base of a rock wall with a dark horizontal crease twenty feet above him as the only indication of an opening. Seeing the ghosts passing through the rough stone, he asked the captain, "Are you sure this is the right way? We can't pass through solid objects as you can."

Every chuckled. "Don't worry. I'm sure this is the right way. Remember, when I came here before, I had a solid body like yours. Now, up ye go."

The climb was even more challenging than it looked as the wall was steep and wet, with only an occasional rounded nodule for hand and footholds. Not until he was near the top did Alex see that the crease was actually an opening to a large chamber beyond.

Once he got to the top, he took a breather, silently admitting that Jane's warnings about his health had been spot-on. He stayed in the opening and helped Diana and Jane over before swiveling around on his stomach and following them down.

The way down was even scarier, as the slope was just as steep and slippery, but he couldn't see where he was going. As he descended, the shadows grew longer inside the hidden cavern, so it was a surprise when his feet finally hit level ground. He pushed away from the wall and turned to see what they'd entered, but the light coming through the narrow opening above wasn't enough to illuminate the chamber.

"That was lovely," Diana said, stepping beside him. "My nails are worn to the nub, and I've got bruises over nearly every inch of my body."

Alex just grunted, then pulled out his flashlight and shone it around. Even though he'd gone spelunking in several caves before, he'd never seen a cavern like the one they were in. There were no stalagmites, and instead of stalactites, the ceiling resembled a light-colored wasp's nest, with open-faced pockets covering most of the surface. "This is so cool."

Diana put her hands up behind her ears and flipped them outward. "What did you say?"

Alex turned and put his flashlight under his chin so Diana could read his lips. "I said it was cool. Come on. The captain is motioning for us to follow him. Stay close to me and speak up if you need anything."

"Hold on a minute," Diana said. "Let me conjure some light so I can see where I'm going." She moved a little way off, then stretched a hand out while chanting,

"Dragon's blood and parchment burn

Bring the fire for which I yearn."

When the flames had sprung to life above her hand, they headed across the chamber and through a short tunnel to a second, much larger room. Numerous short, thick, rounded stalactite columns on the ceiling made it look like a bizarre upside-down mushroom field. Alex shone his flashlight around the room, but the light's beam hardly made a dent in pushing back the darkness. He lowered the beam and swept it back and forth across the boulder-strewn room and saw that the walls nearest him were pockmarked limestone, stretching for as far as he could see. Alex stopped his inspection when he saw Captain Every standing beside a large azure-blue pool.

Pouring sweat, Alex walked over and dropped his pack near where the captain stood. He flipped his braids over his shoulders, then bent down and splashed water on his face.

"Ye should've spoken up sooner," Every said. "We could've lifted the three of ye into here, but I've been dead so long I didn't think about the discomforts of the living."

"I'm always freezing on your ship, so I needed this tropical heat and some exercise to thaw out." Seeing a scowl on Jane's face, Alex quickly added, "But we'll take your offer to lift us over on the way out. How far is it now, Captain?"

Every grinned. "We're close. We're very close."

"Where is it?"

The captain pointed at the water. "Down there. I dropped my treasure chests into this pool."

"So, how are we going to get the treasure out?" Alex asked.

"Don't worry," the captain said, motioning Alex back. "Ye need to stand aside, as the men are going to need room to stack all the treasure."

Realizing neither Jane nor Diana could hear the captain, Alex relayed the information to them, as two sailors dove in. Staring down into the water, he asked, "Is it deep?"

"I don't know," Every replied. "I was looking for a good hiding place where the chests wouldn't be visible.

So, when I found this place, I didn't bother checking how deep it was. I figured I could always find divers to go down and get it."

"Aren't you worried that the chests might have deteriorated and your treasure is sitting on the bottom?" Alex asked.

Guessing as to what they were talking about, Diana interjected. "It depends. If this water is full of organisms, then the wood won't last. If not, then perhaps they'll have survived."

As if on cue, two ghosts popped out of the water and set a large chest down a few feet away.

"How much is down there?" Alex asked.

The captain took off his hat and wiped a sleeve across his forehead. "A fair amount. It'll take us several trips to load all this onboard the ship."

For the next half hour, a steady stream of spirits dove into the pool, emerging moments later with a chest. By the time they finished, Alex counted more than twenty containers lying around the pond. "Holy cow! How much is this worth?" Alex asked.

The captain shrugged. "I don't know in modern terms, but it was literally worth a king's ransom in my day."

"Can we see inside one of them?" Alex asked.

The captain shook his head. "When we're back on board. Until then, we need to focus on safely getting it out of here."

"What are we going to do with all this?" Diana asked.

"It's not ours," Alex replied. "It's the captain's. You can't go around and take something that's not yours."

"Yeah, but he stole it. Besides, he's dead. What's he going to do with it? I think we should take it back and use some of it to fund our missions to find the Maqlû. Then we could distribute the rest throughout the order. So many of us have almost no money and are living off the charity of others."

"There are international laws about treasures like this," Jane said. "In reality, we'd get to keep very little of it. But I'd suggest we discuss what to do with it once we get it out of here and onto the ship."

Alex felt the ankh start thumping against his chest. He looked around, trying to identify the cause of the warning.

"What's wrong?" Jane asked. "Ye look nervous."

"Something's not right," Alex replied.

Diana groaned. "I hate it when you say things like that."

A second later, a series of explosions echoed throughout the cavern.

CHAPTER 23
WHAT THEY CANNOT ANTICIPATE

The echoes and darkness made it impossible for Diana to hear what Jane and Alex were discussing. She gave up trying to understand and held her flames aloft to see the far side of the pool. A motion off to the side caused her to turn. She saw Jane diving to the ground. Before she could react, Alex slammed into her.

Diana hit the ground so hard that it knocked the flames out of her hand and the air out of her lungs. As she gasped for air, Alex drug her behind a couple of treasure chests. Hearing muffled explosions and screaming, she tried sitting up, but he pushed her back to the floor and shouted, "Stay down."

The sulfurous smoke swirling around the darkened cavern stung her eyes, making it impossible to see what was happening. Diana lay huddled against the chest, mentally kicking herself for following Alex into yet another debacle. She dimly heard a nearby explosion and felt a blast of hot air blow past her.

Several more explosions, followed by thudding sounds in the chests, drove Jane to crawl over and ask, "What's going on?"

When Alex didn't reply, Diana shook Alex to get his attention and shouted, "What's happening?" As soon as she touched his arm, she heard the cries and screams of men fighting each other.

Alex turned back to her and held his flashlight under his chin. In a low, urgent voice, he said, "The same ghosts that attacked us yesterday are at it again. I'm not sure why, but they've brought living-world weapons with them." He popped his head over the chest briefly before ducking down and adding, "Remember, they can use any object in our world against us, so don't try to be heroes. Whether you can see them or not, they're here, and they're real."

Wanting to know what was going on in the battle, Diana kept a firm grip on Alex's arm. She saw several ghosts moving around to her right. An instant later, there was a piercing war cry as they charged. She heard a few pistol shots and saw two of the *Fancy's* sailors jump up and fight the attackers with swords. Shrieks and screams mixed in with the sound of metal clanging on metal, sending shivers down Diana's back. A few seconds later, she heard someone shouting, "Retreat," but had no idea which side had said it.

Her hands were trembling so hard that she couldn't control them. Reaching down, she grabbed one of Alex's hands and squeezed it, seeking comfort in his warm, firm grip. "How are we going to get out of here?" she asked. "It was hard enough to climb in here without anyone trying to kill us. It's impossible now."

Before he could answer, Captain Every flew up, handed Alex an old flintlock pistol, and said in a low voice, "They're massing to our right front. We're running low on men and ammunition, so make yer shots count. Unfortunately, this pistol isn't very accurate, so wait until they're close. Then aim for their hearts. It's the only thing that will stop them for sure." He paused, then added, "Ye'll only get time for one shot before it's every man for himself."

"What about us?" Diana asked. "We can help."

"Not if you can't see them," the captain replied before flying off to a group of men hiding behind a large stalagmite.

Alex shoved the pistol into Jane's hands. "You keep this for self-defense."

"How am I going to see a ghost?" Jane asked.

"If you see a sword or pistol hovering in the air near you – shoot it," Alex replied.

He turned to Diana, but she held up her hand before he could say anything. "Don't worry about me. I'll create my own weapon. But what about you?"

"I'm going to go find me a weapon. Remember, I can see them as they glow in the dark. Don't worry about me, though. Focus on staying safe." He paused, then added, "I know it's a little late for this, but I'm sorry for getting you two into this mess." He then switched off his flashlight and crawled away before either girl could argue.

Unable to see in the darkness, Diana conjured up magical flames. The small light glowing from her hand gave her a small amount of comfort. She looked up at Jane. "My magic isn't going to work on spirits in here, so what do we do?"

Jane eyed the chest they were hiding behind and said, "Ah, but we have something that might distract our attackers and help Captain Every."

"What's that?"

Jane's eyebrows shot up, and a mischievous smile crossed her face. She looked down at the lock on the chest and said, "Gold."

Diana smiled at the thought of all the spirits scrambling after gold they couldn't use. A roar echoed through the cavern, followed by a scattering of gunfire and a second wave of sulfurous smoke. She looked down at the fire onyx stone lying in her hand, then stretched her arm towards the lock, closed her eyes, and chanted,

> *"Magic forces black and white*
> *I call upon the powers of Asteria and Perses*
> *Show thy light and thy thunder*
> *Come thee here and break it asunder."*

She felt a tingling in her fingertips as the first threads of magic coalesced in the air around her. A second later, a small lightning bolt shot out of the air and hit the lock, causing a miniature explosion.

Before Diana could react, Jane had knocked off the lock and flipped open the lid. She shoved both hands into the pile of coins, precious stones, and gold bars, then flung them into the cavern as far as she could while shouting, "Gold!"

As soon as Jane's hands were clear of the chest, Diana shoved her hands in to grab two fistfuls of coins. Following Jane's lead, she threw the coins into the cavern and shouted, "There's gold here!"

She thought the cavern grew a little quieter, but just then, she saw a cutlass raised above her. A bright flash, followed by a deafening explosion next to her ear, caused her to jump. She slipped on the slick rocks and fell backwards, hitting her head hard on the floor. For an instant, she saw stars in front of her eyes. Then all the sights and sounds of the battle disappeared as she blacked out.

CHAPTER 24
WHO COMPELS MY STRENGTH

Confused and angry that her brother had helped the three children and old man move on without doing the same for her, Deborah left Port Royal and flew to the top of Blue Mountain Peak to calm her nerves. But as she kept replaying the events in her mind, she couldn't identify anything Alex had done to help them – except encourage them to trust in the unknown.

She drifted off to the netherworld without having resolved anything and didn't return until the next day. As soon as she reappeared, she headed after the *Fancy*, despite the ridicule she'd experienced from Captain Every's crew.

Deborah flew northeast all that day, finally catching up to what she thought was the *Fancy* at dusk. She flew down, but as she was about to land, she saw it wasn't the right ship. Fearing it was another pirate crew sailing after Alex, she flew closer and surreptitiously worked her way along the side until she reached the mid-deck area, where she heard voices. Wanting to listen to what they were saying, she put her ear to the gunwale and stuck her arm through the hull to hold on.

Even though she wasn't flesh and bone, she soon felt seasick, as the ship's rolling made her uncomfortable. Its creaking and groaning only exacerbated her queasiness. She was about to let go and fly away when she heard one of the sailors ask, "How soon will we catch up to 'em, Cap'n Tew?"

"I don't know. They appeared to be undermanned, which means they can't tack very easily. But given the damage in the last battle, I'm not sure our tiller will hold up if we hit rough weather. All we can do is hope they put into some port."

One sailor said, "We outnumber 'em, Cap'n. Maybe we should fly after them and attack before they get a full crew in another port. Once they've got a full complement, we won't be able to beat them with their superior firepower."

"Believe me. I want to catch them even more than you do. Besides wanting to get my hands on that magical staff, I have an old score to settle with Captain Every."

Deborah gasped when she heard Every's name. One of the men heard her and looked over the railing. Spotting her, the man grabbed Deborah by the throat and yanked her upwards.

She screamed, not from pain but from fear of what might happen. The man who'd caught her was a beast, standing head and shoulders above all the other crewmen with arms and legs that looked like short tree trunks and a beard that made him look like a wild monster.

A thin man dressed in a long black coat floated across the deck, and said, in a chilling voice, "What have we here?"

The man's grip on Deborah's throat tightened, preventing her from speaking. All she could do was point at her throat and gurgle some inarticulate sounds.

"Release the girl," the man in black said. "I want to know who she is and what she's doing here."

Figuring it was her only chance to escape, Deborah launched herself over the side as soon as the man's fingers uncurled, diving as deep as she could go.

She waited for quite some time before she finally poked her head above the surface. When she saw the ship had passed out of sight, she breathed a sigh of relief, popped out of the ocean, and headed inland, wanting to put as much distance between her and the ship as possible.

A short time later, she reached a trash-strewn shoreline. Deborah winced at the sight but kept flying inland, passing over a crowded city before reaching the countryside. She didn't stop to think where she was going until she encountered a dense forest on the side of a mountain.

Looking up, she saw the most massive fortress she'd ever seen sitting on top of the nearby peak. It was such an incredible sight that she temporarily forgot about the ghost ship she'd escaped and flew towards it. Deborah stopped at a pointed section of the outer wall that looked like the bow of a ship and took stock of her surroundings. Jagged, heavily forested mountains surrounded three sides of the fort. On the fourth side was the valley she'd just flown through.

The view was so stunning that she didn't see the two ebony-skinned soldiers in blue coats and white pants coming towards her until they'd grabbed her arms. Startled, she struggled to get free, but they had too firm a grip on her. She cried out to release her, but they ignored her protests and hauled her into the fort stopping when they reached an aristocratic-looking Black man with graying hair. He was of medium height and wore a high-collared dark blue coat with a red front and long tails over white pants tucked into calf-high black leather boots. "What have we here, Sergeant?" the man said in heavily accented French.

"General, we found this girl sneaking around the battlements. She looked suspicious, so we thought you'd like to question her."

The general cocked his head to one side. "Well, mademoiselle, what do you have to say for yourself?"

Deborah was too frightened to reply and stood, mute, staring up at her captors.

The sergeant shook her. "Out with it, girl. Why were you skulking around outside?"

Having never been a prisoner before, she was scared witless and blurted out, "I was searching for my brother, who's on the *Fancy* when …."

She didn't get to finish her explanation, as the general exclaimed, "What! The *Fancy?* Captained by Henry Every?"

As soon as she nodded, the general turned to his fellow officers. "After all this time, could he finally be going after it?"

Deborah didn't hear the rest of their discussion as it became a whispered conversation. When they were finished, the general turned back to Deborah and asked, "Where were they headed?"

"I don't know. The ship I was following was heading east. I can only assume they were following Every."

The general slapped his thigh and shouted, "Hah. Finally, our patience is going to be rewarded." He turned to the officers standing behind him. "Gather the men. We're going treasure hunting."

"How will you find them?" Deborah asked. "There's a lot of ocean out there."

The man stopped in the middle of buckling his saber to his side.

Sensing an opportunity to help Alex, Jane, and Diana, Deborah said. "If you release me, I can show you the way."

"How can you be so sure of yourself?" the General asked.

Deborah smiled. "It's easy. All I have to do is follow my brother's aura – it's very distinctive. But you have to promise not to harm the living people on board the ship."

The man looked confused. "Wait, I thought you said it was Captain Every's ship. How can there be living people involved?"

"It's a long story. Would you rather hear it or find them?"

A party of 100 well-armed men followed Deborah out of the fort minutes later.

CHAPTER 25
TOUSSAINT L'OVERTURE

The sudden quiet unnerved Alex so much that he jumped when the captain flew up and drew his cutlass. Every leaned close and whispered, "Most of my men are out of ammunition, so it'll be hand to hand from here on. It's not right for ye three to be a casualty to an old feud, so I'll try to distract Tew and his men while ye escape. Ye'll have to be quick about it, though, because I doubt we can hold out very long. When ye get Jane and Diana out of here, take them to the jungle. Once ye get there, hide, and don't move until ye see their ship leave the bay. Understand?"

Alex shook his head. "That's not going to work. Diana's unconscious and there's no way we can get her out of this place on our own in the middle of a battle."

"Well, ye'll have to do the best ye can. But no matter what happens today, know that we're all thankful for the opportunity to go out on our terms. Now, if ye'll excuse me, we must prepare for the next attack."

Alex nodded, then told Jane what Every had said. "So, what do we do?" he asked.

Jane grabbed Alex's hands. "It doesn't help us if yer discouraged too. I need ye to tell me we'll get out of here okay, then do yer thing. Understand?"

The ankh thumped steadily against his chest, giving him a tiny sliver of hope that things would turn out okay. He squeezed Jane's hands and, with false bravado, said, "You're right. We'll be fine. Just think of the stories you two can tell your classmates about what you did over summer break." He nudged Diana to see if she was awake, but he didn't get a response.

Alex saw Every and his men move off to their left and told Jane, "Stay here and keep your head down, but be ready to move as soon as Diana wakes up."

"Where are ye going?" Jane whispered.

"I can see them, and you can't, so I'm going to go fight with Every to buy you some time to get out of here. Besides, if my hunch is right, they're not interested in you, so you should be safe."

Before she could argue him out of the foolhardy move, Alex slipped over the chests and dropped to one knee. He heard yelling and swords clanging, along with pistol and musket fire. Not being able to see much, he headed towards where he'd last seen Every. He'd taken only a few steps when a deafening roar from the chamber entrance caused him to look up. Dozens of spirits rushed in, firing muskets at Tew's men. Smoke swirled so thickly around him that it soon made it impossible to see anything.

The repeated cry of "Retreat!" joined the cacophony of explosions and screams, followed by an eerie silence. Not knowing what was happening, he clambered back over the chests and plopped down between Jane and Diana.

"Is Diana okay?" Alex asked.

"I don't know. Ye were gone for such a short time that I didn't get a chance to look at her. Why don't ye check her breathing while ye tell me what's going on. I'll check the rest of her for injuries."

Knowing he was incapable of multi-tasking, Alex paused and decided the information could wait. He brushed the hair off Diana's face, bent down to listen to her breathing, then sighed in relief when he felt her warm breath against his cheek. But, when he called out to her, he didn't get an answer. Alex gently started probing for injuries but didn't find any blood on her head or neck.

He moved his hands down to her neck and fell backwards when Diana said, "Watch it, bub."

Mortified, he mumbled some unintelligible words before asking, "Are you all right?"

"I think so, except I've got a splitting headache. Everything's so quiet. What's going on?" she asked.

"I don't know, but I think the battle's over. Someone else arrived and chased Tew's men away."

A smaller group of spirits carrying torches flew through the opening, illuminating the chamber with their dancing lights. The ghost in the lead floated down, landing a short distance away. He wore a black tri-corn hat with feathers and a fancy uniform with a dress sword hanging from a gold-colored sash, making him resemble a Napoleonic general.

Alex noticed the ankh was strangely silent and whispered, "I don't sense any danger, but all the same, stay down until I tell you it's clear." He stood up and walked towards the man he assumed was the officer in charge, saying, "What's going on?"

The unknown ghost was startled but pulled himself up to his full height and, with a pompous air, responded, "I am Francois Dominque Toussaint L'Overture, Governor for Life of Saint Dominique. I have come to claim this treasure in the name of my country."

Captain Every jumped out of his hiding place and flew over. Hovering only inches from the newcomer, he said, "It's mine. Now back off, or I'll send ye straight to hell."

Toussaint L'Overture smiled and motioned with his hand to someone at the back of the cave. Dozens of armed men came pouring through the opening and surrounded them. "Then, I'll have company." He looked at how few men Every still had and said, "But I fear you'll come off the worse for it, though."

Alex stepped between the two men and thrust out his arms. "Enough. There've already been too many deaths."

"I have no desire to fight," Toussaint said, "but I do want this treasure for my country. It's why I brought my men. Besides, I think we've earned it. If we hadn't come along when we did, none of you would be here to argue with me about whose it is." He turned to study Alex more closely. After a few seconds, his eyes widened. "So, you're the one she was talking about."

Alex stumbled backwards. "Who, who are you talking about?" he asked, fearing the answer.

Toussaint waved to the men behind him. Two guards floated down from the opening holding Deborah between them. Alex started running towards his sister, but a soldier stopped him. Before he could figure out how to get to Deborah, Jane and Diana stumbled up. They immediately linked their arms through his so they could see the ghosts again.

"What's going on?" Jane asked as the ghosts came into view. "Who are these people, Alex?"

Alex held up a finger. "Shh. I'm trying to figure it out."

Every leaned in until he was just inches away from L'Overture's face and said, "Well, we have it, and we're not going to just hand this fortune over to you."

Toussaint studied the captain closely for a moment. "You must be the infamous Captain Every."

The captain's eyes narrowed. "I am, but how do ye know? I've never met ye before."

"I've dedicated my entire existence to helping my country. The men with me today are some of a dedicated group of souls who have postponed moving on to stay loyal to the cause. I grew up hearing stories about pirates like you and that you hid a vast fortune somewhere in the Caribbean. My men caught this girl lurking around the Citadelle earlier today, and I convinced her to tell me where she was headed."

Alex turned to Diana. "You usually know this type of stuff. What is Saint-Dominque? I've never heard of it."

Jane looked at Diana and asked, "What are they saying? I don't speak French and don't understand what's happening."

Diana held up her hand to stop Jane from talking. "I'll tell you later. Right now, I need to listen." She turned to Alex. "The French used to call Haiti, Saint-Domingue. It used to supply much of Europe's sugar and coffee and at one time was the richest French colony in the New World."

Alex nodded and turned back to L'Overture. "This isn't Saint-Domingue, and you're not governor here. So, release my sister and stop telling us what to do."

"I can't. My country desperately needs what this treasure can buy. Have you seen how poor my people are? Ever since our revolution, my country has spiraled deeper and deeper into poverty. We were already one of the poorest countries in the world when devastating natural disasters hit us again a few years ago, making things even worse. Please help us."

"Don't listen to him," Every said. "This treasure is mine. He has no right to it."

There was a long silence. Looking around, Alex saw everyone looking at him, as if he would referee the dispute.

Diana nudged Alex. "Hear him out."

Alex turned back to Toussaint and asked, "Why do you think you deserve this treasure?"

Toussaint took off his hat and sat down on a boulder. "You need some background to understand my country's situation. The French imported thousands of slaves a year for decades into Saint-Dominque. My father was one of them. I got lucky, though. The man who owned the plantation I grew up on allowed me to get an education and eventually freed me.

"However, I chose to stay on. There was a lot of talk that everyone would be equal in the new French Republic, but we soon found out that's all it was – talk. None of the European powers, much less the plantation owners, were interested in abolishing slavery here. There was too much money involved. Seeing things were not going to change, many enslaved people started fleeing their plantations. I, too, took to the hills, where I joined one of the maroons. The white plantation owners retaliated, and soon we were at war."

Alex frowned. "Did you just call them morons?"

Toussaint shook his head. "No. Maroons were groups of enslaved people who banded together to fight the plantation owners. At first, most were undisciplined groups of men who only wanted revenge. I became a leader of one of the maroons and trained my soldiers to fight as an effective guerilla army. More groups joined us, and eventually, we drove the French out of Saint-Domingue.

"I switched my allegiance back to the French when they finally granted equal rights to all free people of color. Taking advantage of our new allies, my men and I turned on the Spanish and drove them off the island, thus abolishing slavery across all of Hispaniola. We fought the British army a little while later and forced them to depart the island, too, leaving us free from imperialists for the first time in centuries.

"After that, I turned my efforts to ensuring prosperity for my country. I worked to get trading treaties with the United States and Britain and bring back some of the knowledge we lost with the revolt. Many of my contemporaries objected, and alas, the French kept meddling. When Napoleon Bonaparte became First Consul of France, he decided he needed the money from our island to pay for his European wars.

"Realizing he was in danger of losing the island's riches, he sent soldiers to regain control. Two of my lieutenants turned traitors and helped the French capture me. They took me back to France, where I died in prison. The only good thing those traitors did was complete the revolt against France and drive them off the island for good. Shortly afterwards, I heard

Napoleon sold another part of the French New World Empire to finance his wars. I believe they called it the Louisiana Purchase. It's rather ironic. Despite their efforts to keep their colonies and slaves here in the New World, the French eventually lost everything.

"Alas, my country never became prosperous. Poor management and too many corrupt dictators destroyed my country. We achieved democracy only a few decades ago and need everything we can get to help us overcome our extreme poverty. That's why we need this treasure."

"I saw the pictures of what the earthquake did to your country. It looked horrible." Alex turned to Captain Every. "What are your plans for this treasure?"

"To be honest, I hadn't thought that far," Every said. "I gave up so many years of my life because of it, that all I could think of was getting it back. I was planning on giving some to ye three, though, to help fund yer quest."

"Well, if you don't have any good plans on how to use the treasure, why don't you give it to Haiti," Alex said.

Speaking in fluent French, Diana said, "I agree with Alex. I can't speak for Jane, but I'm sure Haiti can put it to better use than we can. Besides, as cool as it would be to keep it, treasure hunters only get to keep a small portion of the treasure, what with all the competing claims and lawsuits."

Are you okay with that, Captain?" asked Alex.

"I can't believe I'm saying this, but fine. Take the damn treasure," Every said.

"I know you have a ship that could hold all this, Captain," Toussaint said. "Would you do us the honor and carry it to Cap-Haïtien? My men will help you load it and escort you to ensure there are no more attacks. Once there, I will make sure it gets into the right hands."

Captain Every glared at Toussaint. "I've dealt with too many scoundrels in my life just to hand it over to you. And my name is at the top of that list. How do ye think I managed to take this entire hoard from the rest of the pirate fleet I sailed with? I accept yer offer to help carry this haul and escort us, but my men and I will personally take the treasure to the proper authorities. If I don't like the looks of 'em, we'll take it away."

"I've no problems with that," Toussaint replied. "I'm confident you'll approve of the person I have in mind."

"Why don't we worry about those details later," Diana said. "Right now, we need to think about these chests. They've been down in that water for so long that I'm concerned about them falling apart with the weight inside them. You'll need to make stretchers, or something similar, so you can carry them out. Then, when you get to the entrance, you'll need to wait until it's dark before moving it out to the ship. I don't think we want anyone seeing what's going on."

The two ghosts looked sheepishly at each other, then began organizing the men.

CHAPTER 26
THE HARDER THE CONFLICT

Getting out of the cave was much easier than getting in, as Every's men carried them to the outer chamber. For the next two hours, Alex watched as the spirits flew in and out of the cave, bringing in materials to carry the chests, then reversing course and hauling the treasure to the outer chamber on improvised litters. As the ghosts set down the last chest, the one Diana had broken open, Alex felt the ankh start beating gently against his chest. He'd learned enough about his necklace's strange messaging system to know they weren't in danger, but he was curious what it was trying to tell him. He got up and walked to the cave entrance to check if he'd misunderstood, and something outside was causing the little looped cross to come alive. But all seemed normal.

Putting it down to being overly excited, Alex turned and was about to head back inside when he noticed Jane and Diana sitting against the wall on the far side of the chamber, both looking tired and disheveled. Guilt about dragging them into his messy life overcame him. He looked away and noticed the last chest they'd brought out was so rusted and rotted that he could see gold through some of the holes.

Thinking there was no harm in looking, he limped over and bent down, wincing at his body's reminders that he'd overtaxed himself. He lifted the lid and started sorting through it, looking for gifts. Most of the contents were gold and silver bars, but there were also dark red rubies and brilliant sapphires intermixed with rupees, doubloons, guineas, and akce.

None of those interested him, though, and he kept searching. Halfway down the box on the left-hand side, he got a shock. Curious about what had caused it, he grabbed the object and pulled out a gold ring in the design of a woman's head with a sprinkling of diamonds all around. But what caught his attention was the large tear-drop-shaped emerald in the middle of the woman's hair. It was so different than any other ring he'd ever seen that he thought Diana would be interested in it for its history.

He stuffed it into his pants pockets, stuck his hand in again, and rummaged around some more. Seconds later, he received another jolt. Grabbing the offending item, he pulled his hand out and saw he was grasping a slim gold necklace with a silver dragon curled around a flaming red pearl. Thinking it would match Jane's hair coloring, he stuffed it in his pocket.

When he looked up, he saw almost every ghost in the cavern had crowded around, eager to see what was inside. Embarrassed at being caught, he closed the lid and walked over to where Jane and Diana were sitting. He gave them the two pieces of jewelry, saying, "After all you've been through, I thought you should at least get something out of this adventure. I couldn't have made it this far without you two."

"These aren't yours to give away," Diana said.

Alex waved a hand at all the chests. "Do you really think anybody's going to miss these two trinkets? Besides, all this would still be sitting at the bottom of the pool if it wasn't for us."

Jane studied her necklace intently, then asked, "Out of all the jewels in those chests, why did ye pick this one?"

"Don't you like it?" Alex asked. "I can get you another one."

Jane grabbed his wrist, stopping him from walking away. "I do like it. It's jest so different than any other piece of jewelry I've ever seen. It even feels different, almost like it's got a soft static charge to it."

"I know what you mean," Alex said. "It gave me a good jolt when I first touched it, which is why I pulled it out."

Jane cried out the instant the clasp closed around her neck. A moment later, she started shaking. Before either Diana or Alex could help her, she stopped. "Are you all right?" Diana asked.

"Strangely, yes," Jane said in a faraway voice. "It gave me quite a start when I put it on, but …." She turned to Diana. "I'm curious what'll happen when ye put yours on."

"I'm not sure I trust it," Diana said. "I mean, think about it. This stuff has been buried for centuries, and he just happens to choose something that shocks you. That's not a coincidence, and I'm not sure I'm willing to try my luck." She held it out for Jane to see. "Besides, have you ever seen anything like this ring?" she asked. "It's like a beautiful Medusa's head except with precious stones instead of snakes for her hair."

Jane looked it over and shook her head. "No, but I'm still interested in how you'll react when ye try it on."

Diana hesitated, then slipped it on. She yelped and rounded on Alex. "Did you think it would be funny to shock me like that?"

"I didn't mean to hurt either of you. Here," Alex said, reaching out for the ring. "Give it back, and I'll find you something else."

Alex was surprised when Diana clutched both hands to her chest and said, "No, thank you. I'll keep it."

"But, a minute ago, you were ready to bite my head off."

"I've changed my mind," Diana said while staring at the ring. "It's such a strange piece of jewelry that I've decided to keep it."

Deborah flew into the cavern just then and landed nearby. She plopped down and leaned back against the cavern walls.

"Are you all right?" Alex asked. "I've been looking all over for you."

Not knowing who Alex was talking to, Diana jumped up and grabbed his arm. She nearly fell when she saw who it was. "Deborah? Is that really you?" she cried out.

Jane jumped up and grabbed Alex's arm, shrieking in delight upon seeing her best friend. She lunged forward, intending to hug Deborah, but saw her disappear as soon as she pulled away from Alex. Forcing herself to calm down, Jane stepped back and linked arms again with Alex.

Deborah's mouth dropped open. It took her some time before she collected herself enough to say, "I thought my brother was the only one who could see our world. When did you get the ability to see ghosts?"

"We can't unless we're holding onto him," Diana said.

"Or when we're on a ghost ship with him," Jane added.

"You'll have to explain all this to me later. I came over because I wanted to apologize to all of you for not coming to help you earlier. But, as you saw, Toussaint's men captured me and forced me to lead him to you."

"Don't apologize," Jane said. "We should be thanking ye. If it weren't for ye, well, I don't want to think of what would have happened to us."

"I've been thinking about this quest of yours to help me," Deborah said, "and I believe it would be best if you quit and went back home before it gets too dangerous. I'll find some other way of moving on."

"But, Deb," Alex protested. "I promised I'd find one of those Maqlû to help you. And that's what I'm going to do. Besides, I've got a promising lead."

Captain Every floated over, cutting off the conversation. "It'll be dark outside soon, and time to move. I suggest ye bring up the rear so my men won't knock ye over with the chests. So, do what ye have to do to get ready."

"What if our attackers come back?" asked Diana. "We'll be sitting ducks, having to move all these chests."

"My men will be moving the treasure while Toussaint's will fan out over the area to make sure no one surprises us again," Every said. "Besides, we can always pull everyone in and concentrate our forces if we need to defend ourselves, but I doubt we'll need to. We gave them a pretty good beating this afternoon."

Captain Every flew off to where Toussaint and his aides were standing. They talked in hushed tones for several minutes before breaking up.

"It's raining hard outside," Jane said. "We're going to get drenched when we leave here."

Alex looked down at his mud-soaked clothes. "I don't mind. I'm miserable now, but it'll be even worse when my clothes dry, so it'll be like getting a shower."

"I agree with Alex," Diana said. "It would feel nice to get all this mud off of me."

Even though they were exhausted from everything they'd been through, the three got up and trudged out of the cavern before sitting down again on the beach. As Alex let the warm rain wash off the caked mud, he noticed Jane running her fingers through her long ginger-colored hair.

He didn't realize he was staring until Jane asked, "Are ye okay?"

Alex's face turned a beet-red color. "Yeah," he stammered. "I was just zoning out for a moment."

Jane smiled and chuckled, "Uh, huh."

Diana suddenly huffed, turned, and knocked into him on her way back into the cave.

Dumbfounded by Diana's brusqueness, Alex looked blankly at her receding back, and asked, "What did I do?"

Jane shook her head and patted him on the back. "Ye need to pay more attention to the feelings of those around ye," she said before heading after Diana.

When he finished his makeshift shower, Alex returned to the cave and sat away from the two girls. He stared at the sky, lit by the lights of towns around the bay reflecting off the cloud cover. The rain beating on the leaves gradually drummed his embarrassment away to the point where he was surprised when his sister joined him and asked, "You like her, don't you?"

"Who? What are you talking about?"

Deborah shook her head. "You can't be that clueless, can you? I'm talking about Jane."

Hoping the darkness hid the blood rushing to his cheeks, he replied, "I tend to like everybody – unless they're trying to kill me. Now, if you'll excuse me, I have to see if they're ready to move out. Be back in a minute." Alex got up and rushed off before his sister could ask more embarrassing questions.

A few minutes later, armed soldiers appeared and fanned out in all directions, followed by a double column of spirits carrying the treasure.

The work to move the treasure continued through the night and didn't end until the eastern horizon had turned a light blue. Captain Every didn't dally, ordering his crew to weigh anchor and unfurl the mainsails. Minutes later, the *Fancy* was sailing eastward towards the mouth of the bay.

CHAPTER 27
FORGET NOT OLD FRIENDS

Anxious to see her best friend again, Deborah returned from the netherworld early the next morning. Remembering the crew's treatment of her in Port Royal, she hesitated to get closer to the *Fancy*. But when she spotted Jane standing on the ship's bow alone, she cast aside her doubts and flew in, landing a few feet away. She stayed silent for a few moments, unsure if her old friend would be able to see her without Alex around. Deborah saw Jane fiddling with a pendant and floated closer, as she'd never known Jane to wear jewelry. Curiosity got the better of her, and she blurted out, "What's that?"

Deborah was surprised when Jane turned and tried engulfing her in a bear hug. But her friend's arms just passed through her.

Jane stepped back with a sheepish look on her face. "I forgot that even though I can see a ghost on this ship, I can't touch them." She waved her embarrassment away and said, "It doesn't matter. I'm glad to see ye."

"I too wish we could've hugged, for although I would never turn down the opportunity to move on, seeing you again is the next best thing," Deborah said. "Besides, it would've been nice to feel a person's touch again." A puzzled look crossed Deborah's face. "I've seen Alex touch spirits. Why can't you?"

"There's a lot about him that I don't understand. My guess is that it has something to do with his ... necklace."

"Relax, I know about the ankh," Deborah said. "I was there when he took it. I have often wondered how different things would be if I'd taken it when my dad offered it to me."

"Do ye resent him for it?" Jane asked.

"At first, I did, but after seeing what he's been through, I wouldn't wish it on my enemies. Speaking of the devil," Deborah looked around the deck and asked, "Where are my brother and Diana? I don't see them.

"They're still sleeping below. Diana got a concussion yesterday, and yer brother has been hurt several times recently and needs rest. He's pretty beat up."

"I've got to ask," Deborah said. "How did he rope you into helping me?"

"He didn't. When I realized he was still alive after that temple collapse, I convinced Diana to come with me to find him. At first, all we were trying to do was rescue him, but when he told us what he was trying to do for ye, well, we both volunteered to come."

"Why do all this just to help me move on? It's a lost cause."

Jane looked out to sea and, in a faraway voice, said, "Maybe it's because both Diana and I are looking for something that we couldn't find in the Bandruí."

Deborah studied her best friend, who she'd never seen act this way. "What's gotten into you?" she asked.

"I don't know."

"Don't you think you're going way beyond the call of duty?"

Jane smiled. "Maybe, but I think both of us are loving the adventure. It's like nothing we could've ever dreamed of."

"But you're putting your life at risk."

"I know. But it also feels like I'm living for the first time. I'm not jest Lady Yvaine's favored aide out here. And ye should see how Diana's changed. She's overcoming her fear of heights and keeps charging into danger. She's not the shy wallflower we knew back in Stormhold. Heck, I even caught her lying back in Lamanai to cover up things she'd gotten involved with."

Deborah looked down at the water curling about the bow. After a lengthy silence, she asked, "Do you think my brother's after the Maqlû for himself?"

Jane shook her head. "It's too bad ye haven't had time to get to know him. I believe his sole goal is to help ye move on. Diana's more suspicious of his actions, but even she's starting to come around."

"Do you think he has a plan on how to find the Fountain of Youth?"

Jane burst out laughing. "Ye don't know yer brother. But the short answer to yer question is that it would surprise me if he did."

"Are you saying you're comfortable just wandering around the Caribbean, hoping to find it?"

Jane frowned as she thought about the question. "Of course I don't like aimlessly wandering around, but that's not what this feels like. I mean, if I hadn't gone on this journey, I'd never have known what it's like to fire a cannon or find a treasure. We're making a difference. I guess it goes back to what I was jest saying about living."

Deborah pointed at the necklace Jane was fiddling with and asked, "What are you wearing? I've never seen you wear any jewelry before. It's stunning."

Jane stared at the dragon surrounding the flaming pearl for a moment before saying, "Yer brother dug it out of one of the treasure chests back there."

"Are you sweet on him?"

Jane blushed. "Of course not. It's jest that out of all the amazing pieces of gold and jewelry in this treasure – he chose this necklace for me and that strange ring for Diana. They're…."

"What are you trying to say?"

"This is not normal jewelry. It feels odd." Seeing the puzzled look on her friend's face, Jane said, "The best way of explaining it is with an example. I watched Diana with her ring. At first, she didn't want it, but now she's acting very possessive about it. And I hate to say it, but I feel the same way about mine. It's like these inanimate objects are somehow tapping into our emotions."

"That makes no sense."

"I know. And that's what's so interesting."

Just then, a burly sailor flew up and growled, "Scram, ye two. I've got work to do up here and don't want ye getting in my way."

As Deborah walked towards the quarterdeck with Jane, she could hear the sailor grumble, "We've got enough bad luck with two girls onboard. We don't need another one."

CHAPTER 28
BY THE TRACKS WE LEAVE

Later that morning, the *Fancy* sailed across the mouth of a bay with a large Chilean warship lying at anchor in the middle of it. Diana was so fascinated by the strange sight that she didn't notice Toussaint fly up to the quarterdeck. It wasn't until the Haitian general's voice grew to a shout that she turned to see what the commotion was about.

"Captain Every, why aren't we putting into Cap-Haïtien? It's a straight shot from there to the Citadelle, our destination," Toussaint said.

"I want to find a more remote landing site where we won't attract any unwanted attention," the captain replied

"But every minute of delay allows those scoundrels who attacked you to catch up with us," Toussaint said.

"If I were ye, I'd be more worried about living bandits stealing the treasure than Tew's men. We should be able to repel any spirit attacks on land or sea with our combined forces, but I'm not as confident we could repel an attack by the living. As you've reminded me many times, Haiti is a poor country, and poverty can cause men to do some pretty desperate things. And that's why we need to be secretive."

Diana interrupted the heated argument between the two spirits by asking, "Are you sure this money will be put to good use, Mr. L'Overture?" "Will this really help the Haitian people? I don't have a lot of faith in politicians and other powerful people. From my observations, they tend to only look out for themselves, so how can we trust anyone with this treasure?"

"I share your concern, but the man we'll be seeing today is a good person who puts his country first," Toussaint said. "In fact, he's the only person in Haiti I'd trust the treasure with."

"Does he know we're coming?"

Toussaint shook his head. "No. He can't speak to spirits as you and your friends can. But I know his schedule. He's so invested in helping our country that he rarely sleeps and has become a night owl."

"So, what's your plan?" Diana asked.

Toussaint looked uncomfortable. "I didn't plan anything since I never expected this to happen. I'm counting on you and your friends to figure out a way to get him to listen."

"That sounds too much like Alex's planning methods – and that's not good. Where is this place you're talking about?" Diana asked.

"The Citadelle Laferrière. It's one of the largest forts in the Americas."

"So, are we just going to have your men fly the chests up– like they did last night?"

Toussaint shook his head. "That was a short distance on a level surface with boats transporting the chests most of the way. The chests are too heavy for spirits to take very far, and the Citadelle is miles inland at 3,000 feet."

"If your men can't carry the chests to this Citadelle place, how were you planning to get all the treasure there?" Diana asked.

Toussaint shrugged.

"Well, since we have to travel miles to our destination, we'll need a truck. Do you know anyone we could borrow one from?"

"No. Even if you get one, you should know we can only get as far as Milot with ground transportation. The authorities have blocked off the last part of the path up to the Citadelle, which is why I wanted to anchor in Cap-Haïtien," Toussaint said.

"How far is it from Milot to the Citadelle?" Jane asked, joining the discussion.

"It's about four miles to the top."

"Are there pack horses available?" Jane asked.

"There are plenty of horses near the start of the path, as that's how many tourists get to the Citadelle," Toussaint replied. "But you'll have to figure out how to appropriate them."

Diana stomped her foot. "That's not right. You say you want to help your people, but the first chance you get, you want to cheat them. We need to hire a truck driver to take us there and rent the horses. We have plenty of treasure to pay for transportation."

Toussaint opened and closed his mouth several times. "You're right. But, how are we going to arrange for this transportation?"

"It's pretty obvious," Diana said. "Jane, Alex, and I will have to go ashore this afternoon to arrange for a truck rental and a meeting place for tonight. You can move the treasure then."

"That sounds reasonable," Toussaint said. "I'll get a few of my men to fly you ashore so you can procure a truck."

"I don't think it would look good for us to fly through the air in broad daylight with no visible means of support," Diana said. "People will freak out. I think the best way is for Captain Every to get us close to shore so his men can row us in without looking too suspicious. And remember, we'll have to use some of the treasure to pay our way."

"Very well. You know this century better than I do," Toussaint replied.

They continued sailing west until they spotted an isolated shoreline on the western side of the hill outside of Cap-Haïtien. As soon as they dropped anchor, Diana, Jane, Alex, and the captain, stepped into the dinghy and rowed ashore. It didn't take long to find a driver with a truck large enough to hold all the chests, as the gold coins made negotiations quick and easy. After arranging a rendezvous time and place with the driver, they headed back to the beach, where they waited until shortly after dark to meet up with the owner of the two-and-a-half-ton truck they were going to use.

The man looked around at the dark, deserted meeting spot and, in heavily accented French, said, "I'll have none of this. I told you I wouldn't get involved in drug running. You'll have to find another way to move your goods. I'm heading back to town."

Diana stuck out her hands to stop him. "Please don't leave. We're not doing anything illegal. In fact, we're going to be handing over our cargo to government officials. It's just that it's sensitive material, and we didn't want people to get too curious."

The man grunted but seemed to relent a little. "You're just kids. How could you be involved in something like this?"

"It's a long story, but I can assure you, this is only an aid mission," Diana replied.

"You better be telling the truth," the man said.

"We are, but there's one other thing I should warn you about."

"What's that?" the man asked warily.

"When the men with our cargo show up, I'd suggest you stay in the cab and don't look at what's happening." Seeing the panicked look on his face, Diana hastily added, "I told you, we're not doing anything illegal. It's just that I'm afraid you'll freak out if you see the cargo."

The man stuck out his chest. "I'm not afraid of anything except thugs, gangs, and drug lords."

Alex nudged her and whispered in English, "I'm not sure what you guys are talking about, but he already looks pretty nervous. When he sees the chests floating through the air, he's going to freak out. Why don't you try to convince him to loan us the truck for the night, and we'll pay him more."

"That's a crazy idea. Who's going to drive that truck?" Diana asked.

"I will," Alex replied.

Diana rolled her eyes. "We'll be fine. I've already told him not to look at what's happening."

"I hate to be a buttinsky, but Alex might be right," Jane said. "Think about how we've reacted to spirits at times."

"For once, let's stick to the plan." Diana dug into her pack, pulled out the three additional large gold coins they'd agreed on as compensation earlier in the day, and handed them over. "Our delivery should be here soon. Then you can take us to Milot."

Captain Every appeared. "Ah, I'm glad your driver is here. The men should be arriving in a few minutes. Is everything ready to go?"

"Everything's fine so far," Alex replied, "but this is the easy part."

Diana didn't hear the rest of the conversation between the captain and Alex as she shifted her attention to watching the moonlit waters of the Atlantic. She heard a scream, turned around, and saw their driver clap his hands to his head, a look of horror on his face as the first chest floated towards the truck. The driver jumped out and ran off.

"Wait, don't go," Diana shouted. "I promise you. You'll be safe." As he disappeared into the night, she turned to Alex and said, "Well, there goes our plan. I don't know how to drive, and I'm sure none of the ghosts can."

"I told you, it's not a problem," Alex said. "I drove some big trucks when I was bucking hay the last two summers back home. I was the smallest of the crew, so I drove the truck in the field and helped stack off when we got back to the farm. For my age, it was good money."

Diana shook her head. "I don't understand what you just said. I just hope you're good enough that we don't get pulled over for underage driving."

Alex grinned. "I'm not worried about that. Remember who's coming with us."

"Good point," Diana replied.

When the spirits had finished loading and strapping down the treasure, Captain Every gave the signal to Alex, who started the truck and headed up the rough dirt road. Unfortunately, the truck was older than what Alex had driven before and poorly maintained. It took a lot of ground gears and a few snide comments from Diana before he got the hang of driving it. Even then, it wasn't an easy drive, as the bouncing beams of the truck's headlights, a few dimly lit houses, and the faint greenish-yellow outlines of ghosts running interference were all they had to see the road leading to Cap-Haïtien.

The way was also much rougher and slower than Diana expected, as the road over the mountain ridge guarding Cap-Haïtien's western flank was in poor condition. Sitting between Alex and Jane, she rubbed her butt and said, "This has got to be the worst ride of my life. The seat is like a wooden plank, and the road is the worst I've ever been on. I hope it isn't going to be a long drive."

"It might not be far," Jane said, "but I'm worried about the whole road being this bad. If it is, we might not get there till tomorrow."

Diana didn't say anything as she tried distracting herself by fiddling with the strange new ring on her finger. After several minutes of silence, she said, "Thanks again for this ring, Alex. My mom could never have afforded anything like it."

"But she went to Harvard and has traveled around the world. And you go to that Druid school overseas. Don't you have money for all those things?"

"Our school is free of charge for those who qualify," Jane said, "but appearances aren't all they're cracked up to be. Quite a few of our members live with others to help make ends meet.

"But, what about the yacht and the dig? I thought my grandma was funding those, and they must cost a fortune."

"Some of our members are wealthy, but most of what ye see are for the order's business, and…."

Jane never finished her sentence as Alex slammed on the brakes to avoid running into a roadblock. As soon as the truck came to a stop, armed men jumped out of the forest, brandishing guns.

CHAPTER 29
THE CITADELLE LAFERRIÈRE

One of the bandits walked towards the driver's side waving his pistol and speaking in a language Alex hadn't heard before. "What's he saying?" Alex asked. He'd been concentrating so hard on driving the big truck safely over the dark, rutted roads that he hadn't noticed the ankh thumping wildly against his chest until then.

"I think he's speaking in Creole," Diana replied. "But whatever language it is, I'm pretty sure he's telling us to get out of the truck. So, let's do what he says. This treasure isn't worth dying for."

Alex took her advice, jumped out, and raised his hands. Diana joined him as Jane got out on the other side. Despite the warm, muggy night, he felt a wave of cold when Every bent close and whispered in his ear, "Stay calm. We'll handle this."

Seeing a dozen spirits converging on the unsuspecting bandits, Alex called out, "Please don't hurt them." His words trailed off as he saw Toussaint's and Every's men attack the brigands. It was all over in seconds.

He watched in horror as their attackers crumpled, blood spouting from their wounds. Alex turned to Diana, who stood, with her mouth agape and tears streaming down her face. Not wanting her to see the carnage, he turned her away from the bloody scene and held her in his arms as the spirits drug the bandits' lifeless bodies into the woods.

Jane came running around the truck, asking, "Are ye guys all right?"

Alex nodded. Toussaint came up to them and, in a calm, matter-of-fact voice, said, "It's time to move on."

With the deaths of the bandits still fresh in his mind, Alex exploded. "Did you have to kill them? Couldn't you have just knocked them out and bound them up?"

The Haitian general's eyes narrowed. "Did you think they were going to let you go after discovering what you were carrying? Believe me, my friend, I know their type and can assure you they would've had no misgivings about killing you. Desperation drives men to do despicable things. I hope and pray this money will help alleviate some of the poverty in the area so others will not join them. Now, let's go before other bandits find us here."

Alex helped Diana back into the truck and waited until Every gave him the signal everything was ready. Except for the roar of the truck's engine and the occasional gears grinding, they made the rest of the way to Cap-Haïtien in silence.

Despite the late hour, there was still a fair amount of traffic in the city when they finally arrived. Alex, who'd only driven trucks in open fields, found it more difficult than he'd expected to navigate the city's crowded streets, constantly shifting gears to weave through the other trucks, motorcycles, and crowds of pedestrians.

After finally clearing the city, they headed south along a country road with very little traffic. Without the stress of driving through the city, Alex's thoughts drifted back to the ambush. He choked back a sob and, in a husky voice, said, "I'm so sorry about what happened back there."

Jane reached across Diana and gently placed her hand on his arm. "It's not yer fault. It was horrible, but it would have been us instead of them if yer friends hadn't intervened. But ye can't focus on that. Instead, think about all the good that will happen because of what we're doing tonight. Ye saw what it was like down in Cap Haïtien. I've gotten goosebumps just thinking of the difference this treasure will make for some of the people there."

"What about what lies ahead?" Alex asked. "I don't know if I can take much more of this death and destruction everywhere I go. I'm thinking maybe I should give up on this quest."

"But, what about yer sister? I thought ye were doing all this for her," Jane said.

Diana cleared her throat. "I can't believe I'm saying this, but all I ever worried about before I met you was why Gaia chose me to be hard of hearing and whether the Druid way of life was for me. But for the first time in my life, I feel like I can make a difference. So, let's get this done, then go find the Fountain of Youth and see what else we can do to improve things."

Alex grunted but didn't say anything. A short time later, they turned onto the Citadelle La Ferrière road in Milot. For a moment, he thought he'd made a wrong turn, as the street looked more like a narrow alley. But it soon became a broad paved road that quickly started rising.

A ten-minute climb brought them to a large parking lot. Toussaint popped his head in through the window.

"This is as far as you can go in this vehicle. So, if you turn around and back up to the far side, we'll start unloading. While we're doing that, you three need to arrange for horses to help carry the chests up."

"Where are we going to find someone to rent horses at this time of night?" Alex asked.

"I don't know. I could have my men drive the locals out of bed, and you could question them," Toussaint suggested.

Knowing Alex was talking to a spirit, Diana grabbed Alex's arm and heard the last part of the conversation. "Why can't your men carry the chests? It's late, and I don't think it's right to go around waking everyone."

Toussaint shook his head. "It's still too far for us, and you need to be off this mountain by daybreak. If you don't want us to scare the owners out of bed, you need to find another means of helping us carry this load."

"I'd suggest we get a handful of money and start checking," Alex said. "Since you know French, Diana, you lead the way."

They knocked on several doors before they found someone willing to talk to them, but the man was unwilling to rent the horses even though Diana offered him half a dozen gold coins.

Seeing how the man looked greedily at the money, Alex said, "Come on. We'll find someone else." He then turned and walked away.

Jane caught Alex's arm. "We have more money. Why not give it to him?"

"I don't want to work with someone who's greedy. What we offered was more than fair."

Jane and Diana reluctantly followed him away from the house, but they'd only gone a few steps when the man caught up with them and grabbed Alex's arm. "Please, sir, I'm a poor man. I must feed my family. Surely you don't want to take advantage of me."

Alex pulled free. "So, you can speak English now. We might be young, but we're not stupid. Take the coins, or we'll go somewhere else. If you go to a reputable dealer, you'll find they're worth a small fortune. This is a good deal for you."

The man grumbled but said, "Wait for me at the entrance while I get the horses ready."

As he walked away, Diana ran after him and had a quick conversation. When she returned, she said, "By the way, I asked him to get horses for the three of us."

Alex shook his head. "No thanks. I'm not riding one of those. I've been bucked off and thrown off a horse in every imaginable way, including being drug with my foot in the stirrup. So, I'm walking."

"I don't want to ride a horse either," Jane said. "Seeing the poverty around here, I worry about how well they care for the horses."

Diana huffed. "I can't believe you're making me walk. It's a long steep climb."

"No one's saying ye have to walk. If ye want to ride, do it."

"I'm not going to be the only one riding. I just hope you two are up to it." Jerking a thumb over her shoulder at the owner, Diana asked, "What should we do about that man? I don't think we want him coming with us, but he insisted on coming to ensure we didn't steal his horses."

Alex started chuckling as Toussaint's men took the first chest off the truck. "I wouldn't worry about it. The only question I have is how long will he last."

The owner and his son brought the horses just as the second chest was coming off the truck. As it floated towards the horses, the man crossed himself, grabbed his son's hand, and ran away.

Without the owner's help, it took much longer to strap the chests on the horses' backs than planned. As a result, they didn't start up the rough-hewn stone pathway until nearly midnight. They'd only gone a short distance when Diana asked, "Do you think it'd be okay if I use my magic to conjure up some light? Without no moon and only a few house lamps giving off any light, it's really dark here."

"I'm sorry," Alex replied. "I wasn't thinking. I've got plenty of light to guide me, what with all the ghosts around, so I don't see why you can't use your flames. Besides, who's going to see us? I'm guessing they'll be more surprised by a bunch of horses walking by with chests strapped on than anything you'd do."

"I wonder if the people along this path can sense the spirits," Jane said. "The few people I've seen have scurried inside when we've gone by and doused their lights." As soon as the words had left her lips, an old woman climbed onto the path and stared at them.

When she'd passed from view, Jane asked, "Did either of ye get a creepy feeling from that woman back there?"

"Yeah," Diana said. "It felt like her eyes were boring a hole into the back of my head."

Alex kept quiet as he didn't want to tell them he'd felt his ankh thrumming against his chest when walking past her. He soon forgot about the woman as the climb became as tough as Toussaint had warned it would be. Before long, it started drizzling, making the ascent even more challenging.

Shortly after one, they broke out of the forest canopy and paused for a break. The rain stopped just then, and the clouds parted, allowing the light from the rising moon to shine over the surrounding mountains and make the fortress visible for the first time. Alex looked in awe at what appeared to be the prow of a giant stone ship cutting through the hilltops.

Despite the short distance, the rest of the climb was the toughest, as the path rose steeply towards the fort. Alex was relieved when Toussaint finally halted the column near the double doors leading to the Citadelle. "How are we going to get in?" Alex asked as he tried to catch his breath while craning his head to look up at the walls towering over them.

"Don't worry," Toussaint replied. "I have a couple of my men inside unlocking the doors." Moments later, the two great doors swung out, and the former Haitian Governor whistled for the pack train to follow them in.

After passing through, Alex was surprised to find they were still outside the central part of the fortress and had to continue climbing. He saw a large dark stone building off to his left and towering walls to his right. They made a sharp turn to the left, climbed some more, then doubled back towards the bulk of the fort.

Toussaint stopped the column near the inner entrance and ordered his men to unload the horses.

While Alex was waiting for the spirits to get the treasure, he noticed a stack of hundreds, if not thousands, of rusting cannonballs lying off to his left. Alex didn't have much time to gawk at them, though, as the inner doors soon opened, and Toussaint moved through the opening into the inner fort. Despite the dim light, Alex could see four-story-high walls surrounding him. They took a right and climbed up a flight of steps through a large tunnel that emptied onto an upper courtyard.

Turning left, they walked a short distance to a smaller flight of steps that led down to the central courtyard, where they turned left again. Toussaint motioned his men to put the chests down, then waved Alex forward. He led them down another set of steps and through a smaller tunnel that emptied into a walled enclosure.

Toussaint stopped and pointed to another short set of steps that led up to a pair of arched mahogany doors near the guest officer quarters, where armed guards stood on both sides. "Behind those doors is the man I told you about," Toussaint said. "His name is Dutty Boukman. I have done as much as I can to get you here. The rest is up to you." He looked down and, in a quiet voice, said, "I can't thank you enough. I never thought I'd see such generosity." Then he motioned them forward.

Alex took the lead, but as soon as he put one foot on the stairs, one of the guards brought his rifle up and yelled, "Arrêt!"

"Let me handle this," Diana said, gently pushing him aside. She pulled several silver coins from her pocket, handed them to the guard, and asked him in French to show them to the man inside. The soldier looked skeptically at the coins but motioned for the other guard to watch the three intruders.

"I hope this works," Diana said. "Otherwise, we'll have done a lot of work for nothing.

The guard came out a couple of minutes later and handed the coins back to Diana. In halting English, he said, "Go away. You're not wanted here."

Diana sighed. "I can't believe he doesn't want free money," she said. "I guess we'll have to do this the hard way." She brushed a lock of hair off her face, grabbed the talisman from her leather pouch, and chanted,

"Let your minds drift
Dream of things desired
And wake with the rising sun."

Both guards' eyelids drooped as they slowly slid to the ground.

Two more armed guards were waiting inside, standing beside a scratched and dented door. Before they could react, Diana cast her sleeping spell on them, and they too slid to the floor.

Alex walked up and knocked. When he didn't get a response, he pounded on the door and called out, "Open up. We have something for you."

When there still wasn't a reply, Alex slid the latch back and entered. The office was large but Spartan-like. An old desk, a couple of chairs, some lamps, and a large dog-eared map of Haiti hanging on the back wall were the only furnishings in the office. Both windows were open, and an ancient ceiling fan lazily circled in a vain attempt to cool the office.

A small man with silver hair and glasses jumped up from behind the desk and shouted in French, "How dare you. Get out at once, or I'll call the guards."

"Your guards won't be coming," Diana replied in French. "But don't worry, we didn't harm them."

The man stepped back and mopped his brow with a handkerchief. "What do you want from me? If it's money, you've come to the wrong place. I don't have any."

"It just so happens that it is about money," Diana said, holding out her hand. "We came here at the request of one of your countrymen, a Tou…."

Alex elbowed her, not wanting Diana to mention a man who'd been dead for centuries. Diana nodded and continued as if there had been no interruption. "A friend of ours told us you were a man of integrity. We have something that we think you'll be interested in."

The man looked at the three teenagers' dirty, tattered clothes. "You can't possibly have anything that would interest me. Please leave. I have much more important things to do than talk with children."

Alex stepped forward and slammed his hands on the man's desk. "I don't know what you just told her, but I can tell it wasn't very nice. We're not here to hurt you, so get off your high horse and listen to us."

Diana shoved some papers aside and plopped down her remaining coins. "We have twenty chests of this stuff outside. Are you willing to talk to us or not?"

The elderly bureaucrat stared at the gold and silver coins on his desk. He yanked his tie lower and scratched his head. Switching to English, he asked, "Where did you get these?"

"It's an old pirate treasure that no one knows about," Diana said. "We were told that you could put it to good use. Can you?"

Dutty's eyes narrowed. "What do you want? No one would willingly give up such a fortune."

Alex rolled his eyes. "Okay, you got us. There is one thing we want."

"Aha! I knew there was a catch."

"Could you take it off our hands tonight? It's stressful carrying all that treasure around. I haven't been able to sleep well since we found it."

Shocked at the unexpected response, Dutty asked, "Who are you?"

"We'd prefer to remain anonymous," Jane said. "Besides, ye'll have plausible deniability if ye have to answer any questions on where ye got it. But I can assure ye; this is a legitimate offer. Ye'd have to go back hundreds of years and search the world to find the original owners of this treasure."

"This is like a fairy tale come true, but I don't understand. Why are you doing this?"

"We've got more important things to do than sail around the Caribbean with a treasure on our hands and every pirate around wanting it," Alex said. "So, do you want it or not?"

For the first time since they'd entered the room, Dutty let his guard down.

He walked back behind his desk and slumped into his chair, gazing at the coins. "I don't know what to say, but I can assure you I'll put this to good use."

"What are you going to use it for?" Alex asked.

"I'll have to think about it because never in my wildest dreams could I imagine someone dropping a fortune off at my door with no strings attached." Dutty scratched his head and started talking to himself. "I can't trust the official government. They'd take a large portion for themselves, then hand out the rest of the money to their friends, who'd line their pockets, then use whatever's remaining for pet projects to make sure they get re-elected. No, I'll probably use this money for microloans. It'll be hard to trace where it came from, and I'm sure it will help the people more than official government programs." Realizing he'd been talking to himself, Boukman shook his head to clear his thoughts and asked, "How much did you say there was?"

"We don't know exactly," Diana said. "There are twenty-some chests outside with ancient coins, gold and silver bars, and jewels. Each one probably weighs a couple of hundred pounds. I'd imagine that what's left is worth in the tens, if not hundreds of millions, of U.S. dollars. You're going to need someplace bigger than this room to store it, though, because they won't fit in here."

Dutty seemed to come to life. He slapped his hands on his desk and stood up. "Come with me. I have a place they can be stored safely." He stepped outside the door and gasped when he saw his guards lying on the floor.

"Don't worry," Diana said. "Your guards are unharmed. Unfortunately, they didn't want to let us in, so we had to take matters into our own hands. It'll be a few hours before they wake up, but they'll be okay."

Dutty shook his head and led them down the hallway to a small door with a huge padlock. He pulled out a set of keys and opened the lock. The hinges squealed in protest as he opened the door and flipped on a switch.

A dim yellow light flickered on. Alex stepped in after Dutty and looked around. Except for the small door, the room had no other opening. He stepped back out and let Jane and Diana peak in. "There's one thing I should warn you about," Alex said. "I'd advise you not to be around when we bring the treasure in."

Dutty's eyes narrowed. "Why not? What are you up to?"

Jane stepped between Alex and Dutty. "Nothing, but we're concerned our transportation method will upset ye, so it would be best if ye're not around."

"Nonsense," Dutty said. "I can handle anything."

"All right, but don't say we didn't warn you," Alex replied.

Toussaint, who'd been hanging back, disappeared, and returned in a few minutes with his men, carrying the treasure chests.

Dutty crossed himself and started muttering. He kept clenching and unclenching his hands while staring at the long line of chests floating through the hallway and into the room. Unlike the other men they'd met that night, he didn't run away. He waited until the ghosts had stored the last chest before going over to the one Alex had already opened and knelt. Dutty stretched out his hand but hesitated before sliding the bolt back and opening the lid.

Wanting to return to the ship, Alex turned to Toussaint, "I assume you and your men will make sure it's safe here?"

Dutty looked up. "I'm sorry. What did you say?"

"Uh, nothing," Alex replied.

Ignoring the interruption, Toussaint replied, "I'll have my men guarding this fort twenty-four hours a day. I can't thank you enough. We're forever indebted to all of you. I wish I knew how to repay you."

"Maybe, we'll need your help some other time," Alex replied. "If we do, I hope we can count on you."

Toussaint bowed. "You can. I think Diogenes would've been pleased to meet you three." He then returned to the room, instructing his men to guard the treasure.

Dutty absent-mindedly waved them goodbye as he was too preoccupied running his hands through the coins and jewels to notice them leaving.

CHAPTER 30
THE VODOU WOMAN

Captain Every was waiting for them at the gates to the Citadelle. With their loads gone and Every's men clustered about, the horses became restless and kept sidling into each other. Jane grabbed the reins of the nearest horse and called out to Diana, "Grab the more skittish horses' reins. If we don't calm them down, they could bolt." She looked at Alex. "I don't know if the captain is here, but tell him he needs his men to start down the mountain – to get them away from the horses."

Alex relayed the message, then grabbed several horses' leads and started down the mountain, despite his misgivings about the animals.

A mile down the hill, Diana said, "I thought coming up was tough, but this is even harder. My knees ache, and my toes feel like they're getting jammed into the back of my foot."

"For me, the worst part is how parched I am," Alex said. "I ran out of water some time ago because I didn't realize how hard a climb this would be and that it would take all night."

Captain Every looked back and said, "This is a good lesson for you. Always think ahead and make sure you have enough drinkable water. Many a sailor has died of thirst surrounded by water."

The captain's lecture only made things worse. Soon, all Alex could think about was getting more water. Luckily, an hour after they'd left the fortress, they started meeting people coming up the path carrying boxes and bags. Seeing a young girl with a cooler, Alex handed the reins of his horses to Diana and bought a half dozen Gatorades.

After a quick drink break, they continued down the path at a faster pace. A short time later, they encountered the horses' owner, anxiously waiting for them. With memories of the previous night still fresh in his mind, the man and his sons quickly gathered the horses, then hurried down the mountain.

As the sun rose above the nearby peaks, Alex sighed, relieved at not having to deal with the treasure and horses. Feeling chatty, he said, "Can you believe that fort? It was amazing. How do you think they built it up there?"

"I'm sure it was literally built on the backs of the poor," Diana replied. "They must have had the locals build this road, then carry everything up."

"What I don't get is what were they defending against?" Alex said. "The fort's not that close to the ocean nor any good-sized city. Besides, who would attack them? Look at how steep the slopes are around here."

"Remember – the British, Spanish, and French all wanted this island," Diana replied. She hesitated, then added, "I know I haven't always been exactly happy about this adventure, but can you believe we've gotten to see two UNESCO World Heritage sites on this trip? Would you mind if we stopped at Sans Souci on the way down?"

"I'm not sure what Sans thingy you're talking about, but we can't stop," Alex said. "We have to get back to the ship before we attract any attention, especially since I'm driving a truck illegally."

Diana deflated a little. "I understand. Sans Souci is that destroyed palace we passed last night. The guy who built the fort also built the palace. I remember seeing pictures of it. At one time, it must have looked magnificent, but sadly most of it burned down over a century ago."

"I don't get it," Alex said. "Why would you want to visit some burned-down place?"

"Because it still looks amazing," Diana replied.

They lapsed into silence until they passed the first tourist group on its way to the fort. A short time later, they came upon a few houses scattered alongside the path. Some were cinder blocks, but most were little more than sticks supporting corrugated tin sides and roofs. Further down the trail, Alex heard some unique music and was trying to figure out what instruments three teenage boys were playing when a short elderly woman grabbed his arm. He jumped and tried to pull away when he saw she'd painted the top half of her face white in contrast to her ebony skin. In her right hand, she held a carved wooden staff topped by a miniature skull with giant rubies in the eye sockets and a pair of horns curling out of the ear openings. But the most startling aspect of her appearance was her necklace of human teeth and bone fragments.

She tilted her head slightly and studied him a bit before saying, "I've been waiting for you, Alex Scire. Come. I need to talk with you."

He tried pulling away from her, but despite her frail stature, he couldn't break her grip.

Diana reached for her talisman as she stepped towards the woman. "Let go of him."

Alex felt the ankh vibrating softly against his chest, telling him they were safe. He held up his free hand and shook his head when he saw Captain Every start to pull his cutlass out. "I'm okay. Don't do anything rash."

"You can't trust this woman," Diana said. "You don't know anything about her."

Alex looked down to where she was still gripping him and said, "Trust me. It'll be okay."

She let go of Alex's arm as if it had suddenly become too hot to handle. "I'm sorry. I was so excited to talk to you that I forgot my manners. My name is Marie Laveau, and I assure you that I have no wish to harm him. Come," she said to Alex while nodding at Diana. "You girls stay out here. I'll talk to you later."

He followed Marie into a nearby building that, on the outside, looked like all the other shelters nearby – except for the small bright red door with chicken's feet hanging on it.

Once inside, Alex saw candles burning everywhere, giving the small windowless room an eerie feeling. A long table covered by a white lace tablecloth sat in the back with a bouquet of dark purple orchids, a golden monstrance standing in the center, and elaborately decorated bottles lining the edges. Behind the table was a shelf with a hideous wooden mask with streaks of dried blood running down its face and, in stark contrast, a framed picture of Mary holding the baby Jesus.

As bizarre as the room was, what caught Alex's attention was a small table with two stools off to the side. In the middle was an exquisitely crafted clear crystal skull. Forgetting about his bizarre surroundings, Alex ran his fingers over its smooth, cold surface. Smoke immediately filled it and began to swirl around. Startled, Alex jerked his hand away, causing the skull to become clear again.

Marie's eyes were as large as Alex's. "What did you do?"

"Nothing. All I did was touch it," Alex replied as he bent over to look under the table. Satisfied that there were no hidden wires, he stood and looked around at the strange objects scattered about. "I must say, this is the strangest place I've ever been in. And that's saying a lot."

Shaking her head, she waved to one of the stools. "Please sit down. I want to talk with you."

Refusing to move, he asked, "How did you know who I am? I've never seen you before."

Marie motioned towards the crystal skull. "I foresaw your arrival and have been waiting for you since Fet Ghede."

"I don't understand. How could you know I'd be coming? I didn't know I'd be in the area until yesterday."

Marie pointed at the skull. "This shows key future events. I saw you with an ankh and have been most anxious to meet you."

Alex's right hand flew to the little looped cross underneath his shirt. "How do you know about it? Only three living people know I have it."

Marie stroked her chin while studying Alex. "That's a curious choice of words. But it doesn't matter. Would you like to look into my crystal skull?"

Alex shook his head.

Marie's eyes grew round in surprise. "What! Everybody I've made that offer to has accepted. Why don't you want to see your future?"

"A year ago, I probably would've answered differently, but after what I've been through, I'd rather not know. I don't think I could keep going if I knew what lies ahead."

Marie smiled. "You're not at all what I expected."

"Well, you haven't seen people going crazy over power as I have," Alex said.

"On the contrary. I've seen far more than you have and hopefully ever will." She sat still for a minute. When she spoke again, she said, "The path ahead of you is dangerous and not for the faint-hearted. People will pull at you from all sides to get you to aid their cause. To succeed in your quest, you must trust yourself and that which you wear around your neck."

"Do you know what it's supposed to do?" Alex asked as he sat down on the stool.

"No. I've only seen it in my crystal skull. Because of that, I assume it must have great importance." Marie stood up, walked over to a small bookshelf, and studied the books. She started tapping her chin while mumbling, "I wonder…."

Before she could complete the thought, Alex jumped up, knocking over his stool. "Forget it. I'm not going to help you with that thing. The last time I saw one of those books, it caused me nothing but trouble."

Marie looked to see what Alex was staring at and gasped when she realized he was looking directly at her *Sibylline Book.* "You know what this is?"

"At least one that looked a lot like it. It had the same type of leather cover and metal spine." His curiosity got the better of him. "Which volume is it?" he asked.

"It's got an engraving of a cauldron on the front of it, so I've always thought it was about the Pair Dadeni."

"The what?"

"The Pair Dadeni." She hesitated, then pulled the book off her shelf and took it to the table. I can't believe I'm going to tell you this, but it's for one of the Maqlû."

"Yeah, I know about them. Unfortunately, they're fast becoming the bane of my existence."

Marie's eyebrows shot up. "You are full of surprises."

"That's what the Druids say. So, what can this Pair Dadeni do?" Alex asked.

"Legend has it that the Pair Dadeni will bring the dead back to life."

"So, just like the Fountain of Youth."

"Possibly. Alas, all the secrets are locked up in this book, and no one has ever been able to open it."

"Why are you keeping the book out in the open? I thought those books are super valuable."

Marie smiled, "No one has ever broken in because I've got enchantments all around this house." She grinned. "Besides, my decorations scare away most people."

"I can believe that," Alex replied.

Marie suddenly sat down and pushed the large leather and metal volume across the desk. "You seem familiar with this book. What do you make of it?"

"It looks almost exactly like the Palantir's, except for the drawing on it." He swiveled the book around, then placed his left hand over the same type of concentric circles the Palantir book had before placing his right hand on the clasp. Alex heard the faint sound of the lock moving and flipped the book open. He ignored Marie's gasp as he waited for it to update its language. Like before, the blank pages started as cuneiform writing before switching to Greek, then to several other languages, before finally settling on English. When it had stopped, he flipped to the back of the book, unfolded the map, and glanced at it. "Hmmm."

Marie got up from her stool and came around to stand behind his shoulder. "What are you looking at?"

He flipped the book closed before she could look at the map, ignoring Marie's strangled cry.

She returned to her seat, pulled the book towards her, and tried copying Alex's motions. But the book remained closed. "Why'd you do that?" she asked. "Please open it, so I can put something in it to keep it open."

"Nope. I don't want anyone to misuse this information. Besides, it probably won't help you much even if you did have access to it."

She looked longingly at it for some time, then, with a sigh, she placed it back on the shelf. When she turned back to Alex, she was smiling. "I believe Gaia has chosen wisely."

"What do you mean?" he asked.

"I was talking to myself, but if you ever need that book, it's yours. Now come. Look into my crystal and see what it tells you," Marie said. "It may help you on your quest."

"If you can see the future, why don't you just tell me what's important?"

"I can only see bits and pieces. I saw you coming here and figured the skull was suggesting I help you."

Alex chewed on his lower lip as he considered whether to look or not. He realized the treasure hunt had distracted him from his trip's original purpose – finding the Fountain of Youth. For a few seconds, he even debated whether he should reopen the *Sibylline Book* and look at the map more closely. He glanced from the skull to the book and back again. Taking a deep breath, he closed his eyes and placed his hand over the crystal.

He instantly felt a tingling sensation. A second later, the object started radiating heat. He tried yanking his hand away but found he couldn't. When he opened his eyes, it appeared the crystal was about to melt. The outer surface was a brilliant red, while thick black smoke filled the skull. He was about to cry out in pain when the heat suddenly dissipated. The smoke separated into the colors of the rainbow and began swirling inside the skull, gradually growing clearer until a small island appeared. There were no people or structures, just scattered trees, a rocky hill, and a sandy beach. He wasn't sure whether it was from excitement or fear, but Alex felt his heart pounding against his chest.

The picture stayed for only a moment before it broke into separate colors that swirled around and coalesced into the image of a castle in the middle of the forest. A second later, the skull turned into a dark swirling vortex that seemed to want to suck him inside. Tiny points of light began flying by him so fast that he wasn't sure whether he was seeing them or was dizzy.

He felt like he popped out of the vortex and appeared over a wind-swept desert-like area. There was no sign of life except a solitary figure in the distance. The skull continued to pull him forward until he was close enough to see that the man had dark, deeply wrinkled, leathery skin, pepper-colored hair, and a hunched-back appearance. Beady black eyes and a scar that cut across the man's face gave him a fierce Frankenstein-like look. But, as startling as he appeared, what drew Alex's attention was the necklace he wore with a large golden-colored stone in a bronze bezel setting. The man stared at him momentarily before saying in a guttural voice, "Who are you?"

Surprised the skull was talking to him, Alex jerked backwards and fell onto the dirt floor. With sweat pouring from his forehead, he reached for the handkerchief in his back pocket. But his hands shook so hard that he couldn't pull it out. Alex looked up and saw that the skull had returned to a clear quartz color, and Marie was standing over him.

The color drained from Marie's face. "Are you all right?" she asked.

Alex shook his head. "What just happened? What did all those images mean?"

"I don't know what you saw. The skull went dark as you went into a trance. The next thing I knew, you acted like something had knocked you over." Marie closed her eyes and took a deep breath, struggling to regain her composure. When she opened them, she said, "Please go. I can't help you anymore."

Alex struggled to his feet and backed out, ensuring he kept his eyes on Marie. He stumbled into the door and fumbled with the latch before pulling it open and running outside.

Diana rushed up to him, touched his shoulder, and asked, "Are you okay? You look like death warmed over. What happened?"

It took him a few minutes to shake off the after-effects of what he'd seen in the skull. When he felt the fog in his brain lifting, he replied, "I'm just tired. It's a little creepy inside, but…."

Marie came out before he finished his sentence and walked up to Jane. They stared at each other for so long that Alex was about to say something when Marie turned away and said, "Would you come in, please, Diana? I have something to show you."

CHAPTER 31
THE CHOICES WE MAKE

Diana almost laughed at the comical nature of the stare-down between Jane, who towered over the diminutive elderly lady, and Maria. But she could tell by the looks on their faces that neither thought their encounter was funny. Worried the two might start fighting, Diana asked, "Are you okay, Jane?"

Jane didn't blink as she replied, "I'm fine. Ms. Laveau and I can't quite see eye to eye on a few issues, but we've come to an understanding."

"But you didn't say anything," Diana protested.

"Sometimes ye don't have to, to get yer point across. Ye should still talk to her as ye might gain some valuable information."

"After seeing the way Alex shot out of there and your little stare down here, I'm not sure that's a wise thing to do."

Jane turned away from her silent confrontation and laid a hand on Diana's shoulder. "It'll be fine. Don't misinterpret what you saw.

"You'll be all right," Alex said. "And maybe you'll learn something useful."

"Did you?"

Alex furrowed his brows. "I don't know. Maybe."

Diana looked from Alex to Jane, then to Marie. "All right, but I'm telling you, I'm out of there if I sense anything odd."

"Come with me then," Marie said, waving a hand at her tiny home.

Diana followed her in but wasn't ready for the odd mix of Christian, African, and Caribbean religious artifacts scattered around the room.

Marie sat down at the table with the crystal skull and waved Diana to the other stool. "Come. Sit, my child."

"I don't think so." Diana screwed up her face as she scanned the room again and asked, "What are you doing with that rooster? Seeing it lying on the table with blood dripping out is disgusting. How could you kill something and just leave it?"

Marie ignored the question and said, "I can tell you knew what to expect when you entered. So, why did you come?"

Diana tugged absent-mindedly at her ear lobe and mumbled, "I can't help but be curious. You pop up out of the blue and ask us to come into this creepy place. Why?"

"I mean you no harm. I've only asked you in to help Alex on his quest."

Diana sat down and stared intently at Marie, asking, "How could you know anything about him, especially living out here in the middle of nowhere?"

"I could ask you what you're doing here. I don't remember three foreign teenagers ever coming down the mountain by themselves at this time. Don't you think your behavior is a bit odd?"

"Since you wanted to talk with Alex first, I assume you know about things most people don't believe in."

Marie cut her off. "Give me your arm."

Diana hesitantly laid her arm on the table.

Marie clasped Diana's arm and cried out, "Verum Fulcio." A Tree of Life tattoo appeared on Diana's forearm. "I thought as much," Marie said as she let go. "I find it extremely odd that a member of the Bandruí is traveling with a person who could only be described as a warlock by your kind."

"I know every member of our order in this part of the world, but I don't know you," Diana said. "Which means that you were once a member, and they either kicked you out or you quit. Which one is it?"

"Neither. They asked me to join long ago, but I decided against it. Enough of this idle talk. Your friends must be on their way soon, but you have to choose whether you go with them or not."

"What are you talking about? I told Alex I'd help him, and I've come too far to quit now." Diana furrowed her eyebrows. "What are you really up to? Are you trying to break us up?"

Marie reached over, picked one of the straw dolls off the table, and started absentmindedly playing with it. "Quite the opposite. I wish the three of you to succeed in your noble endeavor more than you can imagine."

Diana wasn't sure what to think of Marie's response, so she asked, "What are you doing with that? Is it a voodoo doll?"

"It's nothing," Marie said as she hastily put it down and pointed at the crystal skull between them. "As I mentioned, you'll soon have to decide whether you help your friends or your order. I make no recommendation, nor will I judge you, but I'm warning you; it will be a tough decision. It's why I'm offering you the opportunity to gain information to help you decide."

"Can that show the future?"

Marie shrugged and gestured towards the skull. "Please, avail yourself of this opportunity. There's no harm in looking and possibly much to gain."

Curious about what the woman was hinting at, Diana couldn't help but reach out and touch the skull. To her surprise, she saw an image of the world appear. The crystal object zoomed in so fast that she didn't get to orient herself before she saw a straight of water between two large islands. The skull continued zooming in until an image of a large white yacht resembling the *Pequod* appeared. Storm clouds darkened the sky, making it difficult to determine if it was Elizabeth's yacht. She didn't notice the giant waves battering the ship as she focused on a familiar-looking sailing ship closing in, filled with armed men crowding its deck.

Diana sat up with a start, breaking contact with her vision. When she looked down again, the skull had turned clear. "Bring it back, bring it back," Diana shouted. "I've got to find out more information to save my mother."

"You only get one chance to see the future. As I told Alex, what you see doesn't determine the future. It is but one possibility."

Diana jumped out of her chair and ran for the door, calling over her shoulder, "I'm sorry, I have to go."

She left so fast that she never heard Marie mutter, "Alea iacta est. So, the die is cast."

As soon as she'd reached her friends, she said, "Come on. We've got to get back to the ship and find a way to warn my mother that she's in danger."

"Calm down. What are ye talking about?" Jane asked as she ran after the other two.

"She's sailing into a storm and an attack by Captain Tew's ship. Now come on. I'll fill you in on the rest of the details as we go."

CHAPTER 32
BRAVE ENOUGH TO SAY GOODBYE

Diana walked in silence until they reached the truck, unnerved by what she'd seen in Marie Laveau's crystal skull. There were only a few vehicles in the parking lot, but there was a crowd of locals, as well as almost two dozen horses spread out on both sides of the stone path, saddled and ready for tourists.

"Hey, before we head back to the ship, I need to make a pit stop," Diana said as she headed towards the restrooms. Just as she was about to enter the women's room, she called out, "Remember the toilet paper restrictions."

When she came out of the bathroom several minutes later, a half dozen women swarmed her, trying to sell necklaces, pictures, dolls, and other things to her. Flustered, she stood in the middle of the group, unsure how to politely escape, until Jane reached in and pulled her towards the truck.

As she was settling into the middle seat, Alex jumped in laughing and tossed some beaded necklaces into her lap. Then, he started the truck and pulled away even though people were still shouting at them through the windows to buy their goods.

"That was crazy," Alex said. "You guys have traveled a lot. Have you ever seen anything like it?"

"I've heard some bazaars are like that, but I've never experienced it," Jane replied. "That was nice of ye to buy some of their wares. I'm sure ye overpaid for them, but I'm also sure they needed the money more than ye do."

They came upon an open field a few miles down the road surrounded by a falling-down chain link fence. Some fifty yards inside was a low white stone wall surrounding the ruins of some long-ago palace. "Sans Souci," Diana whispered to herself.

"What did you say?" Alex asked over the roar of the truck's engine.

"I said that's Sans Souci. It's the palace I wanted to visit. I wish we had time to see it. Even in its current condition, it looks magnificent. Imagine what it was like when it was new. By the way, do you know your way back to the ship?"

"I think so. I'm a little fuzzy on how to find the road on the far side of Cap-Haïtien, but I can always ask the captain for help," Alex replied.

"How come that response doesn't surprise me," Jane said.

Soon, they left Milot behind. For the first time, Diana got to see the Haitian countryside. Concrete block houses, many of them painted bright pink, with tin roofs, crowded the road in clusters. Sugar cane fields and banana plantations took up much of the land, interspersed by a few grassy areas with cows and goats staked out to pasture.

"This is so different than where I grew up," Alex said. It's so much greener, but the farms are much smaller, and there's almost no fencing. I don't understand how they make a living on so little land."

"It's not easy. There's probably a lot of subsistence farming going on. Just look at all the chickens and pigs we've seen roaming freely," Jane replied.

But the rural areas did nothing to prepare them for the sights of Cap-Haïtien. When they'd gone through the night before, the darkness hid much of the city's underbelly. Traffic moved at a crawl as pedestrians, small trucks, motorcycles, and three-wheelers crowded the streets. The roads and alleyways doubled as outdoor markets for goods as varied as rough-cut lumber, used tires, iron goods, and furniture. But trash lay everywhere, with free-roaming pigs scavenging through the piles.

As they passed by the shoreline, Alex asked, "Was there a recent storm that washed up all this garbage?"

Diana shook her head. "Sadly, no. This is what happens in many poor areas of the world. It's expensive to pick up and properly dispose of trash. Many people are so poor that they can't afford what you consider a basic service." Pointing towards a group of people lined up behind what appeared to be a fifty-five-gallon drum on tires, she said, There's another example."

"Is that some sort of gas station?" Alex asked.

"I believe those are water stations," Diana replied. "I'm not sure if they are on some sort of city water or wells because each one of them seems to have a small generator nearby."

"This trip has been eye-opening for me," Jane said. "I never realized how much I took for granted."

It was such a depressing sight that none of the three talked for some time until Diana suddenly turned to

Alex. "When you see a phone, can you pull over so I can let my mom know I'm okay?"

It took a while before they finally found a place Diana could call from. Figuring her mom was on a ship somewhere in the Caribbean and that she couldn't reach her on board, she called Elizabeth back in Salem. After a long and sometimes tense conversation, she hung up and returned to the truck.

"Well?" Jane asked. "Is everything okay?"

Instead of answering, Diana turned to Alex. "What's the plan when we get back on the ship?"

Alex didn't immediately answer as he started the truck and eased back into traffic. It wasn't until he was heading up the mountain on the city's west side that he said, "I remember you mentioning that most of the possible locations for the Fountain are west of here. When I was in Marie's house, I saw a small island in her crystal skull. I think it was trying to tell me to look for it." He glanced at Diana and asked, "That didn't sound like your usual type of question. What's really on your mind?"

"I want to head to Nassau, hook up with my mom, and go home."

Jane shifted so she could get a better look at Diana. "It still sounds like ye're not telling us everything. What did ye learn at Marie's?"

"I saw an image in her crystal skull of my mother sailing into a giant storm with Tew's pirate ship on her heels," Diana replied.

"I'm sure the *Pequod* can weather whatever storm you saw," Jane said. "It's big, new, and has all the bells and whistles to keep it safe. And I doubt a ghost ship could harm them either, so I don't think ye should worry too much about yer vision."

Alex didn't say anything for some time. When he did speak, it was in a thoughtful tone. "If I remember right, you said one of the many rumored places of the Fountain of Youth was in Bimini, which is relatively close to Bermuda. So, we can use the trip to Nassau to develop a good search plan. This way, it'll be a win-win. Diana gets to rejoin her mom, and I get to keep searching."

Diana put a hand on Alex's shoulder. "All your grandmother wants is for us to get home safely. Why don't we all go? You'll probably never find the Fountain."

Alex snorted. "I'm not going with your mom. I bet she thinks I kidnapped you, and as soon as she sees me, she'll call the police and have them throw me in jail."

"You're being overly dramatic," Diana said. "She'd never do that. Besides, she'd have no grounds for charging you because neither of us will press charges. We came after you."

"I'm not worried about you guys, but I don't feel the same way about my grandmother and your mom. They won't ignore the fact that you two disappeared, then show up, out of the blue, with me."

"It won't be as bad as you fear," Diana said. "I'm sure it will all work out. You could ask your grandmother to get some of the women to help you search for the Fountain of Youth."

"Hah. That'll be the day," Alex said. "Can you imagine me asking her to help search for something no one believes exists? Especially since we have no idea where it is?"

"Maybe she'd do it if you told her what happened in Lamanai."

"There's no way I'm telling her I destroyed the object they've spent all that time, effort, and money searching for," Alex said. "Besides, I can't ask anyone else to help me until I have a better plan."

"Ye sound different than yesterday," Jane said. "Did what ye see in that skull change yer mind?"

"Yeah, I've been meaning to ask you what you saw," Diana said. "You've been tight-lipped ever since then."

"I saw a bunch of places I didn't recognize and some creepy-looking guy. The whole experience gave me the chills, but I have no idea how any of it will help with our search."

"So, you're not changing your mind? You'll have the captain take us to Nassau? Thank you. You're the best," Diana said as she threw her arms around Alex and hugged him.

"Watch out there," Alex said as he pulled away. "I still have to get us safely over this mountain."

CHAPTER 33
JUMPING SHIP

It wasn't long before Diana started having second thoughts about leaving their quest. She stayed silent until after they returned to the ship, and Captain Every asked, "Have you figured out where you want to go next?"

Diana looked hesitantly at Alex, who waved the question to her. Taking it as continued acceptance of her wishes, she replied, "Nassau. We're meeting my mom there."

Every's eyebrows shot up, but all he said was, "I'll have the men get the ship ready for sailing."

Several hours after the *Fancy* weighed anchor, the winds shifted and started blowing hard out of the east. Diana, who was standing with Every on the quarterdeck, looked at the dark storm clouds above and said, "Shouldn't we head back to Cap-Haïtien to weather the storm in the bay?"

Captain Every didn't answer for some time as he continued scanning the sky, occasionally sniffing the air.

She nervously looked high above her where Jane and Alex were helping furl the topsail on the mainmast. "Is it as bad of a storm as it looks?" Diana asked.

"The birds disappeared some time ago, and the barometer's been dropping steadily since we got back on board, but the wildlife ashore continues to chatter as if there's no storm coming. Plus, the skies are clear to the north and south of us. I've never seen anything like it," Every replied. "I wished I'd spotted the damn storm earlier, so we could've gotten out of its way."

"What do you plan to do?"

"We'll run with the wind until we pass the northwestern tip of Tortuga. Once there, we'll pray the winds allow us to make the Gulf of Gonâve. If we're lucky, then we'll ride out the storm there. However, if the winds keep blowing as they are, we'll be forced to survive a hurricane on the open ocean."

"What about my mom?" Diana asked. "She's out there somewhere."

"She'll be fine as long as their captain plays it smart. Ye said ye thought they started up the Windward Passage a couple of hours ago. I would think their captain would've spotted this storm and put into the Gulf of Gonâve already, rather than risk heading into this."

"You don't know my mother," Diana said. "She can be pretty stubborn. I can see her pushing the captain to keep going, hoping to catch us sooner. Besides, what if they didn't spot the storm, just like we didn't?"

"Well, we can't do anything about that," Every said. "Now, if ye'll excuse me, I need to concentrate on getting you out of this alive."

No sooner had she left the quarterdeck than the winds started howling, churning the sea, and causing Diana's stomach to grow queasy. She forced herself to stay on deck, thinking the fresh air would be better for her than going below, but soon the rain started pelting down, driving her to head below. But a big wave hit before she could reach the stairs. The ship lurched to starboard and sent her skidding across the deck.

When she got up, she stumbled over to the captain, having to yell to be heard above the storm. "Are we going to make the Gulf?"

Every shook his head. "We've already missed our chance of entering the Windward Passage. This storm has come at us harder and faster than I thought was possible. If we tried to make it now, we'd surely keel over, so we'll keep running with it. I jest hope we're not dashed to bits on one of the islands ahead."

"What about my mom? I was hoping we could meet up with her in the Gulf of Gonâve and save the trip to Nassau."

"That's not going to happen. I'll be happy if we make it to Nassau in one piece."

The rain mixed with her tears as Diana turned away and stumbled towards the steps leading below. She was about to head down when she glimpsed a large white yacht several hundred yards behind, headed straight for the *Fancy*.

She jumped when Every apparated beside her and shouted, "Ye need to get out of this storm, miss. Go below where it'll be drier and safer than up here."

Diana shook her head and pointed east. "That's my mom's ship."

Every turned, raised a hand to shield his eyes from the rain, and stared into the gloom behind them.

Diana watched in growing worry as he leaned forward to peer into the gloom, then abruptly flew to the stern. Despite the rough seas, she followed him and looked in the same direction he was. Her eyes widened when she saw the *Amity* trailing her mother's ship. She sidled over to the captain and shouted, "How'd they find us?"

"Damnation!" Every screamed. "Tew's gone crazy. He's crammed every bit of sail on in this storm. If they don't lose a mast, they'll surely catch us, and we'll have no hope of fighting them off."

"But what about my mother's ship?"

"I fear they're in grave danger, but from the storm – not Tew. Her captain probably thought this was a squall, but this isn't a normal storm."

With a touch of panic in her voice, Diana asked, "What can we do to help them?"

Every turned to face Diana. "We have two issues to deal with. Ye are uniquely qualified for one, if ye're willing."

"Of course. What is it?"

"I need ye to go aboard yer mother's ship and warn them of the danger they're in. Do whatever ye have to, but convince that ship's captain to slow down and let the storm blow past them. If I'm right, he thinks this is a freak natural storm, and he should run with it, like we're doing. But I think some supernatural event is causing this gale. That means he's doing exactly the wrong thing."

"So, shouldn't we take your advice and slow down and let it pass?"

Every shook his head. "I think the storm is after us. So, will ye warn yer mother?"

Without hesitating, Diana nodded. "Of course, but how will I get on board? The seas are too rough."

Every motioned for Deborah to come out of the rigging where she was helping furl the last sail. When

Alex's sister arrived, Every said, "I need ye to lift Diana onto the yacht when they come alongside. Ye'll have to do it by yerself as I can't spare anyone else. It shouldn't be too far of a carry, but ye'll have to make sure we're clear of them when ye do it. It would be disastrous if ye tried it with their ship over the top of us."

"What would happen?" Diana asked, with a note of fear in her voice.

"Remember, as soon as ye leave this deck, ye'll be re-entering the world of the living. I don't want ye knocked into the sea by their ship or appear in the middle of a bulkhead."

Diana looked at Deborah. "Can you make it?" she shouted into the wind.

"I think so," Deborah shouted back.

"That's not good enough. If you can't get me on that deck, I'll end up dead in the ocean."

Deborah looked to Every for assurance, but all he said was, "I'll tell ye when to go, but ye'll only get one chance. They're going much faster than we are, so once that ship passes us, there's no way we'll catch her. Plus, ye won't be able to carry her for long, so if ye can't get her on board immediately, ye'll have to bring her back here."

"Will I have time to tell Alex or Jane what's happening?" Diana asked.

The captain shook his head. "I'll tell them. They'll understand."

Diana turned to Deborah with a questioning look in her eyes.

Taking a deep breath, Deborah nodded. "I can do it."

Every nodded. "Good girl. Now, if ye'll go over there by the rail and standby, I've got to ensure we're in the right position."

Diana temporarily forgot her worries about dying and started wondering what plausible explanation she could come up with for her unexpected appearance on the *Pequod*. When the ships were only a hundred yards apart, she started waving and shouting, hoping to get someone's attention.

"No one can see you until you leave this ship," Deborah shouted.

"It's near impossible to understand all of this parallel world stuff. We're on the same ocean and experiencing the same weather. It freaks me out that they can't see me," Diana shouted back.

"I understand. Now get ready. They're almost on us."

Diana heard the rumble of the yacht's big engines and looked up, just in time to see it plunge into the trough of a massive wave. The resulting spray drenched her. After wiping the seawater from her eyes, she saw the yacht towering over them. Its waves pushed the ghost ship around, sending it bobbing and weaving. Instinctively, she flung her hands up to protect herself from the crash. But nothing happened. A second later, she was inside the yacht's hull and out of the storm.

Time slowed as she passed through the dining room, where she saw half a dozen Bandruí scattered through the room with their laptops open. They disappeared as she passed through the hallway and into the lounge. Diana gasped when she saw her mother bent over the mahogany table in the middle of the room, studying a map. She shouted and waved, trying to get her mother's attention, but she passed through the yacht's walls and back out over the open sea.

Diana was so excited to see her mother again that she'd forgotten what was coming next. She saw the yacht's stern pass by, then felt her stomach drop as Deborah lifted her. A second later, she crashed unceremoniously onto the deck of the *Pequod*. Diana looked around, but Deborah was no longer in sight.

It took her a couple of seconds to get her bearings. When she finally got up, she stumbled across the wildly pitching deck and ducked inside. The dryness and warmth were a welcome relief from the wild weather outside. Using her hands to steady herself against the walls, she started moving along the hallway.

One of the younger Druid women came out into the passageway. Stunned by the unexpected sight, she said, "Diana, how'd you get here?"

"There's no time for chit-chat. Where's my mom? I've got to tell her that this ship's in danger."

CHAPTER 34
WHERE THE WAY IS HARDEST

Chrysophylax used the same portal in Acatenango that he'd come through on his previous trip to Earth. Figuring Alex had left Belize far behind, he immediately headed east, towards the Caribbean. Using the homing device he'd borrowed from his uncle, Chrysophylax was finally able to catch up to Alex on a remote beach outside of Cap-Haïtien. But just as he was about to contact the boy, he lost sight of him in broad daylight.

Despite being unable to see Alex, Chrysophylax continued following the device's signals westward around the north side of Tortuga, hesitating when he spotted a violent storm suddenly rising out of the ocean. Like Captain Every, he thought it was unnatural, but he detected something else – something familiar.

He plunged below the ocean surface, looking for the cause of the storm. It wasn't hard to find the source – a sea dragon many times Chrysophylax's size, thrashing about. Making sure he stayed far enough away so that his fellow Berellian's efforts of creating the hurricane above wouldn't harm him, he shouted, *"Stop! You're going to kill the people above."*

The reply thundered in his head. *"Why should I care? All they do is destroy everything they come in contact with."* There was a pause, then, *"Who is that?"*

"Chrysophylax, son of Abraxas. And I assume you must be Kraken. My Uncle Nabu has talked a lot about

you and said we might meet while I work on this project for him. He...."

"*Nabu! Has he returned to Earth?*"

"*No, he's still on Berellus because he can no longer travel.*"

Kraken grunted. "*Then be gone. I have sensed something on the surface that bothers me, and I intend to invite whatever it is to join me here on the bottom of the sea.*"

"*Please don't. I believe what you're sensing is the ankh – the object my uncle gave to the humans. I don't want the boy who's wearing it harmed.*"

Kraken paused and thought, "*You still haven't told me why I should care.*"

"*Nabu believes we are partially to blame for the mess that's happened here on Earth. So, he sent me here to help him recover the Maqlû,*" Chrysophylax replied.

"*What does that ancient history have to do with me?*"

Chrysophylax felt the boy's signal heading away and wracked his brain to come up with something that might calm Kraken down. The only thing he could think of was something Nabu hadn't been impressed with but had caused Chrysophylax to switch from passive observation to actively helping the boy. He blurted out, "*The boy destroyed the Palantir rather than let someone else get it.*" He sensed Kraken hesitating and added, "*He did something nobody else has – reject the power that comes with those objects. It's why I think the boy may be the key to achieving my uncle's goal.*"

Kraken suddenly stopped roiling the water above him. Chrys knew it would be some time before the storm would die out, but at least he knew it wouldn't get any worse. Wanting to follow up on the pause, Chrysophylax said, *"Please, give him a chance. I have a good feeling about him."*

"Did Nabu ask you to protect the boy?"

"No. Quite the opposite. He was very upset when I told him I'd saved the boy's life. He would've been much more comfortable if I'd eliminated the boy the first time I came to Earth."

Chrysophylax wasn't sure, but he thought Kraken was silently chuckling when he said, *"I bet he did. I'd have liked to have been there when you told him. So, what's Nabu's plan?"*

"He's discarded his original plan for the Maqlû because of the boy's unwitting intervention. And right now, all he can think to do is bring all the objects back to Berellus."

"So, what's your plan, son of Abraxas?"

"It's not much of one yet, but I plan on helping the boy survive, as he seems to act as a magnet for trouble. But I like the choices he makes. From what I know of your history, you would too. So, will you stop this storm and let the boy live?"

"Very well." Kraken then turned and swam away.

Knowing he was running out of time to save the boy, Chrysophylax swam off, heading for the rapidly disappearing signal.

CHAPTER 35
MAN OVERBOARD

Even though he knew he was in another dimension, Alex tensed as he watched the *Pequod* sail through the *Fancy*. He was so fascinated by the bizarre sight that he almost lost his footing when he saw Deborah unexpectedly lift Diana into the air and deposit her on the deck of his grandmother's ship. Within seconds, the yacht had disappeared into the darkness of the storm, leaving Alex perplexed about why she'd departed the ship so suddenly.

He shook off the questions racing through his head and climbed down from his precarious perch high up on one of the yardarms and joined Jane on the deck. Because of the shrieking wind, he had to grab one of the girtlines to stay upright. "What happened to Diana?" he shouted. "She left the ship when the *Pequod* sailed by."

"What! Why'd she do that?"

"I don't know, which is why I'm going to ask Captain Every. But you should go below and get out of this storm. I'll join you in a bit."

The two went their separate ways, but when Alex reached the captain, the spirit shouted, "What are ye doing out here? It's too dangerous for ye. Now, go below."

"I came to see what happened to Diana," he shouted

"She's on her mother's ship. Your sister transferred her there so Diana could convince them to back off and get out of this storm."

Before he could go below, another wave crashed over the ship, forcing Alex to hang on to the railing with both arms to stay upright. The storm grew worse as it sped closer until its deafening thunder and blinding lightning were directly overhead. The rain turned from pounding droplets to sheets of water. He didn't think it possible, but the winds increased in ferocity until he had to bend into the wind to remain in place. When he managed to look up, all he could see was one solid horizon as the sky had taken on the same dark grey-green color as the tossing seas. Then, just when he'd decided to try to go below again, a giant wave, bigger than any they'd encountered yet, crashed over the ship, delaying him again.

His opportunity finally came a few minutes later, but as he made his way towards the stairs, a bolt of lightning hit close by. Temporarily blind, deaf, and numb, Alex reached for the railing for support but tripped and tumbled to the deck.

The ship rolled, sending Alex careening back across the deck. Fearing he would go overboard, he lunged out and barely managed to grab the base of the mizzenmast. When his head finally cleared, he pulled himself up and lurched over to where the captain struggled to keep the wheel from spinning out of control.

Every seemed surprised at Alex's presence and shouted, "Why are ye still here? I told ye to go below."

"I haven't made it down yet because of the storm." Alex was about to try again, when another lightning bolt lit the sky.

He felt the ankh thumping wildly against his chest and looked around to see what it was warning him about. To his horror, he saw the *Amity* only a few hundred yards away and closing fast. "Did you see that, Captain?" he shouted.

"I don't have time to look about. I'm trying to keep this ship afloat."

"Captain Tew's ship is almost on us."

The captain waited until the next lightning bolt, then quickly looked behind him. "Damn, damn, damn. Will he never give up?"

"All your men are busy trying to keep this ship afloat. Why don't Jane and I use the stern chaser to get them to back off."

The captain nodded. "Possibly, but he'd have to be too close for comfort for ye to hit anything in these conditions."

"One can hope and pray, but it's not as good as being prepared," Alex said. "It'll take us time to get ready, so you have to make a call now. If you wait, it'll be too late."

Every hesitated, then said, "Very well, but be careful. It's dangerous jest walking across the deck."

Alex didn't wait to hear what else the captain said. He headed for the steps and was soon below deck, sharing his plan with Jane. When he finished, he asked, "Are you up to braving the storm? It's terrible out there, but we're in a damned-if-we-do and damned-if-we-don't situation. We can either stay down here and hope for the best, or go above and risk our lives to try to chase them off. But if they board us, then we'll surely die."

"It doesn't look like we have much choice," Jane said as she swung her legs out of the hammock. "Let's start carrying up the supplies."

Deborah apparated just then. Seeing her best friend appear, Jane rushed over and asked, "Is Diana all right?"

"She's fine. I'm hoping she'll be able to talk her mom and the *Pequod's* captain into slowing down and letting the storm pass. But we're in worse shape. I just flew past the *Amity*, and she's bearing down on us. I don't think we have much longer before they attack."

"We figured as much," Jane said. "Maybe ye can help us carry supplies for the stern chaser."

Deborah nodded, and together the three started pulling equipment, shot, and powder out. Jane paused before they were about to climb back on deck and asked, "How are we going to make it to the stern in this weather while carrying all this stuff?"

"I haven't wanted to think about that," Alex said.

"Why don't you wait for a lull, then make a dash for it," Deborah said. "Keep one hand free. I'll shuttle what you can't carry, since it's a lot safer for me to get around than you two."

Their break came a few minutes later. Once on deck, they fought their way along the railing until they reached the stern and put their equipment down. The lull quickly ended when another huge wave hit the ship, nearly capsizing it. Seeing Jane start to slip away, Alex lunged and pinned her to the rail until the wave had passed and the ship had righted itself.

"This is crazy. We're going to die out here," Jane yelled.

"Maybe, but if we do nothing, death is a certainty," Alex said. He looked over the railing and saw the sea rushing up to meet him as the *Fancy* sank into the trough of a wave. The pitching motion of the ship knocked him backwards. When he regained his footing, he yelled, "Let's get this thing ready to fire."

Time seemed to slow. He thought he heard the periodic booming of cannons from afar, but he wasn't sure, as the howling winds and thunder quickly blew the sounds away.

Jane had to direct Deborah and him on what to do since they'd never fired the cannon, but Alex was surprised how smoothly it went. Getting the slow fuse lit in the storm proved to be the most challenging part of the process until Deborah used a magic spell to light it. He watched Jane as she stood with her feet wide apart to handle the rolling of the ship while her hand jealously protected the glowing wick from the rain, wind, and sea spray.

Alex impatiently waited for Jane to light the fuse. When he couldn't take the waiting any longer, he yelled, "Why don't you fire?"

"We'll only get one, maybe two shots, before we're at close quarters," Jane shouted back. "So, we've got to make each shot count. I'm waiting until she bears to ensure the cannonball doesn't plunge into the ocean or sail overhead. Now hold on because I think our chance is coming up."

The *Fancy* plunged into a wave and was righting itself when Jane bent over and lit the fuse. The cannon roared to life, spewing flames. A second later, the top of the *Amity's* foremast toppled over. Alex jumped and shouted, "A direct hit."

However, his elation turned to terror when the *Amity* suddenly veered towards the *Fancy*.

"Hurry, let's get this reloaded and ready to fire again," Jane screamed into the gale.

They pulled the cannon back, swabbed it out, and prepared to fire. Just as they were pulling it back into position, the storm calmed down, and an eerie silence descended over them.

"We must be in the eye of the hurricane," Jane said, pointing to the thick black column of clouds now swirling around the *Fancy* and *Amity* in a nearly perfect circle.

A nearby explosion brought Alex's attention back to the present. He yelled, "Are you ready to fire the cannon?"

Jane nodded.

"Please make it count," Alex prayed silently as he watched Jane sight the cannon and wait for the right time to fire. The ship suddenly jerked hard to port, knocking both to the deck. He staggered to his feet and was shocked to see a giant whirlpool forming below them. The next instant, the *Fancy* shot forward, riding the edge of the swirling waters around in a wide circle. By the time the *Amity* hit the swirling waters, the *Fancy* was on the opposite side.

Jane scrambled back to her feet, bent over the gun sight, and waited till the *Amity* was directly across the waterless pit from them before she lit the cannon fuse. The explosion sent smoke swirling around the cannon, obscuring their view.

The gun jumped back, giving Alex room to swab the barrel down. But before he could pull the swab out, the whirlpool disappeared, sending the *Fancy* skittering across the water and back into the storm, just as another giant wave hit the ship, knocking Alex and Jane once more onto the deck.

A moment later, the full fury of the storm resumed, plunging the *Fancy* into a deep trough. The sudden shift caused the stern chaser to break loose and careen across the deck. Without thinking, Alex lunged for the rope, vainly trying to keep the cannon in place. The ton of metal and wood was too heavy to stop, though. It rolled across the deck and burst through the railing, dragging Alex into the sea.

Jane started running to the hole, but without Alex on board, the ship disappeared. The next instant, she was plunging into the ocean.

CHAPTER 36
WHEN ALL IS FORLORN

"But, Mom, I'm telling you, there was no black magic involved," Diana said, trying once again to get her mother to believe her.

"Then why won't you tell me how you got on board," Sophie replied.

"That's not important right now. I left Alex and Jane so you could convince the captain to slow down. I know that's not normal procedure for this situation, but if he does, I'm confident the storm will quickly blow over and leave us in the calm. I don't know what's causing this, but it's not a typical hurricane."

"How can you know that? Have you suddenly become a meteorologist?"

Diana grabbed her hair and squeezed some of the excess water out of it as she tried coming up with a response that would get her mom to listen. "Think about how fast this came up. Even with all his sophisticated gear, I bet the captain didn't foresee this. Did he?"

Sophie turned to stare out the windows. "No, he didn't. He said he's never seen anything like it. He even made a crazy comment that the storm seemed to be coming after us."

"We can't afford to waste time debating this. Let's go ask the captain what he thinks. He can look at the radar and judge. If I'm wrong, then there's no harm done. But, if I'm right, then this might be the only thing that can save us."

Sophie stared at Diana for what seemed like forever. At last, she said, "Fine. As you say, it can't hurt. At the very least, we'll quash this nonsensical idea of a storm going after someone."

Several minutes later, they were on the bridge explaining Diana's theory to the captain, leaving everything about Alex out. As Diana talked, the captain studied the radar. Before she finished, the captain, without looking up from the radar screen, commanded, "Ahead, slow."

"But, captain, I thought we were trying to run with the storm," the first officer replied.

"I told you, ahead slow. If you can't relay that order, I'll relieve you of your duties and get someone who can follow orders."

"Aye, aye, sir," the officer said before relaying the command.

The captain turned around, a look of disbelief on his face. "It's the damnedest thing. I've never seen any storm so violent, yet so small. I think your daughter might be right, Miss Bennet. If we slow down, it might just blow past us. How did you figure that out, miss?" he asked Diana.

"It was a hunch."

"Well, let's hope you're right." The captain turned back to the console, signaling an end to the conversation.

Sophie took her daughter's arm and led her off the bridge. She rounded on her daughter as soon as they were in the hallway. "Enough of these games. What's going on? And why are you being so secretive?"

"I promised not to say anything, but I can assure you, Jane and I only went along to make sure Alex didn't do anything contrary to our order's goals. And he didn't, or at least he hasn't."

"I don't believe you. There's no way you could have gotten on board unless someone was using forbidden black magic."

"You know there are types of magic in this world that we don't fully understand," Diana replied. "Well, it was one of those types."

"Then why isn't Jane here? Lady Yvaine is worried sick about her."

"I noticed you left Alex out," Diana replied, staring hard at her mom. When Sophie didn't respond, she added, "He and Jane are on a sailing ship a little way behind us."

"That's impossible. The captain told me there are no other ships in the area."

Frustration at her mother's unwillingness to listen caused her to shout, "I don't care what he says. They're still out there in that storm in a ship that will probably founder any minute. Don't you care about them?"

"They got themselves into this situation. They can get themselves out," Sophie shouted back.

A hatch door slammed closed at the end of the hallway, halting their conversation. Diana looked up and saw Jane standing there, a stunned look on her face. "Thank Gaia, you're safe," Diana said, running towards her friend. "Where's Alex?"

Jane held his Army backpack aloft. "He got washed overboard."

CHAPTER 37
THE FOUNTAIN OF YOUTH

The hurricane drove the *Amity* west the rest of that night and all the next day until the storm finally petered out around nightfall. Exhausted from the effort to keep the ship afloat, Tew had the crew drop anchor and fade away to the netherworld to rest.

Early the next day, Tew sent a spirit to scout the small island they'd anchored near. It was a quarter of a mile long, with a few scattered trees and a hill on one end.

The spirit returned a short time later, saying, "The island is deserted, Cap'n, but there's a sea cave on the high end of the island where we can anchor and make repairs."

With only a wisp of wind blowing, Tew barked orders for his crew to break out the boats and tow the ship to the sea cave. But, with so many spirits having moved on since they'd left Rhode Island, the boats were only partially manned. It took the remaining spirits several hours before they finally towed the *Amity* through a thick curtain of vegetation covering the entrance into a small dark grotto.

Tew had to pause to let his eyes adjust to the darkness of the sea cave. When he could finally see clearly, he looked around and was surprised to see a handful of boats of drastically different ages lying along a pink sandy beach. On the opposite side of the grotto, the sounds of a twenty-foot-tall waterfall cascading into an azure-colored pool echoed through the chamber.

But what really caught his attention was a feeling he had of some unseen power radiating across the cavern, unlike anything he'd ever experienced. It pulsed through his ghostly limbs, making him feel more alive than at any time since he'd died.

Tew quickly forgot about the eerie sensation, though, when he saw a pile of coins, jewelry, and bars of gold and silver towering several feet into the air beside the waterfall. Before he could say anything, his men deserted the ship and flew towards the treasure, letting the *Amity* drift aground on the beach. The sounds of men laughing and yelling soon drowned out the sounds of the waterfall and the waves lapping on the shore.

He followed them to the treasure trove, but just as he reached it, a man wearing a full-length hooded cloak appeared and cried out, "Stop. Leave this place at once, or you're doomed for eternity."

While his men ignored the warning and continued reveling in the treasure mound, Tew turned to the stranger and asked, "Who are you, and why do you say that?"

"My name is Pericles. I've been here for over two thousand years because I tried to hide the object that is the source of all the evil in this place. I'm warning you. Leave now, before it corrupts you too."

"Don't try to scare us away with words," Tew said. "It won't work."

"Listen to me," Pericles begged. "Convince your friends to leave now, before it's too late. I'm warning you; there's too much temptation here. It will end badly for all of you if you stay."

"What danger?" asked Tew. "I see nothing except that which excites the greed of all men."

A fight broke out between two of Tew's crewmen over a stunning ruby necklace. It ended quickly when one of the men stumbled backwards into the pool below the waterfall. Pericles clapped his hands to the side of his head and moaned, "It's too late."

A few seconds later, the sailor extended his arm to the ceiling and cried out, "My god. Look! My arm is growing back."

Tew stared as the spirit began growing bones and muscles. Within seconds, the rest of Tew's men had jumped in and were splashing about in the water. Tew was about to join them when he got distracted by the sight of an elaborately embossed bronze-colored cauldron sitting in the middle of the waterfall ten feet up. He could see nothing unusual about the water coming into the vessel. But it seemed to transform inside it, for as the water spilled out of the cup and into the pool, it gave off a mist like a colorful space nebula. His eyes grew wider as more sailors began shouting joyfully at the miracle of coming alive.

Pericles grabbed Tew's arm. "Please, don't indulge in this madness. I'm warning you. Don't be a fool like your men. You can still save yourself."

Tew ignored Pericles and asked, "Why do you want to keep this to yourself. Surely this is the Fountain of Youth." Tew shook off Pericles' grip and dove into the pool with his men. Almost instantly, he felt a tingle in his arms, where he hadn't felt anything in three centuries. He watched in fascination as bones started appearing inside his ghostly body, followed by blood vessels, muscle, tendons, and ligaments. Tew raised his living right hand and shouted in exultation, realizing he'd conquered death.

Pericles stepped forward and threw off his cloak. Tew noted the man wore an Illyrian-style helmet and a simple white chiton, but none of the accoutrements mattered as he focused on the zombie-like man in front of him. Putrid, yellowing skin covered half of Pericles' face and arms. The rest of his body had no skin – exposing the ancient Greek's muscles, veins, and tendons.

"I warned you," Pericles shouted. "This is what you have doomed yourself to."

CHAPTER 38
ADRIFT

As soon as Alex hit the water, a wave pushed him under. He kicked hard to get back to the surface but got tangled in one of the cannon's ropes and struggled to get free. But the more he fought, the more entangled he became. He grew light-headed as his lungs started burning from the lack of oxygen. Just when he thought he had no more fight in him, the cannon broke loose. The next instant, something hit him from below and pushed him towards the surface. He broke clear in a trough and had just enough time to take in one breath of air before the next wave crashed over him.

Having fresh air in his lungs and no cannon pulling down on him gave Alex hope that he still might survive. When he surfaced again, he hit his shoulder on something hard. A lightning flash showed him it was part of the gun carriage that had broken apart when it hit the water. He lunged for the boards but only managed to brush his fingers against the wood before another wave pushed it away.

Alex had to wait until the next lightning flash before he could spot it, but the swells had washed it further from him. Realizing he wasn't going to reach it, he began searching for another piece of flotsam. A bump from below pushed him up the backside of a swell. When the wave fell into the heaving ocean, it deposited him on top of the other half of the gun carriage. Thankful for the providential find, Alex wrapped his arms around the wood and clung on for dear life, knowing he'd drown if he lost his grip.

The churning sea tossed him to and fro for several minutes until he slammed into the side of the *Fancy*. For a moment, his hopes soared. Alex shouted for help, but the howling winds and crashing waves washed his call away. He was about to cry out for help a second time when a wave washed over him, causing him to swallow so much seawater that he immediately threw up, nearly losing his grip on his makeshift raft. By the time he'd cleared the wave and caught his breath, the ship was out of sight.

For the next few hours, Alex clung to the wood, riding it up and down the waves. The storm-tossed him around like he was nothing but a tiny stick floating on the raging seas. He didn't have the energy to think of anything except hugging his life raft and keeping the seawater out of his mouth. As the sun set, his hope of rescue ebbed.

That night was the longest of his life, clinging desperately to his raft amidst the howling storm. His hopes rose the next morning along with the sun, but it only lasted until a large wave carried him high enough that he could see for some distance. Despair washed over him as he saw no trace of land or ships – just the endless sea. Alex lay his head down on the boards and sobbed.

Worries about drowning soon faded, though, as his thirst grew from a minor irritant to a craving. He remembered what Captain Every had told him about sailors dying of thirst and thought it was strange that it looked like he, too, would die of dehydration, surrounded by nothing but water. Every once in a while, he would try to sit up and gulp in some of the precious water still falling from the sky, but he gave up quickly each time, as the waves were still strong, and he feared he would lose his grip.

The wind and seas finally moderated enough by noon that he took a risk and sat up to soak in some of the precious rain still falling. However, that small luxury ended all too soon as the clouds broke up and the sun peeked through the gaps. Throughout the night, he had prayed for the sun to come out, thinking it would comfort him. Now that it had, he realized it could also punish him. His lips quickly changed from puffy and dry to cracked and painful as the sun and wind conspired to drive the clouds away. The sea changed character and started acting like a giant magnifying glass, focusing the sun's rays and slowly burning every inch of his exposed skin.

As the seas calmed, so did his grip on his raft. He was so exhausted that he eventually relaxed enough to fall asleep, with the waves carrying him into the unknown.

Alex woke up an hour later to the grumbles of his belly and the pain from his blistering skin. He sat up and straddled the board. With the sea calm, he took time to think about his survival options. He briefly thought about paddling but quickly realized that it was more probable that he'd head out into the Atlantic than it was for him to encounter an island.

Alex slapped himself on the head – mentally kicking himself for not thinking about asking a ghost to help him sooner. He instantly regretted the action as he hadn't realized, until that moment, how badly sunburned he was. Despite the pain, he closed his eyes and mentally called for help, hoping his sister, or Captain Every, would somehow hear him and come.

He realized he was completely on his own when half an hour passed with no results. His hopes sunk and didn't rise again until he caught a glimpse of a shiny white object in the distance. He got on his knees and waved, but it was soon gone from sight.

Alex began wondering what other people thought about when they were close to dying. Almost as soon as he had that thought, though, the ankh began tugging on him. He looked down and saw it glowing. Momentarily forgetting about his predicament, he gazed at the tiny looped cross, wondering what it could be telling him. His thoughts were so muddled from everything he'd been through that it was some time before he guessed it was trying to direct him. He lay down on his crude raft and started paddling.

It took every bit of energy he could muster to keep up a steady stroke. He kept making adjustments in his direction based on which way the ankh was pulling on him while trying to ignore his thirst for the next couple of hours. During one of his rest breaks, he sat up and spotted what appeared to be palm trees in the distance. He gauged the angle he thought he should take, reoriented his makeshift raft, and started kicking and paddling as hard as he could. When he paused to check his progress, he realized the waves had pushed him further away from the island. He briefly thought about swimming the rest of the distance but realized he was too weak to make it.

Alex lay back down on the board and rested while trying to figure out what he should do. He'd just decided he'd try one more time to make landfall when something nudged his raft, reorienting it back towards the island.

At first, he didn't think anything of it. But his imagination soon got the better of him, and he looked down into the water for sharks. The only thing he saw, though, was a brief glimpse of color. But whatever it was disappeared all too quickly into the ocean's depths.

He tried paddling again but made no headway and laid down. Before he could close his eyes, his raft got another big push that sent him shooting through the sea directly towards the island. Alex looked over the side, looking for whatever was helping him. It must have sensed him watching, though, and disappeared again into the ocean.

Wondering if he was going delirious and imagining it all, he lay back down. Almost as soon as he did, he felt the raft shoot forward. Instead of fighting it, Alex lay quietly on the plank, staring up at the blue sky. His rest was abruptly disturbed when the creature below suddenly threw his raft into the air. Alex felt a momentary sense of weightlessness before crashing back into the ocean.

Sputtering from the unexpected dunking, Alex threw out one arm, trying to grab the wood before it got beyond his reach. Instead of wood, his hand landed on a scaly hide. Seeing what looked like a strange dorsal fin, he wrapped his arms around it. As soon as he did, the creature started swimming towards the island.

It took him a moment before Alex's mind cleared enough for him to ask, "Chrys, is that you?"

There was a long silence before he got a reply. *"Yes, little one."*

Alex's voice was almost a croak when he said, "What are you doing?"

"I couldn't let you die out here. You've struggled so hard to survive that I just had to help you."

"How long have you been with me?" Alex asked.

"Since you went overboard yesterday. I'm sorry for not helping you earlier, but the prejudices of my kind against humans are so deeply ingrained that I debated with myself throughout the night whether to save your life again. I shudder to think what my uncle and the High Council would do to me if they ever found out how much I've interfered."

Alex lay down and wrapped his arms around the dragon's neck. He was so parched that all he could say was, "Thank you."

Chrys swam so fast that the water curled up and around, constantly washing over Alex. He wanted to get a better look at where they were going, but it took all his remaining strength to hold on.

A few minutes later, his sea taxi abruptly turned, throwing Alex off. Too tired to swim, he sank like a rock, but the water was only a couple of feet deep. He hit bottom and flailed around for several seconds before he could right himself.

He finally managed to stand up and waded towards a narrow sandbar a short distance away. As soon as he reached it, he plopped down, grateful he was no longer entirely at the mercy of the ocean.

After resting for several minutes, he decided to make the short journey to the island. He'd only taken a few steps when a wave broke over the shoal and knocked Alex back into the water on the island side of the sandbar. Barnacles cut into his right side, causing his hands and leg to start bleeding, but the pain had the beneficial effect of giving him a shot of adrenaline.

He tried struggling back to his feet, but the next wave caught him and pushed him towards the shore, dumping him unceremoniously on more barnacles. Alex steadied himself once more, stood up, and waded towards the beach. The waves knocked him down several more times before he finally reached the white sandy shore, where he collapsed, exhausted after being adrift for so many hours at sea. Within seconds he'd fallen asleep.

CHAPTER 39
WHICH DEATH IS PREFERABLE

A wave of cold air hit Alex, giving him temporary respite from the blazing heat but waking him from the first good sleep he'd had in days. He wanted to go back to sleep, but someone kept calling his name. The voice sounded familiar, but he couldn't quite place the speaker. Reluctantly, he opened one eye to see who was calling him and was surprised to see Deborah kneeling over him, an anxious look on her face.

"Thank Gaia. You're alive," she said.

Alex tried responding, but all that came out was a barely audible rasp, "What are you doing here, sis?" He immediately regretted speaking as it felt like someone was using sandpaper on his throat. Alex tried swallowing but was so parched that he didn't have any saliva to swallow.

"First things first. You've got to get out of this sun," Deborah said. "There's a bunch of trees a short distance from here that can provide you some shade. Come on. I'll help you."

Alex started to sit up but instantly regretted the move, as all his aches and pains came to the fore. His head pounded, and his skin felt like it was on fire. He gave up and fell back on the sand.

Moments later, he felt the grip of her icy hands on his arm and shivered as she pulled him to a standing position. The short trip across the beach reminded him of movies he'd seen with people stumbling across the desert, dying from lack of water. When he reached the tree, he fell to his knees, then painfully twisted around until he was resting his back against the trunk. He pointed to his throat and croaked, "Water."

Deborah flew over to where a few coconuts had fallen, brought back an armful of them, then searched for something sharp to crack open the hard shells. She floated along the beach until she found a razor-sharp stone, then flew back to Alex and held out the rock. "Here, use this to open it."

Alex shook his head. Despite the agony of talking, he said in a raspy voice, "I don't have the strength. Will you bust it open, please?"

Deborah picked up a couple of coconuts and took them back to the beach, where she propped one up on some rocks. She picked up a heavy stone and said, "I watched a video once on how to open these things. It's nearly impossible to do it with just brute force." She dropped the rock on it several times until she saw cracks appearing. Then she turned it around, smashed it on the bottom, and pried it apart. She pulled off the loose fibers of the core to get down to the smooth inner shell until she spotted three dots at the bottom that looked like a face. Finding the ridge between the eyes, she followed it to the center of the shell, then hit it on a sharp rock.

A few seconds later, she brought two halves of the shell over to Alex, who took one and tossed the sweet, warm, clear liquid down his parched throat. It was less than a pint, but it was the most wonderful drink he'd ever had. He grabbed the other half and tossed the little bit of liquid it had down his throat before motioning for his sister to get another one.

When he'd finished his third coconut, Deb said, "You need to slow down, or you'll get sick. Why don't you eat some of the meat in the shells? They have water in them and will give you energy besides. You can't live on them for long, but they'll keep you alive for now."

Alex picked up one of the discarded half-shells, pried the sweet white meat out of it with his swollen fingers, and eagerly stuffed it into his mouth. After finishing the last of the opened coconuts, he turned to his sister and asked, "Are Jane and Diana okay?"

His sister nodded. "I'm sorry I couldn't get to you earlier, but after I helped the captain get Jane on board the Pequod, it was all I could do to get back to the *Fancy*. Once there, I had to wait until the winds finally died before I came after you."

Alex pointed to the empty coconut shells and mouthed, "Thank you." Then he shifted around to get further into the shade, tucked his hands under his head, and fell fast asleep.

He would have slept through the night, except a light rain started falling and woke him up. Knowing that the rain meant life, he gathered the open coconut shells and set them out to collect rainwater.

The thought of drinking more water caused his thirst to return with a vengeance. While waiting for the shells to fill, Alex stood with his head back, face to the sky, trying to catch every last drop of rain he could. Unsatisfied with the little he was getting in his mouth, he drank the water collected in the coconut fragments and placed them back down to collect more water. The rain stopped all too soon, but the fire in Alex's throat was temporarily assuaged. He lay back down under the tree and fell asleep.

The sun was well above the horizon when hunger pangs and thirst woke him. He looked around for his sister, but all he found was a neat stack of cleaned coconut seeds lying nearby and a sharp rock to crack them open.

After he'd had his fill of coconuts, and feeling better than he had in two days, Alex scanned the island for the first time. His hopes for rescue sank as all he saw was sand and a few trees surrounded by the ocean for as far as he could see. Despite the sobering outlook, he decided to tour the spit of sand, hoping he might find something that would help him get back to civilization.

He stumbled along the beach, wincing from all of his aches. But those were nothing compared to the daggers of pain shooting through him every time his clothes rubbed against his burned skin. Since the island was only a couple of hundred feet wide, he soon rounded the southern tip, barely a hundred yards away, and passed the grove of coconut trees he'd slept under on his way to the north end. The island gradually sloped upward for a quarter-mile to a small plateau covered by shrubs, a few more coconut trees, and ending in a rocky cliff face that plunged straight into the sea. As Alex stood on the cliff edge, looking down at the waves crashing against the rocks a hundred feet below, a wave of dizziness overcame him, forcing him to step back from the precipice or risk falling in his weakened state.

He sat down in the shade of one of the nearby trees and watched the sun light up the western sky with a brilliant array of orange, red, and purple clouds as it slowly set, helping him to temporarily forget his situation.

Alex had thought he'd seen dark skies in the Rockies before, but they were nothing compared to the tiny island's night sky with no other humans around for miles. With a thickening cloud cover blocking out the stars, it grew so dark that his other senses came alive. A faint echoing sound came from nearby, but the surf pounding on the rocks below made it difficult to pinpoint where the noise was coming from. He stood up, cupped his ears, and headed towards where he thought it was emanating. Unsure if he was going in the right direction, he stopped after a couple of steps and listened again.

Thinking he was getting closer, he took a few more steps towards a bunch of shrubs. The sound became louder and clearer, as if a cascade of water was pounding on rocks. Hoping it was fresh water and not the sound of waves crashing ashore, Alex pushed the shrubs aside and found a small cave opening.

He felt the ankh thumping against his chest but was confused about whether it was pulling him forward or warning him. Despite his misgivings, the possibility of freshwater lured him on. He got down on his hands and knees and crawled through the three-foot-high entrance, where he spotted rough-hewn rock stairs a few feet in front of him. He crawled over to them and started down, gradually managing to stand up as the stairs dropped away from the ceiling.

The further down he went, the brighter the cave got until he reached the bottom and saw dozens of torches lighting a large sea cave. On the far side was an opening, covered by vegetation, where the waves of the Atlantic entered and lapped onto a pink sandy beach that rimmed the entire grotto.

A handful of small boats were on the beach off to his left, while a few larger ones rocked gently in the middle. Some were fairly new, while others appeared to be ancient, including one large sloop that seemed vaguely familiar. He stopped his perusal of his surroundings and looked for the source of the sound of running water. His mouth dropped open when he saw a pile of treasure towering ten feet into the air. He only gazed at it for a few seconds before switching his attention to something even more valuable – a twenty-foot waterfall cascading into an azure-colored pool right next to the treasure.

Despite an uncomfortable feeling about the place, the running water called to his parched throat. He walked over to the pool and was about to dip his hand in when a voice from behind said, "Don't do it. Death be preferable to drinking from that accursed pool."

CHAPTER 40
THE PAIR DADENI

Alex nearly fell when he saw what was speaking to him. He'd heard of zombie movies but never had any interest in watching one. What he saw before him made him feel like he was living in one.

"I didn't mean to startle you," the stranger said. "But please, whatever you do, don't drink or even touch that water. If you do, you'll wind up like me."

Alex barely heard the words. All he could do was stare at the man's rotting skin and exposed muscles, veins, and tendons.

"What, what, are you?"

"My name is Pericles. I'm the guardian of the Pair Dadeni – and am one of the living dead. There's black magic here, so please, leave before it entraps you like it has the rest of us. Better that you had died out there in the ocean than ever come in here."

Alex looked longingly at the clear water splashing down only a few feet away and licked his dry, cracked lips. "What are you talking about?"

"Over two thousand years ago, I swore an oath to my love Aspasia that I would destroy the cauldron that causes these waters to be so polluted. Alas, I failed. My ship ran aground on this island in a storm, and I was the only one who survived. I held out for as long as possible, but eventually, I gave in to my thirst, not listening to the warning my love gave me before I left. I used that damned object to purify the saltwater so I could survive – if you call this surviving. And now – I'm stuck here for eternity."

"I still don't understand," Alex said.

"The magic that gives us this life in Hell also traps us here. Everyone eventually tries to leave, but it always brings us back. Since I failed at my mission of destroying the Pair Dadeni, I have made it my job ever since to warn everyone of the dangers of this water."

Seeing Alex's eyes looking over the treasure, Pericles said, "I'm probably wasting my breath, as none have ever listened. That pile has only grown over the centuries. This place lures people with the hopes of immortality and riches beyond their imagination."

Pericles laughed mirthlessly. "Do you know what the irony of it all is? People call this hellhole the Fountain of Youth. Those who don't know what it can do, think of it as a miracle. Please, I implore you. Leave before it entraps you as it has the others."

Alex was so tired, thirsty, and hungry that he couldn't think straight. He looked around at the boats in the little grotto and said, "I can't. I have no way off this island."

Pericles was about to say something when a voice from above cut him off. "Alex Scire, I presume. I'm so glad we finally meet face to face."

Alex didn't recognize the voice, but something in the tone made the hairs on his arms stand on end. He slowly turned around and was horrified to see a person, even more grotesque than Pericles, standing above him on a set of stairs next to the treasure pile. It looked like a living skeleton, with most of its bones and a little rotting soft tissue showing. It wore soiled, raggedy clothes, had matted hair hanging limply over its face, and cold, dark eyes that stared out of bony sockets.

Alex staggered backwards, horrified by the sight before him. "What do you want?"

"Nothing much." He grabbed the embossed bronze cauldron from the waterfall and held it aloft. "All I want is to learn how to control this."

The creature descended the stairs off to Alex's right and sat down on a carved wooden throne-like chair overlooking the pool.

The ankh was thumping wildly against his chest, but Alex was in such a fog that he couldn't think clearly. All he could do was say, "You've got the wrong person. I don't know anything about that."

He eyed Alex and said, "That's not what Pythia told me. Ye know ye've got quite a reputation among both the living and the dead, so please spare me yer protestations. I know ye've already stolen the Palantir and Gambanteinn, and ye converse with the dead. Surely ye know how to operate this. So, tell me what I want to know, or else I'll make yer pathetic existence more miserable than it already is."

"Who are you?" Alex asked.

"I'm Captain Thomas Tew."

"Tew! You're the one who's been chasing us across the seas."

"Of course. I want to live again, and ye're the key to this object. So, enough stalling. Tell me what I need to know so I can use it and come back to life."

"I don't have any idea how it works. Besides, I'd never help you. I've seen what happens with this type of object."

Tew got up from the throne and held up one of his boney arms. "The cauldron isn't working properly. It brought us part way back from the dead, but I want true immortality. I want to know how to finish the process of regenerating."

Alex grew lightheaded and fell to his knees.

Tew shook his head. "What a horrible host I am. I heard yer earlier conversation with our friend here and can only imagine all ye've been through. Ye must be dying of thirst, and here I am with all this wonderful, refreshing water. If ye teach me how to use this cup, I'll let ye have some of it. Without it, ye'll die a horrible death soon enough. And ye're much too young for that."

"Don't listen to him," Pericles shouted. "You're better off dead than be like us."

Tew waved his hand, and several zombies came rushing out of openings Alex hadn't spotted before. The men grabbed Pericles and forced him to his knees, with one stuffing a rag into the former Greek general's mouth.

"I told you I don't know anything about it," Alex croaked.

"Then why are ye here? Don't tell me ye just happened upon it. Come now. I grow impatient with yer childish stubbornness."

Alex didn't have the energy to respond.

Seeing he wasn't getting anywhere with his threatening approach, and realizing Alex wouldn't be useful to him dead, Tew switched tactics. In a cajoling tone, he said," Maybe I was wrong about ye. So, let bygones be bygones, and let us be friends. Come. Drink up. Otherwise, ye'll die if ye don't have some of this wonderful water. And trust me. I've seen men die of thirst, and I can tell ye it's not a pretty sight." To emphasize the point, he dipped the cauldron in the water and drank deeply from it. He held out his arm and watched intently as a piece of putrid flesh appeared on his forearm, covering up a small amount of his skeleton.

Tew gazed at the additional flesh for a second before turning to Alex. "It wouldn't be the worst thing to ever happen to ye. Pythia told me yer mother and the other witches are ashamed of ye and that yer father kept ye hidden from the world because he knew others would fear ye. But I won't forsake ye as your parents did. I want ye as an ally. If ye work with me, ye could achieve more power, fame, and wealth than ye can imagine. Partake of this water now, so ye can live."

Alex tried shouting, but it came out as little more than a croak. "I'd rather die than join you."

Tew's face grew thunderous-looking. "Ye can only live so long on coconuts. Even if ye did find other food, there's no way off this island without joining me."

Alex looked longingly at the water. He knew he couldn't trust Tew, but he was so thirsty that he felt he was on the verge of fainting again. Despite his avowed intentions, he got to his feet and stepped toward the sparkling blue water.

As soon as he did, he heard the same woman's voice he'd heard in his head before. *"You've come so far. Don't lose your resolve now."*

He started to take another step, then stopped as the woman's voice said, *"Trust yourself and the ankh."*

Misinterpreting Alex's hesitance, Tew said, "Don't listen to that old fool, Pericles. It saved his life and let him live for over 2000 years. And look at us. We were dead, but it's brought me and many others back to life."

Tew dipped the cauldron into the water and thrust the cup towards Alex. "Ye're near death. Drink from it, and ye can have not just life but immortality. So what if ye don't look right at first. Ye'll have plenty of time to figure out how to operate this cauldron properly after ye drink from it. Besides, it will take away all of yer pains and make ye feel more vibrant and energetic than ye've ever felt before."

Alex's lips were swollen and cracked from the sun and saltwater, his throat burned, and his gut gurgled in protest at its harsh treatment of late. He'd never felt so miserable in his life. And all he could think about was the water. He could hear Pericles struggling with his captors, but the cavern started swirling.

In a mental fog, he stumbled over to the pool and rested his hands on the cool stones to keep from falling. He saw the reflection of his swollen face and barely recognized himself. Suddenly, the waters stilled, and an image of his grandfather's face appeared in the water, smiling and motioning him forward.

In a trance, Alex started to dip towards the beckoning water. He cupped his hands and extended them towards the pool, but just as he was about to touch the water, Tew knocked his hands away. "I must not have been clear. The deal is that ye agree to figure out how to operate this object and share that information before ye get a single drop of this water. No deal. No water."

Alex's mouth was so dry that he only managed to croak, "I'm telling you, I don't know how it works."

"Ye might want to reconsider yer answer," Tew said. "I understand dying of thirst is rated just below being burned to death and being flayed alive as the most painful death there is."

Alex looked longingly at the water, only a foot away.

Tew leaned over and whispered, "I'll make it easy on ye. All ye have to do is promise me that ye'll teach me the secrets of the cauldron, and ye can have yer fill. Say yes, and ye avoid a horrible death. There's no need for someone as young as ye to join your family in the afterworld. Come. Let's not be enemies."

Alex stood motionless, staring at the fountain. He didn't know if he could endure much more.

"I see ye have a lot of willpower, but if ye're not willing to help yourself, think about your sister. I understand ye're going through all this suffering just for her. How will ye help her if ye don't learn the secrets of the cauldron? All ye have to do is tell me ye'll figure it out, and I'll let ye drink. Ye don't have to die."

The thought of slaking his thirst was so overpowering that Alex began thinking of lies he could tell Tew about the cup. Just then, a longboat entered the grotto and glided to a stop on the beach. A dozen men jumped out, followed by a wild-looking woman. They wore tattered clothes and looked like living skeletons with exposed muscle tissue, boils, and sores all over their faces and arms. All of them had listless expressions and peered out of dull black eyes. They sloshed through the water and up on the beach, heading towards Tew.

The woman pushed to the front of the group and said, "We couldn't find the *Fancy*, Cap'n."

"No problem, Miss Dieu-le-Veut. Poseidon is with us today, as the boy graciously decided to show up at our humble accommodations on his own volition."

Anne Dieu-le-Veut came up to Alex and studied him. "Is this what you've been so worried about, Cap'n? I don't understand what all the fuss is about. He don't look so high and mighty to me."

Alex couldn't take any more. He nodded and moaned, "I'll do it, but you have to let me have some water." Without waiting for Tew, Alex reached a hand towards the water. He never touched it as a small grey furry animal that had blended in so well that he hadn't seen him, bit his hand.

CHAPTER 41
NIGHT OF THE LIVING DEAD

"Ow," Alex screamed as he jumped back from the waters and shook his hand. He looked at what had bitten him and thought it looked like a miniature furry grey dragon. A stream of images suddenly flitted through his mind, but they flew by so fast that he could only make out a few of them – all showing pictures of men like Pericles and Tew.

The crowd of rough-looking men, who'd continued growing in numbers, broke out in laughter. Tew turned to some zombies near Alex. "I'm tired of this. Get the boy to drink the water. I'll be damned if I let him die of thirst and take his secrets with him. He'll be much more committed to helping us regenerate once he's in the same state we are."

Dieu-le-Veut said, "I think I can speak for all the men here, cap'n. We'd be honored to add some fresh blood to our august assembly."

"I'm telling you, I don't know anything," Alex wailed.

Tew ignored Alex and roared, "Get him."

Alex ran for the stairs he'd entered on, but half a dozen zombies broke from the crowd to stop him short. He turned and raced towards a nearby boat, where he picked up an oar and began beating on the zombies closest to him.

None of them flinched as his swings were too weak to hurt any of them. One grabbed the oar and snapped it in two.

More zombies crowded around, closing their circle ever tighter. The scent of rotting bodies became so overpowering that he thought he'd faint. A burning sensation on his chest caused him to glance down and see that the ankh was glowing underneath his shirt. It became so hot that he felt like his skin was on fire. He yelped and started dancing around, trying to cool off.

Dieu-le-Veut pushed through the zombies and reached out to grab Alex. "Come, lad. Let me welcome you to our club." The instant she touched Alex, though, she screamed and yanked a blackened arm stump away.

The other zombies froze. Seizing the opportunity, Alex charged towards the stairs leading out, bowling several over. Everyone he touched screamed out in agony. The smell of burning cloth and skin filled the grotto with a terrible stench, making it hard to breathe. He broke through the first ring but found a second group had encircled him holding him back with oars, pikes, and swords.

Tew flew over and pushed his way inside the circle. He pointed at Alex and yelled, "He's only a boy. Don't just stand there. Get him!"

Dieu-le-Veut, who'd run to the pool, and shoved her arm in, shouted, "Stay away from him, men, or you'll suffer my fate. He's cursed; he is." The rest of the zombies stepped back, leaving Tew standing alone.

Alex looked around for a weapon but found nothing handy. A wave of cold air washed over him, and an instant later, he heard his sister shouting, "Hold on, Alex. Captain Every's men are coming."

Several zombies ran towards her, brandishing their swords and cutlasses. One fired a pistol at her, but she flew away, causing the bullet to harmlessly pass by her, just as Captain Every and several dozen spirits flew in. Every's men spread out, surrounding the zombies, then dove, crashing into the massed group of half-dead men.

Alex thought he'd stepped into something out of the twilight zone. He didn't know how it was possible, but he figured that the Pair Dadeni must have something to do with the zombies and ghosts being able to see and fight each other. The sound of metal on metal, guns going off, and the cries of wounded and dying men echoed deafeningly through the cavern. Every once in a while, he'd hear a different type of scream and see a zombie on fire from one of his sister's magical fireballs.

He watched in horror as some of the zombies broke from the battle and ran towards the fountain to heal their wounds before rejoining the fight. Seeing their opponents rejuvenated by the waters, some of Captain Every's crew broke from the battle to drink from the fountain and rejoin the fight as zombies.

Not every combatant, though, made it to the Fountain. The spirits who died turned into a fine dust that settled on the beach, while the dead zombies fell to the floor. Limbs and bodies soon littered the cavern floor, making it hard for the combatants to keep their footing.

Alex stood in the middle of the melee, feeling helpless, until an arm with a cutlass still in its hand skidded across the beach, stopping at his feet. The ankh shocked him into action. He pulled the weapon out of the bony hand and charged the two men who held Pericles prisoner near the fountain. Pointing the sword at one man's heart, he lunged, wincing as the metal struck bone and slid further in.

Pericles took advantage of the second man's surprise and pulled free. He snatched a nearby sword, lopped the man's head off, and charged into the fray. Alex was about to follow when he saw the cauldron sitting on the edge of the pool. He grabbed it with no clear idea of what he would do with it and headed down the steps.

It wasn't until he was near the bottom that Alex realized the battle had stopped. He halted and looked at the carnage all around him. Several dozen zombies were still standing, but just as many were dead or severely wounded. But what caught his attention was seeing Every kneeling before Tew, a sword at his neck.

"Tell me the secret to the object, boy, and I'll let yer cap'n go."

"Don't do it, lad," Every called out. "I'll gladly die and take my chances of going to perdition rather than have ye give him the object."

"Are ye going to let yer friend die like this?" Tew asked. "I'm willing to let him live. Seeing him on his knees in front of me is revenge enough for deserting me in the Indian Ocean. As I told you, all I want now is the knowledge of how to use that which ye hold."

Alex looked around and saw he was alone, as Every's crew had either moved on or turned into zombies and died. A half dozen living dead surrounded Pericles while Deborah sat huddled on the steps leading out, exhausted from using so much magic. "I've told you; I don't know how it operates. And even if I did, I'd never tell you."

"I think ye will, boy," Tew said as he swung his cutlass with all his strength and cut off Every's head. Before the body had time to fall to the sand, it had turned to dust.

"No!" Alex cried out.

He was so shocked that he barely heard Deborah cry, "Watch out!"

Too late, Alex realized that while his attention had been on Captain Every's situation, two of Tew's men had been sneaking around the side of the grotto to outflank him. Both carried oars to make sure they kept their distance.

When Tew yelled, "Get him, boys," the two zombies ran at Alex. One used his oar to knock the cauldron out of his hands, while the other used his to knock Alex down.

Alex tumbled down the remaining stairs, hit the cave floor, and rolled across the loose rocks towards the cauldron, tearing his clothes and ripping open his tender sun-burned skin. He stopped close enough to where the Pair Dadeni had rolled to a stop that he was able to reach out and touch the object.

Tew dropped his sword and scrambled for the cauldron. He tripped on a severed arm and fell but managed to grab one side of the bronze vessel before Alex could pull it to him. Pericles broke away from the other zombies and jumped on Tew, giving Alex enough time to leap for the cauldron. He landed on the two, his exposed hands and arms quickly burning through their skin and bones, turning one arm of each man into a blackened stump.

Pericles cried out in agony, rolled free, then got up and ran to the pool, thrusting his ruined arm into the water.

Despite his pain, Tew jerked the Pair Dadeni free and rolled to the other side, tucking the object under his good arm, and headed up the steps to the fountain.

Alex struggled to his feet and stumbled after Tew, praying for the ankh to devise a magical solution to stop the zombie. Instead, he felt the heat from the ankh fade away. Panicked, he pulled it out and shouted, "Don't give up on me now, you blasted thing."

It did nothing. When Alex looked up, he saw Tew with his ruined arm in the fountain pool and a grin on his face.

"So that's your dirty little secret," Tew said. "I always thought ye had some magical powers, but it doesn't look like it's going to help ye now." Tew dipped the cauldron into the water and drank deeply from it.

Alex jumped up the steps and grabbed the cauldron just as Tew finished drinking. The two wrestled with it for some time. Despite having two hands to Tew's one, it was an equal struggle in Alex's weakened state. As they fought, the ankh swung freely and landed in the cauldron.

Alex was in such a daze that it took him a second before he realized Tew had stopped fighting. He looked around for the cause and nearly dropped the Pair Dadeni when he saw the cauldron glowing a brilliant golden color. Strange markings appeared on it, similar to the alien symbols he'd seen in the *Sibylline Books*. Light shot out from the cup, bouncing off the walls and ceiling, while a cloud of psychedelic colors spilled over the object's rim.

Tew let go, jumped off the stairs, and backed up, joining the rest of the zombies on the far side of the grotto.

The tiny dragon-like animal he'd seen earlier alighted on Alex's shoulder. No sooner had the claws of the winged creature dug into his shoulder than an image of a small motorboat suddenly burst into his head, blocking out everything else. It took him a moment before he realized it was meant to be his way out. He turned to head back down the steps, but the light from the object was so blinding that Alex couldn't see anything. He stumbled and fell but had such a tight grip on the Pair Dadeni that he didn't lose control of it.

Deborah flew up and guided him down the remaining steps towards the boats on the beach.

The cauldron started pulsing in his hands, all the while glowing ever more brightly. The image of the motorboat fought with the object's brilliance for dominance in his mind – until the little dragon leaned over and pulled the ankh out of the cup.

Freed from the spell, Alex dropped the cauldron and let Deborah drag him through the shallow waters until he bumped into a boat and fell in.

CHAPTER 42
ADRIFT AGAIN

Tew rushed forward and grabbed the Pair Dadeni, holding it up and jubilantly shouting, "He did it." He danced around for a few seconds, then ran towards the Fountain of Youth, with all the zombies following him, except Pericles.

The Greek general and statesman waded into the water but stopped short of the boat. "Why did you unleash the Pair Dadeni's powers? You have let an evil out upon this earth – an evil I gave my life to stop."

"I'm sorry. I didn't mean to," Alex replied.

Pericles glared at Alex for a minute, then slumped. "At least you've done something no one else has. You've resisted its temptation." With his one good arm, he pushed the boat further into the water. "Go," he said, "while you still have a chance to escape. They will undoubtedly come after you once they drink from it and rejuvenate."

Before Alex could reply, the ankh started pulsing so hard that it felt like somebody was pounding his chest. He pulled the little looped cross out and saw it was glowing even brighter than the Pair Dadeni. A humming sound from near the fountain caused him to look up. He saw the cauldron's light pulsing at what seemed like the same frequency as the ankh.

A nip on his hand, followed by an image in his mind of the vegetative covering, drove him to channel his thoughts towards escaping. Only then did he realize he'd stumbled into the small motorboat he'd pictured earlier.

With Deborah urging him to hurry, Alex managed to get the engine started just as Pericles gave one final push to the boat to get it free of the beach.

"Aren't you coming?" Alex asked.

"I can't," Pericles replied. "I'm tied forever to that cauldron. Besides, I have to stay here to limit the harm you've caused."

A commotion from the back of the cavern prevented Alex from replying. When he looked to see what had caused the ruckus, he saw the Pair Dadeni had burst into flames. Tew dropped it and screamed, "After him. He's tricked us."

Deborah grabbed Alex's shoulders and shook him. "We must get out of here. Now!" she shouted.

Alex shifted the tiller and pointed the little boat towards the opening. A shudder went through the cavern as they reached the curtain, sending loose rocks and dirt tumbling into the water.

The boat hit the vegetative mat and stopped. Alex gunned the engine, but they didn't move. Deborah floated to the bow, spread her arms, and chanted an incantation Alex couldn't understand. An instant later, the thick fibrous strands caught on fire. He gunned the engine again, and they shot through.

They had only gone a short distance into the ocean when Alex heard a long, low rumbling sound. An instant later, part of the hillside came crashing into the cave, sending a billowing cloud of dust high into the sky.

Alex looked back and saw Pericles standing at the entrance, a broad smile on his face. He saw several boatloads of zombies heading after them, but as the first boat approached the opening, the entire island shuddered. Large chunks of the hill above the opening came crashing down, trapping everyone inside.

Another rumble shook the island. An instant later, the whole northern half of the isle collapsed, sending a massive wall of water out into the ocean. It hit a few seconds later and picked up their tiny motorboat as if it were nothing more than a leaf and carried it hundreds of yards out to sea. When the wave had passed, Alex looked back and saw half the island had disappeared below the surface. He stared back at the cloud of dust still rising into the sky, too tired to think or act.

Deborah was the first to break the silence when she suddenly gasped. "Are you all right? In all the commotion, I didn't realize how badly you were hurt."

Alex looked down. His shirt and pants were little better than rags, and he could see numerous dark stains where his blood had discolored them. He felt something trickling down his arms and saw blood running over and through the sand coating on them. "I guess there's one benefit of being in this shape – I barely feel anything except my throat."

"We need to get you to land as soon as possible," Deborah said. "I know there are some nearby islands to the north and south of here, but I'm not sure where, so I think it best to head due west. That way, we're bound to hit Florida. If we go any other direction, we might end up in the middle of the Atlantic."

Alex slowly turned the boat in the direction she was pointing. It was some time before he spoke. "I'm sorry, sis."

"For what?"

"I know you thought that if I helped your order find one of the Maqlû, you'd move on, but I don't think you can trust anyone with those objects. So, I won't go in search of them anymore. We'll have to find another way."

He was surprised his sister didn't argue with him. Feeling a need to explain his decision, he added, "This is the second, no, make that the third, magical object I've destroyed. But I don't regret what happened. All those objects have caused so much suffering that I couldn't live with myself, letting them continue to exist. And I'm no better because I've killed and destroyed while searching for them."

"You didn't do anything wrong," Deborah said. She paused, then added, "I've done some thinking about this whole situation and can't help but believe there's a lot more to all that's happened since we met than we understand. So, if you can bear my company, I'd like to see this through with you."

Alex tried smiling, but between his sunburn, cuts, and bruises, it looked more like a grimace. "That sounds wonderful, but you know what's really on my mind right now?" he asked as they headed towards the setting sun. Seeing the questioning look on his sister's face, he grinned and said, "I would really have liked it if you had brought some of those coconuts along."

***

Enjoyed *The Pair Dadeni*?

If you enjoyed this story and have a moment to spare, I'd appreciate a short review on Goodreads or the site where you bought this book. Your help spreading the word is greatly appreciated, as reviews make a huge difference in helping new readers find the series. Thank you!

ALSO BY THE AUTHOR
The Maqlû Series

After mistakenly taking his dad's magical ankh, Alex Scire suddenly sees ghosts everywhere, including his sister, who's stuck in the afterlife. To help her move on, he joins an expedition headed to the ancient Mayan city of Lamanai to search for a magical object. But to succeed he has to battle a tyrannical ghost king's army and survive assassination attempts by those who killed his family.

After destroying The Fountain of Youth, Alex Scire finds himself adrift on the ocean, until he stumbles upon a ghost who holds the secret to the Holy Grail. Thinking he has one last chance to help his sister move on, Alex embarks on a quest that takes him from the dungeons of the Spanish Inquisition to Dracula's haunts in Transylvania to find the Grail.

After taking the Holy Grail to Avalon, Alex Scire encounters the ghost of William Wallace. The former Scottish warrior is stuck in the afterlife and asks for help finding his scattered body parts so he can move on. Alex agrees and begins searching throughout Britain to help Wallace. But Alex's sudden reappearance, after everyone assumed he was dead, causes his enemies to redouble their efforts to kill him.

AUTHOR'S NOTE

Historical accuracy of *The Pair Dadeni*

The Pair Dadeni was originally part of my first book – *The Palantir*, but I split it off because it was a separate story, and I wanted to write a pirate adventure.

As I've done in all my books, I've drawn inspiration for some of the characters and events from fascinating historical people, places, and events because **'Truth is stranger than fiction.'** For instance:

Although I have taken literary license to portray their **characters**, many of the ghosts were inspired by real people.

- The most fascinating person I learned about was Toussaint L'Overture. Born into slavery, in what is now Haiti, he rose to lead Haiti's army in throwing out the French, Spanish, and British armies. In the process, he helped free the enslaved people not just in Haiti but all Hispaniola!

- The pirate Henry Every is one of the most interesting pirates in history. Some of his more fascinating exploits were:
    - He stole his ship, one of the most fearsome pirate ships of its time, from the British Navy and renamed it *The Fancy*.
    - After stealing the Grand Mughal's treasure, he talked the rest of the pirate fleet (formerly led by Thomas Tew, who died in the fight)

into letting him protect it (which he promptly sailed away with).

- o His theft of the Grand Mughal's treasure caused the British East India Company to organize the first worldwide manhunt to try to capture him.
- o He is one of the few successful pirates who lived (i.e., not hung or killed in battle). No one knows what happened to him as he just disappeared.

Many of the **locations** in the book are places I've visited, including;

- The fortress on the book's front cover – the Citadelle La Ferrière is the largest fort in the Americas and a UNESCO site.
- Port Royal, in Kingston harbor, was once one of the most populated and wealthiest cities in the Americas. An earthquake and subsequent tsunami sunk most of the city and killed thousands. It is now a small town and UNESCO site. And the Lewis Galdy story is based on history – he was swallowed up by the earthquake/tsunami and spit out by the ocean.
  - o The picture I used on my 'About the Author' page in the book is of me standing in front of Fort Charles in Port Royal.
- The grocery store Alex visited in Kingston is based on one we shopped at – the most interesting store situation I've ever been in.

- The extreme poverty we saw in Haiti was sobering. From what I've read of L'Overture's story, it sounds like the U.S. could've made a difference in the country's trajectory two hundred years ago – but we chose to look inward.

- The mythology in this book is based primarily on Druid, Mesopotamian, and American Indian mythology, but I've also included some Caribbean influences. When my youngest daughter and I were in Haiti researching this book, we tried tracking down signs of Voodoo/Vodou influence in the country, but nobody would talk to us about it. My takeaway is that it's nowhere near as prevalent and wild as the movies make it out to be.

For more information on the historical places, events, and characters included in this book, go to my web page, where I have posted a glossary about many of the interesting historical facts included in the book.

ABOUT THE AUTHOR

JC Holmberg is the author of the Young Adult Fantasy Adventure series – *The Maqlû*. He and his wife, Mari, live in *The Kentucky Wildlands*, surrounded by nature. John splits his time working on his forestland in the mornings, writing in the afternoon, and continuing his travels to research settings for future books.

The picture below is the author at Fort Charles in Port Royal, Jamaica.

FOLLOW THE AUTHOR

Although *The Maqlû* is a fantasy series that includes ghosts and magic, the books are set in the amazing real world with fascinating historical characters. To learn more about the author, the background of each story, and some fascinating fun facts included in the books, go to,

www.jcholmberg.com

www.ingramcontent.com/pod-product-compliance
Lightning Source LLC
Chambersburg PA
CBHW061103190726
48286CB00006B/1866